Knaves Templar

PREVIOUS MATTHEW AND JOAN STOCK MYSTERIES

Knaves Templar

Leonard Tourney

St. Martin's Press New York

Design by Guenet Abraham

Library of Congress Cataloging-in-Publication Data

Tourney, Leonard D.
    Knaves templar / Leonard Tourney.
        p.   cm.
    "A Thomas Dunne book."
    ISBN 0-312-04961-7
    I. Title.
    PS3570.0784K6   1991
    813'.54—dc20   90-49297
                                                    CIP

First Edition: February 1991

10 9 8 7 6 5 4 3 2 1

Knaves

Templar

Prologue

T he old curate dreamed, and in his dream he saw himself laid out in his winding sheet. His visage was stark and marmoreal; his pale white hands reposed prayerfully on his chest, and beside them lay the little silver crucifix and chain his mother had given him when he had been ordained thirty-four years before. From somewhere above, the solemn strokes of the passing bell floated down; the pious murmur of last rites whispered like the sea at a distance. Yet he did not smell the brine of the sea, but the sickly sweetness of putrescent flesh.

The dream struck terror to his soul and wrenched him from sleep. For a long while he lay in a cold, quicksilver sweat, too struck by the vision to pray, wondering what it had meant, the terrible dream, and fearful of sleeping again lest the vision proceed from mere death to something more awful—judgment, hellfire, eternal torment. Then from far off he heard the complaint of the aggrieved milk cow and the two cantankerous geese, though the weathered shed that housed the beasts stood beyond the stream and the church itself.

"Cursed fox," he said aloud, yet half-glad for the distraction. Or worse, a thief. Either way, the curate was not to be deprived of what was his by a lesser creature. He struggled to free himself from his bedclothes, groped in the darkness for his boots, and hastily dressed. He struck a match to his lantern, and all the while the geese honked. He expected a scene of feathery carnage to meet his eyes when he came to the shed. He had dreamed of death. Would he not find it waking?

An oak cudgel was in his hand before he emerged into the night. The moon was full and looming, and over the churchyard a thin layer of new snow shrouded crypt, monument, and cross, while beyond the iron pickets marking consecrated ground he could see the dark mass of the church where he preached and administered the blessed sacrament on sabbaths.

He moved quickly for his years. A thirst for vengeance upon fox, wolf, or whatever other lawless scavenger had violated the stillness of the night and threatened to make a meal of what was his, thickened his blood and hardened his spirit. The geese were still fussing when he pushed open the door of the shed and held the lantern high in one hand and the cudgel in the other, demanding to know who or what was there before there was anything to see. His heart raced. His eyes shifted to every corner of the shed, which smelled of hay and ordure and animal fear.

His appearance silenced the animals, who knew his

scent and had no fear of cudgels. Then, between the cow and the geese, their long necks turned toward him inquiringly, he saw the intruder.

It was no beast. It was a woman. He almost laughed with relief.

She lay upon her back fork-legged in the foul, matted straw. Between her bare thighs lay a bloody infant, still and curled as though yet in the mother's womb. He could see the foulness of the straw, blood, womb blood. He could smell it with the other smells. The cord still linked mother and child, but the child was still. The curate knew that it was dead.

Seeing no danger to himself, he cast the cudgel aside and approached. Yet there was something awful about the vulnerable female form, the dead babe, and the solitude of the untoward birthplace, and perhaps because of those things or because his dream had been fulfilled in part, he approached uneasily, as though there remained more to fear than met the eye.

He raised the lantern for a better look at his uninvited guest and recognized the woman, although he had not thought to find her in so humble a place or so wretched a condition.

"You've fallen very low, madam," he said with a mixture of respect for her station and disapproval of her history. "No marvel your child was born dead."

"He would have lived, had his birthing been otherwise," said the woman. Her voice was low and husky, the enunciation perfect. As he might have expected in a woman of her breeding. "He was a man-child. He would have lived to avenge his father."

The curate wagged his head with disapproval and set the lantern down on the straw. "He who violates God's holy ordinances shall by God be destroyed."

"Foolish old man," the woman said. "Were such the

3

case, who would be alive? All have sinned. This poor child did no wrong. Nor was bill of particulars laid at my feet. As for my husband, even he was innocent, a victim of corrupt lawyers and judges."

The curate started to remind her that her husband had been condemned by a jury—honest men and true, whom the curate knew by their first names. Then, recalling his higher duty, he began to pray over the dead infant, for he supposed the child to be innocent enough, save of Adam's curse.

"Spare me your prayers, you whited sepulcher."

The accusing voice interrupted his thoughts and stung worse than the cold. He opened his eyes and looked at her directly. Even in her present circumstance, it was a striking face, as fair as any in Norwich or its environs, with arched brows and high forehead and, beneath the straight nose that was her father's endowment, the full, sensuous lips that would have tempted a courtier to an eternity of kissing.

Her beauty moved him.

"Let me help you up," he said.

"Don't trouble yourself. I'll lie where I am."

"Will you? To what end—to come to your grave like this miserable child? Live and repent."

"Of what? Loyalty to a husband?"

"He wasn't your husband—at least not in the eyes of the law or the Church."

"I'll not quibble with you," she said in a stronger voice. "You've taken my husband and my child, you lawyers and priests. May God's curse be on you all, vipers and hypocrites."

After the curse, she turned her face away from him.

"At least let me bury your child," he said softly.

"In the churchyard? With his grandfather and great-grandfather and great-great-grandfather from time out of mind?"

"You know that's impossible."

"Is it?"

"You know it is. Look, I'll make a grave for him outside the pickets. I know a place."

"I'll wager you do," she said. "Where the bastards of the town's high and mighty are hidden so as not to sully the reputations of their fathers."

"It's a peaceful place, beneath a hawthorn," he said.

"Without monument or epitaph—"

"The law's explicit on the matter," he said.

"Damn the law," she said. "Don't you touch my son." Then she said, more gently, "If you have any mercy in you, let me and my child stay the night here. My son's dead, as you can plainly see. No earthly care can trouble him now. As for me, it's warm enough in the straw. See how the cow has settled herself—and the clamorous geese. Your coming has calmed them, for which I thank you. I pray you let me stay."

"But what of the child?"

"I'll bury him myself."

He thought to ask where, but he did not. He wished he had not heard the alarm of cow and goose. Had not come foolhardy to the shed. Not seen mother and child. He wished for bed and sleep. In the light of the lantern she was looking at him strangely, and somehow her calmer manner filled him with more dread than her blasphemies had done.

"Where will you go now?"

"Where no one knows my name—or my history."

"Then you must travel far."

"Yes."

"Are you able?"

"I am. Thank you."

He saw her lips part in a half smile, but there was no friendliness in it, no womanly yielding to man or necessity, only a knowledge of something beyond his own knowledge, and that unnerved him too. She hadn't moved all the while they had talked. She remained in the position she had been in when giving birth, too exhausted to move, he supposed, and now too defiant. Then she said: "There's yet another thing you might do for me, if you will."

He was almost afraid to ask what it was she wanted now.

"I want you to witness."

"Witness—what?"

"An oath."

"What manner of oath?"

"Why, an oath to God, sir priest."

"Well and good if the oath be godly and faithfully observed."

"It will be both, I assure you."

"Then speak it."

She seemed to draw a long breath before speaking, thinking the oath through, he thought, searching for the particular words. The silence was heavy in the shed, a heavy weight upon him. He was almost relieved when she spoke. "I swear—"

"Yes?"

"Before Almighty God . . . to avenge my husband's murder and my child's. And may I be the instrument thereof. So help me God."

The curate shuddered at her words. "You sin in making such an oath," he said sternly.

"Then I sin," she said. Her eyes narrowed and she waved her hand a little, as in a gesture of dismissal—as though she were still a daughter of the gentry and not a fallen woman whose husband had been hanged dead that morning with half of Norwich looking on, the curate among them.

Despite his detestation of her wicked oath and sins, the curate was tempted to leave her with a blessing. His impulse was not so much a sudden rush of charity as it was a desire to placate, for he feared the half-naked woman in the shed, the woman who had no regard for him or for his God.

The curate returned to his cottage and his bed but not to sleep. Visions of the defiant woman and her stillborn child haunted him and he tossed restlessly, nor did all his prayers bring relief. At dawn he rose and went out to see how she had passed the night. Opening the door of the shed, he almost expected to see her still there, her legs spread, the dead child nesting in between them, the woman's eyes burning like coals with her hatred.

But she was gone. Only the bloody straw remained as a testament to her presence, or to the vengeful oath she had sworn.

A week later he found where she had buried the little body. Beside a noble monument memorializing the remains of one of Norwich's most respected families, the earth had been disturbed. The curate wondered at the determination that could have driven the woman to claw frozen earth to make the shallow grave—love, hatred, madness? But he did not disturb the grave. He remembered the woman's oath and did not want her vengeance to fall upon his own head.

1

Almost five years to the month after the woman gave birth in the curate's cow shed, a young man stood a lone vigil on the banks of the Thames, many miles to the south. His name was Edward Litchfield, and as he looked down into the dark, swirling water, he contemplated not the river, but the depths of his own foolishness. For he had been outrageously cozened—cheated, gulled, fleeced. Choose what word you will, it all came to the same mortifying end. And for that reason, the cold and the dark and the terrible solitude of the riverbank all seemed a fitting punishment for his folly.

He had come to the appointed place as agreed. The

Temple Stairs, half past ten of the clock, unarmed, alone—and most particularly the latter. And not by agreement but neglect, without so much as a torch or lantern. And upon what security? The word of a seeming friend, well motivated to turn traitor? The promise of a return of a tithe of what he had lost? Pulling his cloak tightly around him, he remembered it was his birthday. Self-pity momentarily replaced his anger. Regret stung more than the wind. His seventeenth year, it was—by virtue of which he was the youngest of the apprentice lawyers of the honorable and ancient Society of the Middle Temple, chief of England's Inns of Court.

He knew his present mission would confer no credit on that ancient institution, nor upon his doting father in Suffolk, who having studied law in the same Society in the first decade of Elizabeth's reign, had spared no expense that the son of his old age should follow in his footsteps. A modest, churchly youth in Suffolk, Litchfield had turned prodigal in London. He had become a haunter of taverns and cockfights, bearbaitings and theaters. He had spent more time reading lascivious verses than the grave treatises of Perkins or Plowden, more hours rutting in the stews of Bankside and Southwark than listening to dull lectures upon the grating machinery of the law, which, as one wit had said, was wont to gnaw upon its victims mightily before gobbling them up.

All this he had done and more, in part from natural depravity, in part from a desire to keep pace with his comrades.

But now, blasted by an ill wind and worse experience, he was ready to repent. He had concluded that the law was not for him, nor the life of a wastrel. Like the Prodigal of the Scriptures, he had fed too long at the trough of swinishness. Now he was ready to eat humble pie at his father's beneficent table.

But repentance would not come easy. The worst would be his father's insistence that the trick had been as transparent as its depravity. Why had he not seen it?

Standing by the river, Litchfield thought resentfully of his chamberfellow, Peregrinus Monk. It had been Monk who seduced him to the mischief in the first place. Yes, it had been Monk's fault entirely. And it had been Monk whom Litchfield had asked for his money back.

He had suggested to Monk that he might whisper in the ears of certain persons of the Temple just what was going on behind their learned backs, in chambers and passageways and Hall while the law was being piously intoned. Knights Templar indeed! Was not *Knaves Templar* a fitter name for such a crew?

He remembered how earnestly Monk had begged him to keep their little secret. "Keep faith with us," Monk had said. "You've sworn an oath."

"An oath? A thing writ upon water," Litchfield had answered. "What I have given freely, I may take again with equal freedom."

Litchfield remembered his words, repeating them to himself as he stared into the river's turbulence.

It was upon the heels of that thought that he became aware he was no longer alone on the Stairs. His friend appeared at last. Monk, as heavily muffled as Litchfield, raised his arm in greeting and flung a curse into the watery chaos before them.

Litchfield came at once to the matter. "You've brought my money, then? As you promised?"

"In good time, Edward," Monk said through the woolen scarf he had wound around his neck so that only his eyes and forehead could be seen. "First a little something . . . to strengthen the bargain."

"I am already strengthened."

"So I see," Monk answered, drawing a bottle from inside his cloak and handing it to Litchfield. "But no fort can be too strong. Ask any engineer. Here, take it. 'Twill do you good."

Litchfield decided there was no harm in taking another drink. He had had many already that night. He took the proffered bottle and pressed it to his lips. A great draft he took; the liquor burned his gullet as it dribbled down. He swallowed hard and coughed. Wiping his mouth on his sleeve, he said: "My money, Peregrinus. No less than you promised."

Monk reached into his cloak and pulled out a leather purse. He dangled it before the younger man. "Last chance to change your mind. But say the word and you're still with us."

"My mind's made up, curse you," Litchfield replied.

He heard his own speech slur and thought it was the numbing cold. He reached out for the purse, but Monk pulled it away just as his fingers were about to close around it.

"Come, Peregrinus. Let's not play cat and mouse—"

Litchfield did not finish his admonition, nor did he try again for the purse. His head swam and his vision clouded over. God's blood, had he drunk that much?

He looked at Monk, but saw only the outlines of a man. "Peregrinus?"

He reached out blindly, his head swimming. He felt his fingers touch the purse, the slippery leather. Then he felt himself falling forward and caught, smelled the damp wool of Monk's cloak and the smell of the man himself. For an instant he remembered when the two of them had challenged each other as to how many stoups of Ned Hodge's strong black ale the other could drink. Monk had carried Litchfield home then in his arms. The same smells then of cloak and man, the same not unpleasant sensation of being borne in another's arms. But not the same dizziness, or the terrifying blindness.

At the time Monk had assured him that although he was a boy in years, he was a full man in his cups.

The old memory faded beneath the burden of his agonizing pain, and then Litchfield felt nothing, thought nothing, was nothing.

At dawn, Henry Sherlock, with nearly thirty years on his back as a Thames waterman, nosed his wherry into the Temple Stairs, thinking he might find a little morning business. Some Inn of Court gentleman to haul upriver or carry over to Southwark.

"God save you, sir!" Henry cried, perceiving that there was indeed someone waiting on the Stairs. "Upriver or down, it's all one to me, sir."

The lone figure on the Stairs made no answer to Henry's invitation. His curiosity aroused, Henry stepped ashore for a better look. He thought the gentleman sitting with his back to the wall might have fallen asleep or frozen to death. It had happened before. In Henry's thirty years on the river, he had seen almost everything.

His second supposition proved to be closer to the truth. The gentleman was no more than a boy, really. Perhaps sixteen or seventeen, Henry reckoned. Glassy-eyed and stiff as a mackerel, he was sitting without complaint on the hard, wet stones, his white face turned upward and toward the east as though in expectation of the dawn, or a glorious resurrection.

Henry crossed himself and was about to exercise his salvage rights on the dead man's earthly goods when he realized the poor devil at his feet had more than the cold to blame for his demise. The corpse's arms were stretched out along the legs, and the palm of the right hand was open, as though its owner expected some charity from the next passerby. Several inches of wrist were exposed as well, and all bloody, and now Henry could see that the dead man's stockings were soaked with blood and that there was a great pool of blood the dead man sat in. Clutched tightly in the right hand of the corpse was the apparent instrument of this violence—a bloody razor with an ivory handle.

Henry crossed himself again, and being a devotee of the old religion, he muttered a quick prayer to the Virgin and to whatever saint looked kindly upon suicides.

Henry was tempted to take the razor as well as the purse, which he was pleased to see contained a handful of coins, but when he tried to open the dead man's clenched fingers, he could not.

Later that morning, the body found by others and duly reported to those authorized to handle such matters, a constable's man, just sworn that day to his office, had to break the fingers of the dead man to release the razor.

2

A fortnight after Litchfield's body was discovered on the Temple Stairs—and not more than a quarter mile from the scene of the crime—Matthew Stock, a clothier of Chelmsford, Essex, and constable of the same, relaxed before a fire banked high and red, enjoying a pleasant conversation with his wife. He was a man of about forty with a plain, honest face, brown complexion, and black hair only beginning to show a little gray about the temples. Somewhat below the middle height, he was plump, although by no means corpulent, and quite well spoken for one whose people had risen to prosperity and public honor only in his own generation.

Joan Stock appeared younger than her husband, yet their christenings had not been more than two months apart. Her coloring was similar to his, and twenty years of marriage had blessed them (or cursed them, however one regarded it) with common mannerisms. Joan had a winsome oval face and dark eyes full of expression and a thoughtful cast that, when she was angry or resolved, erased every impression of the softly feminine. Like Matthew, Joan was short, but more trim, especially since a recent illness had shriven her of some of her former weight.

The Stocks were guests of Master Thomas Cooke and his bride, Frances Challoner Cooke. Matthew, having performed valuable service for them both in the way of discovering the murderer of Mistress Cooke's uncle not a month before, had now been prevailed upon to remain in London to inquire into an even more mysterious enormity at the Middle Temple, where Thomas Cooke was a prominent member.

At the moment, however, Matthew's discourse did not touch upon enormities. Rather, he spoke of the delights of the palate and the ear—hearty victuals and the joys of music—having never been able to tell which in life he loved the more. Joan listened attentively, even while her fingers busily stitched and her eyes remained fixed upon her work as though to look away for a second was to spoil all.

"Tender meats succulent beyond belief," he continued with unconcealed relish and staring into the middle distance as though what he described were at the very instant being borne into the parlor by a troop of ghostly servants. "Pheasant and godwit, pig and pudding, fruits, cheeses, candies, and confections. What you will and as much and a plenty of drink, draining every cellar in Burgundy or Spain."

His recital caused her to look up from her stitchery. "Humph," she said. "Fine fare for gluttons and wine-bibbers."

"Not so," he protested. "Sufficient, rather, for any honest stomach."

She laughed. "God bless us, like yours, I warrant."

"I'll not deny I like to eat," he returned defensively.

"Well, then, proceed," she said in the same good-humored vein. "Let us have the rest of the tale."

Matthew shifted in the high-backed chair with the elegantly carved arms, and smiled broadly. The vision floated back into his head. "Imagine, then, all this plenty stretched out through practically the whole month of December and into January as far as Twelfth Night. With one of their number crowned Prince d'Amour, as he has been called from time out of mind."

"Go on."

"With as much ceremony, display, and feasting as one might wish. Plays, masques, jousts, pageants, performed almost nightly."

Joan said: "You make the Inns of Court sound like academies of pleasure rather than colleges of learning. I supposed these young gentlemen went thither to learn the law."

"Oh, they study, according to Thomas, but they play as well, especially at Christmas."

Joan pondered the delights her husband had described. Then she remembered the other things not so merry or pleasant. "I suppose Thomas did not darken this vision of Christmas revelry with more sad stories about suicide deemed murder, did he?"

"Marry, I have learned the name of one of the dead—the circumstances of one other. The first was the son of a Suffolk gentleman, a former member of the Temple himself. The poor boy had just turned seventeen."

"Ah, that would be he who slashed his wrists," she said, putting her stitchery aside. "What of the others?"

"A hanging and a poisoning."

"Jesus preserve us!" she exclaimed. She was not sure of the wisdom of continuing this morbid topic so near to bedtime. Would not such thoughts stir up dreams of equal horror, of white, bloodless faces of hanged men with broken necks, bulging eyes, and blackened tongues? And the poisoned. Would those images not be of equal horror? "Thomas *thinks* they were all murdered?"

"So he does," Matthew answered. "For reasons he has promised to explain in greater detail when I meet Master Hutton tomorrow."

"Master Hutton?"

"The Treasurer of their Society, the chief officer."

"Three dead men in as many weeks—very suspicious unless suicide is contagious."

Their conversation yielded to a companionable silence. Matthew rose from the fine, comfortable chair to crouch before the fire. He laid two faggots on the charred ruin of earlier ones and maneuvered them into place with a poker. Then he remained there, staring into the rising flames. Joan returned to her stitchery, thinking. She recalled the strange concatenation of events by which they had come to know the Cookes and be their guests. It had begun at Bartholomew Fair, nearly half a year before, when Matthew's success in apprehending a would-be murderer of the Queen had brought his unusual talents to the royal attention. Next, to service on behalf of Frances Challoner, then one of the Queen's Royal Maids, and immediately thereafter to a dangerous sojourn in Derbyshire in a decaying castle, and more murders discovered and prevented.

That mystery unraveled to everyone's satisfaction, comes young Thomas Cooke with another. And at the very moment when Joan could think of little else but getting home again to Chelmsford for Christmas. For she had grown weary of castles and great houses, of royal courts and all the bowing and scraping. She yearned to be mistress of her own house again, no matter how humble, and dreamed of her kitchen with its orderly ranks of utensils and its sooty ceiling, her own good pewter and neatly arranged cupboards, where she could find whatever she wanted. And most of all she missed her daughter, Elizabeth, and her little grandson, who Joan feared would be gangling and bearded by the time she laid eyes on him again, so fast did children grow these days.

And then, even as they were readying themselves for the journey home, Matthew had come to say that Thomas had invited them to remain in London for Christmas.

"Remain in London!" she cried. "Whatever do you mean, *remain* in London?"

Thomas had told Matthew about the suicides.

"What!" she declared, working herself up into a fine frenzy of opposition. "A pox upon all laywers! Do they not stir up enough trouble in the courts with their quiddities, their suits, and their gibberish comprehensible only to their own breed, that they should murder one another and draw simple, honest souls like ourselves into the fray?"

But Joan's longing for home had succumbed to the powerful demon of curiosity. Besides, the Cookes had proved generous hosts. Joan now counted Frances Cooke a friend, who had seemed so aloof before when she was a Queen's Maid and Joan had been sent in disguise into Derbyshire to play housekeeper. Even Frances's handsome young husband, with his good humor and hospitable nature, had advanced in Joan's esteem.

And so Joan had given her consent, and now, by God, it was two weeks before Christmas itself, London as cold as a witch's teat, and Matthew hobnobbing with lawyers and beginning in some of his phrases to sound like one too!

Leaving her to stay at home.

There, indeed, was a bone to gnaw upon! She asked again, breaking the silence, was there not a place for her in Matthew's new adventure? After all, had husband and wife not always shared all, bed, board, and yes, danger too?

"Impossible. The Inns are a man's preserve, a precinct as sacred to the sex of Adam as was the island of the Amazons to females."

"Stuff and nonsense," she snorted. "Of course women go and come. Has not the Queen herself stooped to enter these sacred masculine precincts you speak of? Was she not present when Master Shakespeare's *Twelfth Night* was performed only last year? Tell me, is Royal Elizabeth a woman or no? Answer me that! And has she set foot within the Middle Temple or no?"

He conceded that the Queen had, got up from his crouching, and returned to the elegant chair.

"Then she's a woman and so am I, and my rights of passage follow as the night the day. Let us speak no more nonsense about male precincts."

"Great ladies come to the entertainments," Matthew said, "but even the laundresses must by House rules be beyond the age of forty to enter there. As for Her Majesty, she is, after all, Queen of England. That office guarantees her certain privileges that might reasonably be denied to mere mortals like Chelmsford housewives whose husbands are no more than clothiers and constables. A fine lot of searching out we'd get done together. Why, we'd be as conspicuous as ravens in the henhouse."

"More like sheep among wolves," she said.

"No, sweetheart, as much as I would like your company and good counsel, you must keep the home fires burning on this occasion. Trust me. You'll know my heart; I'll keep no secrets from you. You'll know everything."

She regarded him skeptically, but she decided against further protest—at least for now. Her exclusion was no small annoyance. Didn't she deserve some compensation for being denied Chelmsford at Christmas?

Later, in their bedchamber, perched cross-legged upon the immense four-poster bed, she said: "When is it you begin your scratching for clues?"

"Tomorrow," Matthew answered, avoiding his wife's glare. "I'm to meet Master Hutton, the Treasurer. A very learned gentleman, I'm told."

"Oh, he is learned, is he?" Joan remarked. "Then a great wonder it is he cannot solve these mysteries himself, else what good, pray, is his learning?"

Joan put her question indifferently, as though she cared not a fig that she had been excluded from the hunt. And all because she was born a woman.

3

ome spring and summer, London would flourish, ripe orchard and garden countrify the town, their exhalations sweeten the air, fetch bird and bee, redeem damp and squalor. It was not so now. London was bleak in December, gray and webbed like an old man's face.

The four Inns of Court—Gray's, Lincoln's, the Inner Temple, and the Middle—were situated on the north bank of the Thames in a ward known as Faringdon Without. Once in the country, the Inns now nestled in the heart of Elizabethan London, the City having grown up rankly about them. They were now a tolerably easy walk from any quarter of the metropolis, given passable weather and the absence of urgency in getting oneself there. Since on this morning neither weather nor time was to be reckoned with, Matthew and his young host, Thomas Cooke, had decided to walk.

Fleet Street was the most direct thoroughfare from Cooke House, but though it was not yet seven o'clock, the street was already thronged with wagons, carts, coaches, horsemen, and pedestrians of every class, with such a rumble and clamor of wheel, beast, and man that Matthew wondered the inhabitants along the street could abide it. At their backs the morning sun shone distantly through a gray haze of smoke that scented the air and stung the eyes and covered the cobbles with a fine layer of soot.

While they maneuvered through the crowd, Thomas, tall, fair-haired, elegantly caped, and in all, a fine specimen of his class, was lavish in his praise of the Society of which he was a member.

"Of the four Inns, the Middle Temple is indisputably the most illustrious, having been founded by the famous Knights Templar in King John's time."

"The Knights were lawyers then?" Matthew asked.

Thomas laughed. "Crusaders, rather. They established themselves near the Holy Temple at Jerusalem, hence their name. They adopted as their battle chant *Non nobis, Domine, non nobis, sed tuo Nomini da gloriam.* Not to us, Lord, but to thy name give the glory. A pious motto. These knights pledged themselves to resign all earthly wealth. To serve only Christ."

"A laudable aim," murmured Matthew to the back of his long-shanked friend and hastening to keep up.

"But there was a falling away. The Knights performed great feats for our Saviour's sake, then acquired the very wealth they scorned. They grew proud and arrogant, and were suppressed at last by the Church they strove to defend. The property that was theirs, where the Temple now stands, was given to students of the common law."

Matthew listened, took the lore in, both what was new and what familiar. It was too early to say what was material to his purpose. He had a philosophical view of his work. Finding truth was not like looking for a lost coin where one recalled having seen it last. It was like thrusting a hand into a rabbit's hole and finding the hole inhabited by a serpent.

The two men passed by Fetter Lane and Chancery Lane, where the Royal Courts of Justice stood and where Matthew saw an assembly of gowned lawyers and judges and their petitioners. Thomas pointed out this exalted personage and that, and then the two turned down Essex Street, and ahead of them Matthew glimpsed the river and, upon its gray surface, a flotilla of barges, tiltboats, and the ubiquitous wherries that bore passengers upriver and down.

They paused while Thomas tossed pennies to a cluster of beggars, none of whom could have been more than ten or eleven. Their grim faces were hard; experience had made them seem older. Matthew gave from his own purse, and while he did he reflected on what a wonderful and wicked world London was. Not all the villages of the realm equaled the sum of its humanity. And constantly growing, too, added upon by rural folk, adventurous or desperate, flocking hither to seek their fortunes. Some never to be seen after; others to return to their native ground with fine clothes on their backs, a new world of stories to tell, and good hard money to buy land and houses and lord it over their old neighbors, who must now call the returned prodigal "sir" and his good wife "madam."

The beggars behind them, Thomas returned to his earlier theme. "We Templars are a close-knit company, as

you shall presently see. We are bound by a common purpose—the noble ideal of justice, without which man
would come at his brother with tooth and claw."

"How many are you?"

"Nearly a thousand men and boys dwell in the Inns.
And that is not to count servants, underbutlers, pannier-
men, cooks, gardeners, and porters. Almost the size of the
Queen's own household by comparison. All are persons of
quality, the students, I mean. Sons of knights, earls, bar-
ons, the upper gentry, although some of our more prosperous merchants are deigning to send their offspring
there. I mention Edmund Morlas, mercer, and Henry
Doubleday, merchant, to name but two. Our chief officer
at the Middle Temple is called the Treasurer."

"He whom I am to meet shortly," Matthew said.

"The very man," Thomas said.

"I pray God he speaks plain English and not Latin or
law French," Matthew said.

Thomas laughed pleasantly. "He speaks plain enough—
too plain for some who have felt the lash of his tongue.
For the rest, I admit we lawyers have our terms of art to
blabber among ourselves to the mystification of the laity.
And, of course, the customs and traditions of the Temple
itself, hundreds of years in the making."

"Must I learn a new tongue, then?" Matthew asked
jokingly, although he feared in part it might be true. For
right there on the busy thoroughfare, elbow to elbow with
strangers, he was gripped by a sudden and fierce homesickness. How he missed the familiar sights and smells of
Chelmsford, and the plain, honest English of buying and
selling cloth.

"Take courage, Matthew," Thomas said cheerfully,
seeming to sense his companion's shift of mood. "Even as
Virgil guided Dante into the depths of hell, I will be your
guide and translator."

Thomas laughed at his own jest, but Matthew prayed the obscure joke might not prove prophetic. He knew little of Virgil and Dante beyond their names, but whether hell was a real place or a figure of speech, he understood the word meant mortal danger.

A shrewish voice with a harsh London accent said, "Come in," and Matthew followed Thomas into the little office with its overly large desk and tall cabinet stuffed with books and papers and smelling of mildew and ink and wood smoke. There was a single lancet window giving view to the desolate garden, and a little hearth with a fire laid. Behind the desk sat the owner of the voice that had so unceremoniously welcomed them—a pale young man with thin blond hair lank about his ears and parted in the middle. He had high cheeks, a thin, straight nose, and a complexion as smooth and hairless as a girl's. His eyes were hard and close-set, and although by Matthew's estimate he could not have been above thirty, there was a sullenness in his expression that made him seem older, as though he had seen much of life and found it wanting in whatever lesser mortals thought worthwhile.

"Is Master Hutton in?" Thomas wanted to know.

"He is, Master Cooke."

There was a silence. For a moment, the clerk's eyes fell to what he had apparently been reading before.

"Well, tell him I and the father of a prospective member of the House would be honored to speak to him. We do have an appointment, Phipps."

"He has someone with him just now."

"Tell him I and Master Stock of Chelmsford await his pleasure," Thomas said impatiently.

The man whom Thomas had addressed as Phipps sighed heavily, slipped from his chair, and went to a closed door opposite the one Matthew had just entered. He knocked softly and then went inside. As soon as he was out of sight, Thomas whispered, "That's Theophilus Phipps, Master Hutton's clerk and secretary. It's his humor to be perverse. Hutton you shall find quite pleasant."

"What's this new paternity you have thrust upon me?" Matthew asked.

"A little invention of my own," Thomas said, his eyes twinkling with amusement. "Since you were so good an actor in Derbyshire, I thought you might play doting father in London. A useful stratagem, I think. Phipps has the longest nose in the Temple. Should he sniff out your present purpose, the whole Temple should know of it before vespers. Discretion is always to be advised. Other than Master Hutton, only you and I will know the real reason you are here."

"I am to be a gentleman, then, for only gentlemen's sons are admitted," Matthew said.

"An advancement in station, over Derbyshire. Be grateful for small blessings."

Matthew smiled and nodded agreeably. The door opened and Phipps came out. He was followed by a student, by his cap and gown, a man in his twenties and strikingly handsome, but at the moment somewhat crestfallen.

"You may go, Master Keable. And next time, use the brain God gave you."

The author of this admonition now appeared over Keable's shoulder. Matthew saw a corpulent personage of about fifty years or thereabouts, with sparse gray hair crowning a large round head in which the eyes seemed almost lost in the rolls of pink flesh. The chastened student passed them without a word or nod. The Treasurer invited Thomas and Matthew in, his large face changing at once from a mirror of stern disapproval to benign hospitality.

The Treasurer's office was large and square, generously windowed and comfortably furnished. A wall opposite was given over to books, row upon row, rising from floor to ceiling. Other walls were hung with portraits of stern-faced men wearing judges' robes and chains of office.

Matthew looked around briefly and then studied the Treasurer himself. When preliminary greetings were past, Hutton said: "Master Stock, that you are skilled in such service as we presently require, I have on the authority of Master Cooke here. His word and also that of Sir Robert Cecil, a special friend of mine."

"Sir Robert does me too much honor if he has commended me."

"Too little if he has not sung your praises to the Heavens," Thomas interjected. "And not just in Chelmsford has Master Stock given good service."

"Quite so, quite so," said Hutton, beaming with approval. "Now, you must understand that you must proceed in this business with haste and secrecy."

"I do, sir."

"Three gentlemen of our Society have met mysterious ends within a fortnight. Should it be made known that these were murders, we'd have blind panic—a cheerless prospect for an otherwise joyous season, to say nothing of the scandal to these hallowed halls, where, if anywhere in England, the law should not be so grievously flouted."

"I understand the first victim left a letter?"

"Edward Litchfield," said Hutton. "Sir Peter Litchfield's son and heir. Foolish boy, quite spoiled. A too-ready recourse to his overly provident father's purse caused him to engage in one escapade after another. The letter claimed that it was the disgrace of his misconduct that was his undoing."

"And so he slit his wrists. May I see the letter?"

"Certainly."

Hutton reached in his desk and withdrew a piece of paper. He handed it to Matthew.

The message written there was brief and composed in a round, childish hand. To Matthew its sentiments seemed forced and calculated, as though written not in a passion of self-loathing, as it proclaimed, but with an ulterior motive:

My disgrace weighs heavily upon my head. Perhaps in Heaven I will receive that grace denied me in this mortal sphere. Forgive one and all the hand raised against itself.

Matthew read the words aloud, after which Hutton said: "Very bad theology, if you ask me. If he really thought suicide a key to Heaven, he was a greater heretic or ignoramus than a prodigal."

Matthew asked where the note was found.

"Stuffed in his pocket," Hutton answered.

"Are you certain the writing is his?"

"I thought so," Hutton said. "Thomas concurred. Yet Sir Peter denied it was written by his son, although he allowed it was a fair imitation."

"Then that point is unsettled," Matthew said. "Of course, the father would prefer to have his son's death interpreted as murder rather than suicide. What other evidence is there that the death was not what it seemed?"

"The razor. It was clutched in Litchfield's left hand."

"And?"

"Litchfield was right-handed," Thomas said.

"We believe the evidence was contrived to make Litchfield's death seem a suicide," Hutton said. "The razor inexpertly positioned in the left hand. The note a forgery."

"We supposed," said Thomas, "that if a stranger had done the murder, he would not have had access to Litchfield's own razor. Nor would he have been familiar with Litchfield's writing. Indeed, would have had no need to make murder seem otherwise. That the razor, a fine piece of cutlery, was left behind at all rules out theft as a motive, even though Litchfield's purse was gone."

Matthew thought for a moment, then said, "Assuming it was murder as you suppose, the killer knew his victim, had access to his razor and his writing, and had good reason to disguise cold-blooded murder as self-slaughter. Suspicion must fall upon his chamberfellow."

"That would have been Peregrinus Monk," said Hutton, looking very grim.

"I assume he has been questioned," Matthew said.

"As much as a dead man can be questioned," Hutton answered. "For he hanged himself the morning after."

"Did he also leave an explanation?"

"A mere phrase scrawled upon the wall. *Sorrow beyond enduring*, it said. That was the phrase, wasn't it, Thomas?"

Thomas said that it was.

"Words that suggest contrition more than melancholy," Matthew observed. "Do you think he killed his friend and then himself from guilt?"

"Perhaps," said Hutton. "The real question is why. Why should he have compounded the crime by disgracing Litchfield's memory with a feigned suicide? These things don't happen without a cause."

Matthew agreed. The heat of passion might occasion manslaughter, even in a well-meaning, law-abiding soul. A case came to mind. One of his own townsmen, and a very decent fellow too, who had covered up his crime for years until later murder had brought it all to light. But Litchfield's murder, if that was what it was, had been cold and calculating. Murder by design. The razor would have had to be procured before, poor Litchfield reduced to insensibility. Then a vicious bloodletting, as in a butcher's shop.

He asked about the third victim.

"Poison," Hutton answered, his round, fleshy countenance even more distraught and disapproving. "One of the benchers, Hugh Giles."

"What manner of poison was it?" Matthew asked.

Hutton shrugged. "The doctor was unsure. No vial or other receptacle was found. The doctor said there were a number of possibilities. Realgar, aquafortis, white arsenic, mercury, powder of diamonds, lapis causticus, cantharides. I mention but a few, being no physician or apothecary. One of the other gentlemen said he thought Giles had received some jellies and tarts for a present, and these could have been contaminated, but not even a crumb was discovered."

"But the doctor was sure it was poison?"

"It was unmistakable. I saw the dead man's face. It was horrible to look upon. A true lesson in the mortality of mankind and the fragility of the flesh."

"And did this Giles, like the others, leave a note behind him?"

Hutton shook his head. "There was none. Only the testimony of those close to him that he had been morose lately. He was of a religious turn, you see. A great reader and reciter of the Sacred Scriptures. Before he died he burned all his papers and many of his books. He is said to have kept a diary in which he wrote regularly. But it evidently was burned too. A heap of ashes was found in the hearth."

"Did he have a chamberfellow?"

"Turner, another bencher, but he's been gone the whole term. At the time of his death, Giles had the chamber to himself."

"If there was no note, why is it supposed Giles took his own life?"

"Only that there was no evidence to the contrary. It was rumored, however, that he was heavily in debt."

"Was the rumor true?" Matthew asked.

The Treasurer looked surprised at the question. "Why, by the mass, I supposed it was. It is not unheard of. What young man has enough money, or the patience to earn it? London is an expensive city, Master Stock, and a lawyer must dress well to be taken seriously."

"Then you don't know for sure that it is true, this matter of debts. Whom he might have owed, how much, and upon what terms?"

Hutton admitted he did not know absolutely. His voice was edged with defensiveness. "After all," he said, "a gentleman may have debts and yet his closest friend be ignorant of the fact. It isn't the kind of thing one broadcasts from the housetops."

"Yet rumor knew it," Matthew observed, as much to himself as to Hutton. "No creditors have come forth since Giles's death demanding their money?"

"Not that I have heard of. What of you, Thomas?"

Thomas agreed. He had heard of no creditors, he said. "The Templars sometimes borrow money from each other. Gambling is a popular, and often dangerous, recreation, you see. It is quite possible that whoever Giles owed erased the slate clean upon his death. It would have been a charitable gesture."

Matthew thought the image of Giles as a debt-ridden gambler mightily incongruous with his reputed piety, and said as much. Hutton grudgingly admitted the incongruity, then supplied Matthew with several instances in which it was otherwise. "Those religiously disposed, to the degree he was, are often afflicted with torments of the flesh, which I suppose compulsive gambling to be," the Treasurer said. "The man was a Puritan of the first water. With talk of disease and death, dressing in sad colors, and speaking lightly of this frail existence."

"Now that I think of it," said Thomas, "I believe I would have called Giles saturnine rather than melancholy. He was respected for his learning. And he knew his Bible, even as Master Hutton has said. But something was eating at him. I noticed it even while I still resided in chambers, before my marriage, and would converse with him familiarly. I considered him my friend, and had invited him to Thorncombe for the nuptials, but he said he couldn't come, and was evasive about the reasons. He said there was something in London he had to see to, and would be no more specific than that. I thought little of it at the time. We were friends, but not such good friends that I should miss him on my wedding day. Besides, I supposed what he had to see to was some suit at law."

Matthew asked if there was anything else then, some piece of evidence not yet disclosed. He looked at the Treasurer, awaiting an answer. Hutton's face was a heavy face of stolid self-government and administrative rectitude, the face of a man who seemed to know passion only by hearsay—a face to be painted and then hung upon the walls like the others around them, serious, intent lawyers' faces. Matthew suspected Hutton's legal practice had concerned wills and deeds, things writ upon paper, and not the passions of the heart, for he had obviously been uncomfortable speaking of these matters.

"As I said," Hutton began, "Giles burned his papers. But not all."

"We found a sort of list," Thomas explained.

"In one of his shoes. Clearly a deliberate concealment. Perhaps he feared it would otherwise be found."

Hutton handed Matthew the new clue. It was a piece of foolscap that had been folded and refolded. On it were written five names in a masculine hand more hurried than careless:

> *Prideaux*
> *Braithwaite*
> *Litchfield*
> *Monk*
> *Giles*

Matthew read the names aloud, unsure as to how to pronounce the first and making the last syllable of the name rhyme with "ducks." He commented, "Three of the five are dead. A sinister proportion. What of the others—this Prideaux and Braithwaite?"

"Prideaux is a mystery," Hutton said. "No one is enrolled in the Middle Temple with that name. As for Braithwaite, he lives—an utter barrister of some accomplishment. I showed him the list and asked him what it meant, but he could make no sense of it. He insisted he had never heard of Prideaux."

"Was he not fearful of being included on a list of mostly dead men?" Matthew asked.

"He made light of it," Hutton said.

"A curious response. I myself would be unnerved to be on the list," Matthew said. "What manner of man is he?"

But the Treasurer was interrupted before he could answer. Phipps stuck his head in to say that Hutton's next appointment waited without.

Hutton nodded, and Phipps closed the door behind him. Hutton said: "Your investigation must be carried out with discretion, as I have said, Master Stock. There can be no public acknowledgment of your purpose. Even among the benchers and readers of the Inn. We three alone will know your true mission here and by whose great authority you act."

"Thomas has already provided me with a guise when he introduced me to your clerk," Matthew said. "I am to be the father of a son who would fain join your Society, and I am here as a scout to see if the Temple be a fit habitation for him."

Hutton smiled broadly and said, "Why, this is an excellent subterfuge. And well within the circumference of belief. For we often have fathers who come here for the very purpose you pretend. Indeed, some fathers who are themselves Templars share their chambers with their own sons. I will have Phipps make arrangements."

Hutton rose, signaling that the interview was at an end, and went to the door. Matthew heard him exchanging words with Phipps. In a few moments he was back again. "It's done, Master Stock. Your accommodations are provided. There is but one vacant chamber and it shall be yours as long as necessary."

Hutton's face seemed troubled. Matthew guessed the cause. "My chamber is the one previously occupied by the dead men?"

"Yes," Hutton said sympathetically. "I'm sorry. I would gladly house you elsewhere were there room. But you see, we are a large company of several hundred souls, like rabbits in a warren."

Matthew asked why the chamber had not been claimed by another, since space was at such a premium.

"Ah," Hutton said as he escorted Matthew and Thomas to the door. "The Kingdom of Fear is more ancient than that of Reason, and it bears greater sway. But surely a man of your practical experience has no fear of ghosts? Besides, it will put you in the very gullet of the mystery. I assure you the chamber is well placed, both convenient to the Hall and commanding a fine view of the river and Temple garden. In spring and summer they are quite lovely."

Matthew thought about the garden. He had passed through it on the way to the Treasurer's office. It might be lovely indeed in the spring and summer, but it was now winter, and viewing it would be pleasing only if one exercised a considerable amount of imagination. As for ghosts, Matthew had no fear of the dead in their narrow subterranean rooms. It was the living that he feared—a cold-blooded murderer not content that his victims die, but that they also be disgraced as suicides. He said to Hutton, "Only tell me how I shall find the chamber appointed me and I will shift for myself."

4

Thomas insisted on walking Matthew to his rooms, then that they stop on the way to view the Great Hall.

Matthew agreed it was an impressive structure. Its lines were austere and vaguely ecclesiastical, with high-pitched timber roof, tower, buttresses. The entrance was imposing. The whole obviously built at enormous cost—and, of course, far more costly to build now than then. Thomas said: "Edmund Plowden, a distinguished son of our House, supervised its construction. Plowden was Treasurer in those days. A good thirty years ago. After the Church of the Knights, the Great Hall is our most famous monument."

As Thomas steered him in, a spacious and stately chamber met Matthew's eye. It was a good forty feet in breadth, somewhat more in height, and twice forty feet in length. It was lighted by six clerestory windows on each side and one at either end, and above was an open hammer beam ceiling of intricate workmanship. At the far end of the Hall was a richly carved screen, a dais, and upon it a long table running crosswise. The lumber for it, Thomas presently explained, had been grown in Windsor Forest, a gift of the Queen.

Lengthwise against the walls were more long tables, leaving the center of the huge chamber open, except for a fireplace there, the smoke of which escaped from a lantern in the roof. Upon the floor, rushes had been thickly laid, and above the wainscoting on the walls were somber portraits, heraldic memorials, clumps of holly hung for the season.

Thomas rattled off dates, names—distinguished members of the House, or their guests, sharers of feasts and theatricals. Matthew grew impatient. The names meant little to him, the dates less. He was not impressed. For all its grandeur, the cavernous Hall was uninviting. It was not *his* England he viewed—his England of towns with single streets, village greens, neighbors one knew by name. He was impatient to begin his work, to have it done. He had not stayed in London to see the sights.

The two men left the Hall and crossed a quadrangle to come to another building. It was very long, with ivy-covered walls and arched doorways and windows. "The bulk of our Society have chambers here," Thomas said.

Gowned students came and went. To Matthew they all seemed very young, many mere boys with cheeks and complexions made ruddy by raw winds and cold. The students talked and laughed and jostled each other, and Matthew concluded that the deaths of their fellows had made little impact on them.

The chambers that had been those of the dead young men and were now to be Matthew's consisted of a sitting room or study and a bedchamber, each with its own fireplace, but very meagerly furnished. Apologetically, Thomas explained that the members of the Inn were responsible for furnishing their own lodgings, and that although some of the Templars lived quite sumptuously, the greater number lived simply, sometimes without servants to attend them.

Matthew looked around the rooms and felt alienated by them. You don't belong here, they said. And in his heart he knew they were right. Cold rooms they were, despite the fire that had been laid and was burning; rooms empty even of the spirits of the dead. He shuddered. His attention was drawn to the open beams on the ceiling. He turned to Thomas.

Thomas said solemnly, "Monk used his bed sheet, which he shredded into strips. He fashioned a sort of rope and then hanged himself with it."

"Who found the body?"

"His servant. A man named Griffin."

"Is he about?"

"Monk's father took him home with him."

"And the words on the wall?"

Thomas pointed to the wall opposite the windows. There was nothing written there now. The wall had been scrubbed. Matthew remembered the words, *Sorrow beyond enduring*, Monk had written. But what species of grief had they expressed—an unbearable loss, or guilt at having murdered and maligned a friend?

Matthew walked over to the window and looked out.

The Treasurer had been right. The window provided a good view of the garden. In the distance he could see the Thames and the Temple Stairs. Had Monk looked out and remembered what he had done and been overcome? Maybe he had thought about Litchfield as he kicked the stool from beneath his feet and swung there, his feet dangling inches above the floor. Or maybe Monk had been hoisted up against his will. That was possible too.

Someone knocked, and Thomas went to answer.

Matthew was surprised to see it was Keable, the same young man Master Hutton had been disciplining earlier. With him was another student.

Thomas was quick with introductions. "Gentlemen, may I present Master Matthew Stock of Chelmsford, a worthy gentleman clothier of that town whose son is considering joining our fellowship. And these, Master Stock, are Masters Keable and Wilson."

Matthew shook each of his visitors' hands and studied their faces. The one called Wilson looked to be about twenty. He was very tall and angular, with wispy red hair sticking out beneath his Templar cap, and his chin and nose disfigured with a crop of pimples. He had large ears that stood outright from his head, and the guileless countenance of a curate. His companion, Keable, was indeed endowed with extraordinary personal beauty. His clear blue eyes were striking, his jaw marvelously sculptured; his skin was taut and bronzed. He was of middle height but broad-shouldered, and he carried himself with the easy confidence of one who knows that he is admired by all who see him. The only detriment to his appearance, as far as Matthew could tell, was his expression, which was somewhat proud and disdainful even when he was speaking pleasantly, as now.

"We heard voices within," Wilson said, "and came to have a look."

"We thought we might have a new neighbor and we wished to make his acquaintance," Keable added.

"We didn't suppose the chamber would be tenanted so soon, given what happened," Wilson said. He looked from Matthew to his companion, Keable, and then back again.

"Master Cooke has told me what happened here," Matthew said, sensing Wilson's discomfort and suspecting it was superstitious dread that had brought Wilson hither rather than a desire to be hospitable to a newcomer. "Suicide is an awful thing—both for him who commits it and the family who must live with the disgrace of it. Yet I fear no ghosts and will rest easy in the bed yonder."

Wilson gave a little laugh, and his ruddy cheeks flushed. "If you can endure the tumult about you, sir. I pray you find these lodgings . . . to your liking—and to your son's as well."

"Master Stock's son is a quiet, retiring young man," Thomas said, glancing sideways at Matthew. "Master Stock is unsure of his son's capacity to endure the rigors of study."

Keable made a droll face, and Wilson laughed outright.

Keable said: "Well, sir, there are in truth rigors to be endured, and such we face at this moment with all the House preparing for the Christmas revels. I doubt any of us will crack a book until Twelfth Night's past. Between now and then we rehearse our parts."

"These gentlemen are preparing an interlude—a masque," Thomas explained. "Marry, these masculine forms you see before you will upon the enactment thereof play women's parts—"

"Not I," Keable protested. "I'm a satyr."

"I beg your pardon, Master Keable," replied Thomas good-humoredly. "But you, Wilson, are a woman, are you not?"

Wilson flushed again, and admitted that he was. "A besieged virgin," he said, "afloat in farthingale and decked with rouged cheeks and fine periwigs to excite the lust of their fellow students."

"Whose lusts are quite excited enough already," Keable interjected, and they all laughed. "Will you join us for dinner, Master Stock?"

"Yes, Master Stock," said Wilson. "Pray, don't prove a reluctant guest."

Matthew had wanted to ask Thomas more questions about Monk and Litchfield, but he knew there was no way to avoid so pressing an invitation. Besides, he thought he might learn something about the murders, and despite his generous breakfast earlier, he was hungry again.

Theophilus Phipps stuck his head into the Treasurer's door and blinked, owl-like. "With your permission, sir, I'll go to dinner."

"Go to dinner, Phipps," Hutton said, looking up from a book to see that it was his clerk who had spoken and then turning his eyes down to the page again. "Oh, Phipps, one moment."

"Sir?"

"You will make sure that Matthew Stock has all he requires while he resides with us?"

"Why, he shall be treated in princely fashion," Phipps said. "A medium-hard bed and the excellent fellowship of us Templars."

"He may make inquiries—about the House. If so, he should be answered readily and truthfully."

"Sir?"

"I mean, Phipps, if he asks to see the Minutes, let him."

"The Minutes, Master Hutton?" said Phipps. "Well, he's a most doting and officious parent indeed to commit to such dull reading, for all there is names, dates, and sums. Most fathers are content if their offspring have no lice or whores in chamber."

"Just do what I say, Phipps," Hutton answered dryly.

"So I shall, sir."

"Get you to dinner, Phipps."

"I'm already gone, sir."

The Treasurer didn't care about dinner, although he was, under normal circumstances, a robust feeder, as his generous girth attested. The Chelmsford constable's visit had upset him—both its purpose and the man himself.

Hutton set his eyes again to his book. It was a work he had been trying to finish for months, a learned treatise on the Roman law. But as his eyes swept the page, its author's Latin seemed an unintelligible tongue. Hutton knew his vision was deteriorating, the result of years of reading by dim candlelight. But that did not explain his present difficulty. The truth was that he could not focus his mind. The murders preoccupied him.

In the face of Stock's impudent questions, he had tried to assume an air of control and imperturbability. He had tried to mask his alarm—and his humiliation. For it grieved him that he, a man of learning and authority, who called every Privy Councillor by his first name and dined with the Queen once a quarter, should be required to submit his great problem to a mere country constable.

Robert Cecil's recommendation of Stock, however, had brooked no denial. It was not that Hutton had been ordered to engage Stock's help; it was that he simply had no reasonable grounds other than his own vanity for refusing it. And Hutton knew that Cecil—a man of great power whom Hutton was honored to call a friend—would be insulted if every courtesy was not extended to his special agent.

Yet if Hutton was to have official help, why could it not have been someone of his own choosing? Hutton would have preferred a man of breeding. In sum, another lawyer, distinguished in his profession and subtle in language and manner. Perhaps a former student of the Temple. Yes, that was it! A man who knew the Temple's ancient customs and traditions and honored them and would revere the reputation of the House even as he revered his own personal honor. Someone who understood the value of discretion—

The Treasurer shuddered as he thought of the word spreading through London. Murders in the Middle Temple! Already he imagined the veiled glee with which the other Inns would receive the news. The hypocritical professions of horror, the self-righteous congratulation that they themselves were free from such a plague.

A plague that, if brought to light, would reflect badly on himself, who was not without ambition for higher honor in the realm.

His book lay open on his lap as he stared out of the window recalling every word of his recent interview with Stock. Had he not been informative, courteous, amiable—all to a fault? Had he given the country constable cause to complain to Cecil that he had been unused? He had not.

Of course, some of Stock's questions had been impertinent. That business of Giles's debts. Was Stock trying to prove his mettle by implying Hutton's negligence in accepting rumor as fact? But what nonsense! What was so unreasonable about assuming that Giles had debts? Didn't practically everyone in London?

He turned his eyes to the page and forced his willful brain to engage the words there. He read a few lines but understood nothing and felt a queer prickly sensation in his legs. The fire on the hearth cracked and smoked, but still Hutton felt a chill. He thought of the dead men—cold now in their graves. He thought of Giles, whom he had known and even liked a little. And he grew even colder and his legs pricklier.

About five o'clock, Hutton having retired to his privy lodgings, Theophilus Phipps, driven by long-restrained curiosity, put down his pen and, finding himself alone and not likely to be disturbed, slipped into the Treasurer's office, leaving the door slightly ajar so that he could hear if anyone entered his outer office. Quietly and efficiently he sifted through the clutter on the Treasurer's desk, contemptuous of the disorder there. It was not long before he found what he sought. He had taken note of the seal of the letter when it had arrived several days before, and having remembered it, now thought it not unlikely to have something to do with the unusual privileges that were to be accorded to a mere nobody from Chelmsford.

He opened the heavy parchment that had been folded so carefully, enjoying as he did the richness of its texture, the fine scent of perfume in the glob of wax that had ensured its privacy.

Phipps's eyes moved quickly past the predictably fulsome honorifics of the introduction to come to the letter's burden: *I have been asked by Master Thomas Cooke to write you of Matthew Stock of Chelmsford who in divers times past has done service good and valuable in my name and may be depended on to do the like in any inquiry into the late and most lamentable murders in your Society.*

The letter was signed by Sir Robert Cecil himself.

Phipps's hand shook a little as he read the name, and his heart beat at an accelerated rate. He reread the line *late and most lamentable murders,* and the phrase stuck in his craw.

He refolded the letter and put it where he had found it,

removing all signs of his tampering. He went at once to his own lodgings, and bolting the door behind him, he fed the cat he kept some scraps he had in his pocket, laid a fire, and then sat before it in a kind of trance. The cat came and curled up in his lap and went to sleep, but Phipps didn't move. Not for a long time. Then suddenly he roused himself, shifted the cat onto the floor, and went to change from his scholar's gown into a new satin doublet with ruff collar. He perfumed himself and then selected from his wardrobe an expensive hat a courtier might have envied, fur-lined and high-crowned with a brave feather. He looked at himself in a looking glass.

His nose was a little too straight and assertive for his tastes, and his lips wanted that voluptuous fullness he so much admired in certain of his friends, but it was not at all a bad face, especially his pallor, which Phipps found very becoming and infinitely superior to sunburned complexions.

Well pleased with his appearance, he donned his best cloak and set forth. A lesser man might have cringed before the prospect of an official investigation of the Templar suicides. Investigations, after all, often went awry. The wrong man was sometimes accused. Then, too, investigations often disclosed a good bit of dirt simply by accident.

But Theophilus Phipps was undaunted. A plague upon the Chelmsford constable, he thought, and the ponderous tub-of-guts Treasurer, and even the great Cecil himself, whom many scorned as the Queen's little pygmy.

5

Dinner in the Great Hall was a disappointment to Matthew. The food was Lenten fare, belying all he had told Joan about Templar feasting. He sat, forsaken and miserable, with Wilson and Keable while they wrangled over some abstruse legal question. Even before the two men were finished eating, Matthew excused himself. He had to return to his host's house in the City to gather his things.

Joan laughed when she heard about Matthew's "son." But then she looked at him shrewdly and said: "I'faith, husband. I wist not you had a son. By some other wife, I warrant, since I recall no male child of my body."

"An offspring of expedience, not nature," he said. "No

daughters are admitted to study, as reason dictates they should not be. The law is most unwomanly work."

"Were it more womanly, I trow, then it would be less work," Joan said pertly. "And pray do not rest your cause on reason. Say *custom*, rather, for I know not why a woman should not be as litigious and full of subtle shifts as any man, if she but put her mind to it."

Matthew laughed and kissed her on the cheek. "Well spoken, Joan. You are a most resolute defender of your sex. I'll give you this, if during my stay in the Temple I find one brain as nimble as yours, I'll dress myself in woman's garb and parade before the Inn's gates with a placard proclaiming woman's right to study law. Yes, and practice it too."

She said she'd hold him to his promise. Then she asked: "But how long will this business keep you? I'll sorely miss you as my bedfellow. Will not you be cold of nights and long for my hugs and kisses?"

"Ah, as sailors long for land when they're three years at sea."

"Good Lord, I hope you do not intend to stay *that* long!"

"Not so long. And I *will* miss your hugs and kisses."

"And my earnest admonitions that you bundle up when you go abroad in this foul season?"

"Yes, oh yes."

"And my sound counsel when you stand doubtful of your course?"

"As much as hugs and kisses."

"Liar," she protested, casting upon him a cynical eye.

"Nay, no liar, but a plain, honest fellow who knows only how to tell the truth. Upon my oath, I'll tell you what I'll miss."

"Say it. My cooking, doubtless."

"Ha, wrong again, Joan. Rather your sweet face as much as I am gone from you."

They kissed again, husband and wife, for they were as private and merry as could be in the fine bedchamber they had been provided in Thomas Cooke's house, and far removed from the somber halls of the Temple where three young gentlemen had met untimely ends.

The shabby tavern was not an establishment that would have earned the patronage of Theophilus Phipps had necessity not deemed otherwise. It was located within hailing distance of the river and at the end of a narrow, filthy lane with an open sewer running down its middle. The house itself was very old and braced up on either side by newer buildings. It had four full stories, the upper of which extended out beyond the first, two bow windows, and a weathered sign that creaked on rusty hinges when the wind blew. A careful eye could still discern the image of the bird that had given the tavern its name, but the creature represented had a predatory look, more like hawk or falcon than seabird, and whether this impression stemmed from the artist's ineptitude or was merely the effect of time and weather was impossible to know.

Now that the Gull came within Phipps's view, he made an expression of distaste as he might have done had his delicate nose been thrust above a pile of rotten herring. Dim light showed from the bow windows and even dimmer illumination from the upper stories, but he could hear the sound of raucous male voices from within. It was well past nine, and the evening's riot was in full swing.

Phipps adjusted his fine hat and prepared himself to enter. He knew whom he would find within. The clientele of the tavern were a motley crew—idle apprentices fearless of their masters' threats, crippled veterans of the wars and foreign sailors, beggars who had found a few pennies for a cup of ale or cheap wine. And, of course, young gentlemen of the Inns of Court, who, in passing their prodigal hours in its dissolute environs, saved themselves the expense of a boat ride across the Thames to the even more depraved Southwark stews.

For it was no secret—except perhaps from the officials of the City who preferred houses of the Gull's character to confine themselves to the outskirts—that the tavern was no better than a common brothel. Ned Hodge, the master of the house, was a quondam pirate who, if his own boast was not a tissue of lies, had once been marooned on a desert island with only the bodies of his dead shipmates for meat. Hodge was fond of telling the story to every new customer of the Gull—especially the young gentlemen of the Middle Temple, for whom Hodge's self-confessed cannibalism raised some interesting legal questions. This same Hodge had an old, fantastically wigged slattern in his employ who kept house for him upstairs, and a bevy of young female lodgers who resided there on dubious terms and had many "friends" among the customers.

These women served all comers but preferred the young lawyers. Their preference was no mystery. The lawyers paid well for their pleasures and were more likely to be free of disease and foul linen, qualities not to be despised even in so grand a city as London was. These same women went out of their way to curry favor with the students. They troubled themselves to learn the names and the places whence they came; they called them "young sir" and "Your Grace," when he so honored was no greater than a linen draper's brat.

It was one such denizen of the Gull whom Phipps had come to see. His purpose was not illicit love, for Phipps's preferences were otherwise, a poorly kept secret at the Inn;

nor was it to consult upon some legal matter, for Phipps despised the law, admiring only those who practiced it, reaping where they had not sown, and making social discord, the bane of ordinary mortals, into a fruitful field. His purpose rather was information—information about one of the young men who even now was the subject of the Chelmsford constable's most secret inquiries.

For the truth was that at the Temple, Theophilus Phipps supplemented his modest income by lending money for a hefty profit, prompting more than one of his clients to refer to him as the "little fair Jewess of Temple Lane," and denigrating, in one fell stroke, his complexion, effeminacy, and usury. Edward Litchfield had been one such client—indeed, in Phipps's view, a quite wonderful one—ever desperate, greedy, reckless, burrowing deeper and deeper in debt, his only security being the oft-repeated and, to Phipps, quite intriguing assurance that there was more than the means to repay in the offing. Some project vaguely alluded to, not to be extracted from the young man for all Phipps could do to have at it. *There's great wealth at hand, Master Phipps, but give me leave to come to it.* So had been Litchfield's words.

For some reason, Phipps had believed. In the course of his surreptitious moneylending, Phipps had heard many such stories, yet Phipps believed.

And now Litchfield's murder made the young man's boast even more plausible. But Litchfield was dead, Phipps deprived not only of repayment but of God knew what other rewards that might have come from knowledge of Litchfield's secret project.

Phipps was determined to know the truth.

Now, Phipps took it as a matter of principle that no man keeps counsel from the woman he beds, for although he have the resolution of Samson, yet some Delilah will wheedle the secret out. And Litchfield, a callow youth weakened by dissipation and hungry for approval, was no Samson. And so Phipps suspected that a certain whore of the Gull had been privy to Litchfield's scheme of enrichment.

The question was, would she reveal the same to Phipps?

Inside, Phipps surveyed the scene, the rude, obnoxious crowd, with disdain and loathing. Seeing several faces he recognized but not wishing to be seen himself, he made for the stairs that led to the upper story.

Phipps ascended, slowly like an angel in a morality play. On the landing was an old woman in a red periwig. He experienced a moment's revulsion at the wrinkled face and thanked his stars for his own smooth complexion, as fair as a girl's.

He placed two coins in the outstretched palm and was gratified to see by the woman's expression that it sufficed. He named her whom he sought, and the woman nodded toward the end of the corridor. "Last door on the right. Enjoy thyself, sweeting," the old woman called after him as Phipps, with grim determination, set out for the place where he should have the benefit of his bargain.

"I know what I shall do to remedy these complaints," Joan said later when they were undressed for bed and Matthew had leaned over to snuff the candles out.

"What, pray?"

"Why, I'll dress myself as a man—in cape and gown— and go with you to the Temple to be this son Thomas Cooke has conjured up."

She heard his chuckle in the darkness. Annoyed, she said, "What, don't you think I appear young enough?"

"By God, you do, Joan," Matthew said placatingly. "As youthful as when we wed near twenty years ago. Yet you are too much woman to appear a man, too fleshed out in bosom, beam, and stern. Moreover—"

"Hold, husband!" she said sharply, wishing the candle were still lighted so she could look him in the eye. "Not another word. I may be no famished figure of famine, but neither am I plump as a partridge. I've lost a good quarter of myself these months from home and my own cooking. Not to mention the devastation of my illness in Derbyshire, where I almost died! Besides, not every young man is as thin as a rail. Why, consider Marcus Gridly, who keeps shop on High Street. He's no hitching post! Then there's William Tower, our good neighbor's son, who weighs as much as any two of his age."

"True, Joan. I only meant that no man could find in your countenance anything but a woman's soul, for it is not clothes alone that make the sex but the soul of one or the other."

"Humph! Sweet flattery to save yourself from my just wrath," she answered, embracing him, loving his firm grasp and the warmth of his body pressed against hers.

"Nay, the naked truth, I protest."

"Spoken like a true philosopher—or a husband desperate to find his way to paradise."

"To find my way there, I'll flatter or philosophize."

"You need do neither, husband," she said huskily. "But be still now and take your fill of me. Then sleep, for the thought of our parting grieves me to the quick."

Afterward, when her husband's soft snores told her he was asleep, Joan lay awake worrying. Their bedtime banter had provided her with only a temporary suspension of her concern, for she had weighed the evidence he had from the Treasurer's mouth, and now it seemed to her beyond doubt that the Templar suicides could be nothing less than subtle murders.

And what risk did Matthew run in meddling in such bloody matters? A father of a young Templar presumptive, indeed! A pleasant fiction, she granted, but the sons of the Inn were gentlemen's sons, high-bred, learned, and proud like their worthy fathers. Could Matthew—good-natured, intelligent, but a simple clothier—succeed in the impersonation?

And if he failed—what then?

The price of exposure would be more than a mere failure to accomplish his mission. Matthew might be murdered too—his death dressed up to seem self-slaughter!

As fearful as the specter of these dangers was, Joan knew she had no power to deny her husband's will. She could not drag him home to Chelmsford by her apron strings, or even bribe him with her favors to stay out of harm's way. He was too far at sea in his perilous enterprise to turn toward shore again.

Tossing restlessly, she prayed she might put the fearful matter from her brain, prayed that soothing sleep would come and in its wake the reinvigoration of day, when all such fears dissolved like the thin veneer of frost.

And then before she was aware, she fell asleep and dreamed.

In her dream she sat before a large, finely wrought desk like the one Matthew had once seen in Theobalds, Cecil's great country estate. The desk was heaped with books and papers, letters bearing seals, writing implements. Directly before her was a heavy tome with yellowed pages open to her view. She strained to read, but try as hard as she might, she could not decipher a single line. She knew no Latin, but she knew its look, and this was not it. Nor was it alien Greek, which she had also seen in her time. The words upon the page seemed like her own tongue, yet although individual words made sense, their sum was incomprehensible.

Her ignorance intensified her growing alarm. She felt she must know what the words meant, where she was and why. Then a new anxiety gripped her. She suddenly sensed the presence of someone standing behind her, looking down over her shoulder.

She dared not draw her eyes from the page to see who the intruder was. Then she heard a deep, hollow voice reciting.

The words recited were the words on the page, she was sure of it. But the voice gave them no further meaning than what she had previously determined.

Then there was silence; soon after, she awoke.

She awoke to the bells of the City and a cold, gray morning. She looked outside, and she could see frost on the sloping rooftops and on the chimneys.

Fearing that her dream had some prophetic content, she revealed all to Matthew as they dressed and he completed his packing. He agreed it was a strange dream and then offered an interpretation.

"The book was a book of law, which you do not understand any more than I. He who read behind you was undoubtedly a lawyer or judge. I see no mystery there, Joan."

"Perhaps not, Matthew, and yet I felt such a vexation that I could not read a jot. And I have a lingering fear that the dream has more significance than you suppose."

"And so it may, Joan. Time will tell. As for now, one last embrace before I go."

She withheld neither affection nor tears at her husband's parting. She watched him from the window of the house until he disappeared around a corner.

Then she sat thinking for a long time—about the dream and where Matthew was to go and what she herself might do. At last she concocted a plan of her own—a plan that, while it might not take her within the Temple gates, would at least bring her to its curtilage. Her spirits quickened at the opportunity—and at the danger.

6

ater that morning, Joan had a long talk with Frances Cooke. It was warm and pleasant in the parlor, and despite the difference in their ages and stations in life, the two women talked familiarly. But when Joan announced her intention to go out alone on the streets, Frances was alarmed. London streets were unsafe, she said, full of thieves, cutpurses, bullies, and obnoxious, rowdy apprentices. She began a graphic recital of recent misfortunes involving unwary strangers in the City.

Frances was nineteen, slender, well featured. Her long, flaxen hair was her glory. Daughter of a baronet and before her marriage one of the Royal Maids to whom the old

Queen had shown great kindnesses, Frances retained much of the aristocratic air of her former position, although as the wife of a younger son of a mere knight, she had fallen somewhat in the social order.

"A servant *must* accompany you," Frances said firmly. "Robert, our groom, knows London like the back of his hand. And London is not, after all, as your Chelmsford is, where everyone knows his neighbor and no doors are locked."

Joan was about to answer that Frances grossly overestimated the civic virtue of country towns, but kept silent. With dismay she thought of Robert. Tall, gaunt, solemn as a gravedigger, Robert had, by Thomas Cooke's account, been in the family for years. Joan could hardly imagine a less pleasing guide for her excursion.

She would have much preferred the company of Edward Bastian. Edward was Thomas Cooke's manservant. A solid, well-spoken youth, Edward had proved his mettle in Derbyshire and had temporarily absented himself from service to fetch his wife and child from there. Lacking Edward, Joan would have preferred to go alone. She felt perfectly capable of navigating the streets of London. Had she not done it before, and under perilous circumstances? Let some brawler or pickpurse or rude apprentice lay a hand upon her and she'd show him what he deserved!

Yet she recognized, now, that concession to Frances Cooke's anxiety for her safety would become her as a houseguest and friend, and she made no further protest, while Frances, satisfaction writ large upon her face, summoned the dour groom.

Robert had wanted to know, quite naturally, where Joan was bound since he had been instructed by his master's young wife to accompany Mistress Stock. But Joan, true to her nature, took offense at the question.

"Why, sirrah, I am bound where I will. If you care to accompany me, you may."

"My mistress bids me go," Robert answered with frigid dignity, "and so I shall." He made a sour expression that implied disapproval of country women who thought very highly of themselves but whose birth was no better than his.

Joan looked up at Robert. She could see he was very angry, and not wishing to make him an enemy, she relented a little. "Very good. I wish to see the sights of the City, if it please you—the Exchange, or Bedlam, where the lunatics are kept. Or the China houses."

"It looks like rain," Robert complained, his long face very pale and his lips thin and censorious.

"And so it does," Joan said, looking at the glowering sky above the rooftops. "Yet we both shall live despite it."

Joan wore the cloak Matthew had purchased for her just a week before. It fit her very snugly. She also wore a fur hat, leather gloves, and a fine woolen scarf. "Come now, or it will be suppertime before we set out."

Joan was halfway to her destination—the Middle Temple—before she realized she had lost her escort somewhere in the crowded street behind her. She didn't stop to look for him; she pressed on, in the direction she had been given, energized by a growing excitement.

She recognized the place well enough when she saw it, and what little doubt she may have had that it was the Temple itself was resolved by a kind stranger who confirmed it was so. She could see also some of the students in their gowns coming and going, but she saw no women among them. It was as Matthew had said, a seeming male preserve. She envied him his admission to such a place and his manly freedom. It was not that she would keep company with lawyers, but to be excluded by reason of her sex! There was an offense hard to endure.

She turned from the gates that, while open, seemed to shut her out, and contemptuous of masculine arrogance, she walked a few yards farther, then turned down a lane at the end of which was the riverbank.

There she stood for a while looking across to the other side. At a distance she could see the houses of Southwark, the round shape of the Globe, steeples of churches elbow to elbow with bawdy houses and taverns of the most disreputable sort, all veiled in the dirty brown smoke of wood and coal fires. Then she turned again, and closer at hand she saw the Temple Stairs, where, according to Matthew's account, young Edward Litchfield's bloodless corpse had been discovered.

Seeing the place, Joan could well believe the death was murder. The Stairs seemed an unlikely scene for suicide. Why walk forth on a cold November night to do that which might as well and more efficiently be done before one's own fire? But Edward Litchfield had gone out, driven by some unknown purpose. What?

She stood a long time in silent witness to the scene, until, overcome at last by the morbidity of her meditation, she shook the image off and prepared to leave. Disappointed by the fruits of her morning's excursion, uncertain in retrospect as to what, after all, she had hoped to accomplish, she started back up the lane but had no sooner taken several steps than her attention was drawn to another who had evidently been sharing her view of the river.

It was a woman in her twenties, Joan judged, garbed in a cloak not so fine as her own but of good solid stuff and showing enough of her face so that Joan recognized in it more than a little to admire. This young woman had an uncommon beauty—arched brows, a finely shaped nose, full lips, and a soft, round chin. The two women exchanged glances and nodded, and then the woman moved up the lane, turned a corner, and was lost to Joan's view.

A few drops of rain began to fall, and since she had no wish to get wetter than she needed to be, Joan decided to find some shelter and perhaps something to eat, for the morning jaunt had given her an enormous appetite. She went the way the woman had gone, turning down a narrow side street, and although it was a shabby neighborhood she had entered, she went in the first public house she came to.

The tavern was very busy for midday, a noisy, dissolute crowd whose company she would have scorned had not the drizzle become a light rain. There were trencher tables all round and hardly a stool to sit upon, but she managed to find a place by the window, and after some time trying to catch the attention of a servingman, she ordered a hot caudle and some bread and cheese. She waited impatiently for what seemed an hour before the servingman returned to present her with her drink and his regret that there was neither bread nor cheese in the larder, for he said the storm had driven such a multitude into the Gull that they had consumed every bit.

"The Gull?" she asked, reaching in her purse to pay for the ale and thinking it ridiculous that a business establishment should be so poorly provisioned for the likely instance of foul weather.

"The tavern's name," said the servingman, who seemed a pleasant enough sort, she decided.

Since Joan's arrival, even more customers had straggled in, coughing, dripping wet, and cursing the weather and greeting their friends in the same breath. Outside, the rain had turned to sleet, and although it could not have been more than three in the afternoon, it seemed already to be getting dark. Inside, the almost exclusively male company that had met her eye when she entered was now diluted by a handful of women. Most were blowsy, rough women of the neighborhood, possibly even the washingwomen Matthew had said were allowed access to the chambers at the Temple. The women were holding their own with the men, laughing and talking, trading jibes and insults, but all in a rough good humor as though they all had known each other for years. There were also young women, some very young, shabbily dressed with bare necks and low-cut bodices and much plump pink flesh showing, to the delight of the leering men. These were going from table to table and seemed to know the men who sat there and treated them familiarly and called to them by names, greeting them with kisses and squeezes and indecent touchings so as to leave Joan with little doubt what sort of women they were. "Filthy tavern and brothel too," she almost said aloud, viewing her situation now in its true light and beginning to regret she had ever ventured abroad, much less taken so precarious a refuge as the Gull.

In the next moment Joan's attention was drawn to a newcomer descending from the upper parts of the house. To her amazement she saw that it was the very young woman she had seen earlier at the riverbank—she who had caught Joan's attention by her beauty. As this same woman made her appearance, a chorus of rough male voices cried out her name in greeting.

"Why, it's Nan, our own Nan."

"Good evening, Nan, what news?"

"Give us a song, Nan, or a kiss at least."

Shocked to find the woman she had admired a denizen of so loathsome a place, Joan gaped, while Nan, returning the various greetings of the tavern's customers, laughed and swung her hips provocatively. She was dressed very much as the other women of the Gull, in a loose-fitting smock that left her white neck and much of her breast open to view. She swaggered toward the bar and threw her arms around the shoulders of several of the unsavory types lounging there, while from other tables men began to move toward her as though there were something quite wonderful in her very proximity.

But Joan was disgusted—disgusted by the lechery, the drunkenness—and dismayed, too, by the spectacle of beauty abused by so foul a condition. She rose to go, but had no sooner taken a step toward the door than she felt a rough hand upon her shoulder.

She looked upward to see a tall sailor looming over her. He was a large, barrel-chested man with round, unshaven face and cruel eyes, and he smiled down at her with a grin that made her blood run cold. He smelled of fish and sweat, and she would have recoiled from him even if he had not taken the liberty of touching her as he now was.

"Mind my company, mistress?"

"I prefer my own," she returned sharply, fixing him with a cold stare of disdain.

"Oh, do you?" he said. "But I prefer yours, so will join you without your leave. I see there's room here."

The man plunked himself down on the stool and then drew Joan into his lap, squeezing her wrist painfully. His thick speech, vacant stare, and foul breath testified to his drunkenness. Disapproval of his impertinent touching of her had now become something more than annoyance. She struggled to free herself, protesting his bad manners and fishy smell, which seemed to grow stronger as he exerted himself. "Don't be unkind, my girl," he said. "I don't like it when my company is scorned. I suppose you think yourself too fine for me—or worse, that I have no money. Well, my purse is full enough, and I'll offer you as much as any man here, for although you seem a bit long in the tooth, yet you are a plump, juicy wench."

Thrusting his hand inside Joan's cloak, he began fondling her breast as though he had a husband's rights. The insult shook her from her previous immobility. She twisted herself from his grip and, standing, swung at him with all of her strength. The blow caught him on the jaw and sent him reeling backward. Her eyes blazing, she said: "How dare you, you dog-face! I am a respectable woman, no whore. Here in these vile surroundings for refuge, not for vice, as you seem to suppose. Nor would I give my body to you were you the last man on earth."

Joan spat out these words as the sailor struggled to his feet, helped by his friends, as unsavory a bunch as he. They were glaring at Joan as though the man she struck had received an undeserved blow. Standing now, the sailor unleashed a flood of insults aimed at her, vile names, some of which were sailors' terms she had never heard before, although she had no doubt from his angry, twisted visage and tone of voice that each was as degrading as the next. Meanwhile, the sailor's friends joined in the abuse, calling her proud slattern and greasy whore, and other filthy names that made her quiver with rage and almost forget the danger she faced from the sailor's violence. Now she hoped for nothing more than to be revenged on these foulmouthed, mean-spirited creatures glowering at her.

"A fine lot are you all to combine your strengths against a lone woman. Base cowards and knaves too! Is there no one here to give me aid in my distress?"

She had no sooner made her request than it was answered. Nan came pushing her way through the crowd and began to appeal to the sailor and his friends to leave their insults and go back to the bar, where she promised them a round of drinks at her own expense. Nan flattered, cajoled; Joan could see what a favorite Nan was. Manipulating, without threat of force or violence, she could have her way, simply by that voice, that face, the body moving beneath the gown.

Yet while the obnoxious sailor's friends were moved by Nan's persuasions, the sailor himself was not so easily placated. With an expression that clearly revealed how deeply his pride had been hurt by Joan's rebuff and blow, he cursed Nan, the Gull, the whole female race. He shoved Nan aside and made for Joan.

Joan grabbed the stool, thrust it outward defensively. One of its legs jabbed the sailor hard in the groin. He howled and doubled over with pain.

Joan stared incredulously at what her quick thinking had wrought; the sailor remained bent, like a broken limb, clutching his groin, his face hideous with rage. But she knew she had stopped him for the moment only; he would be at her again, no question about it, and this time the knife he wore in his belt would be in his hand.

She would have run for the door had the crowd of onlookers not pressed her so closely.

The sight of the sailor undone by a mere woman provoked great hilarity on all sides, even from the sailor's shipmates who before had been so sympathetic to his cause. They laughed and slapped each other and the victim of Joan's stool on the back, as though he were suffering from a piece of meat lodged in his throat, and in all the laughter and jostling a candle was upset on a nearby table and a fire started in the rushes.

Cries of "Fire!" mixed with the raucous laughter as some of the tavern's customers scrambled over tables for the door while others, immobilized by drunkenness, stood there gaping or continued to drink or shouted for the servingmen to douse the fire before the whole house was consumed by it.

Then Joan felt a tug at her sleeve and turned to face

Nan. "Follow me, make haste," Nan shouted above the din.

Thinking that any retreat could only improve her situation, Joan followed without question, allowing the young woman to lead her through the mob and then quickly up the stairs that minutes before Joan had watched Nan descend.

At the top of the stairs an old woman in a red wig appeared to ask what the riot was below. Nan said it was nothing but a jest on one of the customers, and the old woman went away, apparently satisfied with the explanation despite the uproar below and the frequent shouts of "Fire!"

Nan dragged Joan into one of the chambers off the passage and bolted the door behind them. It was the first chance Joan had had to express her gratitude to her rescuer.

"Foul weather breeds foul custom," Nan said, as though the ordeal Joan had just suffered was a frequent occurrence at the Gull and to be borne like any other inconvenience of London life. "You'll be safe enough here, at least for the time being. The good tosspots below will have forgotten all about you in a quarter of an hour. As for the fire, the servers know how to put it out, if they have to piss upon it."

The young woman said her name was Nan Warren, and Joan identified herself. "I thought the sailor meant to kill me, so angry he was," she said.

"Ha," said Nan. "That's Flynch, Will Flynch. He's one of Ned Hodge's cronies. Ned owns the Gull. That's why he offered you no protection."

Nan made further disparaging remarks about the host of the Gull and his friends, and Joan was forced to laugh despite the fact her heart was still racing.

"As for Flynch," Nan said, "you have served his turn. You aimed truly with the stool, for his privy member shall be perpetually limp hereafter. You have quite undone him, for pleasure or procreation."

"The loss of pleasure is his own fault," Joan said, feeling again the indignities visited upon her. "That he will not father a litter of his own kind is the world's gain."

The two women continued to talk, and Joan found Nan of goodly conversation despite her disreputable trade. The girl was pleasant and well spoken and seemed as interested in Joan's life and reason for being at the Gull as Joan was in hers. Joan asked how long Nan had lived in London—for she recognized from the girl's speech that she was no native to the place—and Nan said five years come Michaelmas. She also asked Nan how she had come to her present employment in a house she spoke so disparagingly of, and Nan, without apparent embarrassment at Joan's directness, answered that she had fallen on very hard times since coming to the City and had been forced to thrive as she might.

Then Joan told Nan how she had come to the Gull that day, and how she had been walking in the vicinity of the Middle Temple because her husband was a visitor there. She confessed, too, how vexed she was at having been excluded, and Nan said she understood very well and remarked with some bitterness that men were good for little else but lording it over women and that one's true friends could hardly be found beyond one's own sex.

Joan herself was not quite so hostile to men that she was ready to accept Nan's proposition, but given the girl's account of her own experience, Joan sympathized with it.

"Your husband is a lawyer, then?" Nan asked.

"No, a clothier—and constable," Joan answered.

"Then he goes to the Temple to make an arrest?"

"Arrests are to be made by others," Joan answered. She

wasn't sure how much to disclose of her husband's true purpose at the Middle Temple. Nan was, after all, a total stranger. And yet she was so amiable a person, so open and good-hearted, that Joan felt little need for discretion. "There have been certain crimes within its walls," she confided.

"I'm not surprised," Nan said. "I know many young gentlemen of the Temple who are patrons of the Gull. They all think very highly of themselves, but most are not worth a farthing. As for these crimes you speak of, I have heard of none, save for lawyers' fees, but that's no news. Yet if graver crimes are practiced by lawyers, it's no marvel, for reasonable it is that he who knows the law best is best equipped to break it."

Joan found this response more than apt, and she had an even higher opinion of her new friend than before. Whispering as they were in the darkness, she felt as though she were speaking beneath covers with a sister. She had almost forgotten the danger that had driven her to this place—or that might still remain below.

"It is quieter downstairs now," Nan said. "It is probably safe for you to leave."

"But what of Flynch and his besotted friends?"

"I'll go see the coast is clear," Nan said.

"And what if someone comes? How shall I answer?"

"I have this chamber for the night. You'll not be disturbed. As you no doubt noticed, I have some seniority here amid the flock, having pecked in this yard longer than other of Hodge's birds."

Nan slipped out, leaving Joan alone and fearful again, for despite Nan's assurance that she was safe, doubts assailed her. What if Flynch attacked Nan, who had heroically put herself between Joan and his wrath? The little chamber, a welcome shelter when Nan was by her side, now seemed to Joan a dreary cell, where she faced the prospect of an indefinite and solitary confinement.

She waited for what seemed a long time and was at the point of leaving despite what danger awaited her when she heard a knock and Nan's voice. Joan unbolted the door and let her friend in.

"You were right, Mistress Stock," Nan said when the door was closed behind her again. "Flynch is still at the bar—and in a worse mood. Hodge has been plying him with drink to console him for his humiliation and wound. Flynch is full of threats and has worked his shipmates up into a fine frenzy."

Joan's heart sank at this ominous report. She looked at Nan in desperation. "Is there nothing to be done? I can't stay here forever. My hosts will be beside themselves with worry. And my poor husband, when he hears I'm lost in London, will fear I have been murdered!"

Nan said, "Don't worry. I have a plan that will save all."

Joan urged her to say what this plan was.

"I told them you fled—out a window."

"But did they believe it?" Joan asked.

"Probably not."

"Then how am I to escape? I'm fearful of heights."

"There'll be no windows to climb through, trust me."

Nan went to a little bed that occupied one corner of the chamber and, kneeling down, reached beneath, withdrawing a chest. She opened the lid and searched the contents while Joan watched. Then Nan said: "Here's what will make your escape perfect."

Even in the darkness Joan could see that what Nan had furnished her was another suit of clothes—clothes for a man, jerkin, doublet, hose, and stockings, even shoes.

"Flynch and his friends will be watching for a woman, if not too besotted to see. These clothes belonged to a former customer of mine. A married man, would you believe, who sought his pleasures in strange houses, to his wife's annoyance. He was having his fun one night when his wife and her brothers—all as tall as trees—came to demand where he was. Our honest host, Master Hodge, accepted sixpence for revealing the married man's whereabouts, and wife and brothers all come thundering upstairs without further ado. Each of the brothers had a stout cudgel, and the wife was armed with an iron skillet and the will to rattle her husband's head with it at first opportunity. I barred the door against them, and the married man went out the window, headfirst and naked as a babe, leaving these things in my custody. To this day he has not returned, but whether dead or merely in his good wife's custody, I cannot say. I was going to sell them, then decided on some occasion I might require their use for an escape of my own. Here, let's see how they fit."

Joan hesitated to put on the clothes. They were motheaten and smelly, and besides, they had belonged to an adulterous husband who undoubtedly richly deserved his coxcomb to be rattled for his transgressions. But she recognized the merit in Nan's plan. Flynch and his filthy crew would have their eyes peeled for a farthingale, not for doublet and hose. What was more, she would have to leave sometime.

Joan removed her cloak and gown and petticoats, telling Nan to keep them for her, for they were of great worth. Then she put on the doublet and hose. The doublet fit her tightly, as did the hose. "What about my hair? Will not my sex reveal itself?"

"Never fear. I have a cap. Besides, your hair is short. Many men wear theirs at that length, and some of the gallants of the town at even longer length for fashion's sake. As for the little rouge upon your cheeks, no one will notice. The color will be taken as the fruit of your recent amorous exertions." Nan laughed, and her confidence bolstered Joan's own. Maybe, she thought, the trick would work after all. What had she to lose?

Nan presented Joan with a cap of the kind apprentices were wont to wear in the streets. It was too large for her head, but Nan assured her that its size would work to her advantage in concealing more of her face.

Joan pressed Nan's hand warmly and kissed her on the cheek. She made Nan promise to come to see her at Cooke House. "These surroundings cannot be to your liking."

Nan looked around her and shrugged. "Believe me, Mistress Stock, there are worse surroundings, as you call them. There are poor women within the sound of Paul's bells who live in the street for want of a roof, or if roofed, live no better than pigs in their sty. The truth is that I hate the life I live, but have learned to accommodate myself to necessity, no matter how grim."

"Necessity is a foul word if it leads to a foul life," Joan said. She told Nan where she lived.

Joan went out with her protectress, feeling very awkward and unnatural in her male attire. On their way down the passage, they were passed by a rough-looking sailor and another of the Gull's women, but neither paid any attention to Joan, and she was relieved, feeling that she had passed the first test.

At the head of the stairs, Joan looked down. The tavern was less crowded than before. Her eyes searched for Flynch; she spotted him in the midst of his fellows at the bar. Apparently recovered from his wounds, he seemed to be telling some yarn, for all his friends were looking at him and laughing at regular intervals. Joan held her breath and descended, her arm linked with Nan's as though they had just shared more than conversation in the chamber above.

Joan made her way around the tables toward the door,

Nan still leading her. The customers now seemed too drunk to take notice. Some were asleep with their heads on their arms. She might have been invisible. She felt Nan squeeze her hand encouragingly, and in the next moment Joan stepped out into the night.

It took her little time to reach Cooke House; she ran almost all the way, grateful that the sleet had stopped and her sense of direction had remained true despite the evening's events.

She stood outside the door, knocking frantically, for she was very cold. After a few moments the groom whose protection she had scorned earlier that day thrust his head out to see who was knocking at such an unseemly hour.

"Is that Mistress Stock come home again?" called Frances Cooke worriedly from somewhere within.

"No, madam," replied Robert, turning his head slightly to acknowledge the direction of the question. "Only some strange youth." He turned to look at Joan suspiciously. "Well, what is it, boy? Tell me your business and do it quickly, or be off with you!"

7

Homesickness clutched at his heart. Through the narrow panes of his chamber window, Matthew looked out into the night. The storm had struck with a fury, sleet pelted the glass, and he was glad to be indoors, grateful for a companionable fire cracking and sputtering on the hearth. He thought of Joan and wondered what she was doing. He imagined her sitting in the parlor of Cooke House, cozy and safe, enjoying the warmth of a similar fire and perhaps engaged in some pleasant discourse with Frances Cooke. He was glad that the two women had become friends, but his separation from his wife troubled him sorely.

He turned from the window and sat down in the chair

he had pulled up to the fire in an effort to make his strange surroundings more homelike. The fire had been laid an hour before by the wizened old man with bent back and pinched, scrupulous face. He had made a great fuss about the fire, the old man—as though the positioning of faggots and mounding of kindling were as much an art as the drafting of deeds and quittances. He said his name was Jacob Flowerdewe. He said he was the underporter, a title he pronounced with pride, as though he had come to his station by royal appointment. Jacob bragged that he remembered the name of every Templar he had served, his face and his humors too, and that he knew all the nooks and crannies of the Temple. He claimed he had hardly set foot outside the Temple precincts since good Queen Bess came in to save England from the Whore of Babylon, the wicked Mary.

"Jacob, sir. They all call me Jacob, plain and simple, for *nomen nonsufficit,* as the learned say, and my Christian name *sufficit* very well, I think."

"Jacob let it be," said Matthew, amused at the old porter's prattle and its curious mixture of plain language and legal terms. "I am told the last resident of this chamber died in it."

Jacob looked pained at the thought. "Oh, he did indeed, sir. Bless me, it's as true as God's word. He stretched his neck from the very beam above your head. I saw the body myself, sir—and a cheerless sight it was, with his face all swollen and his tongue extended and his eyes as big as tennis balls."

"Suicide," said Matthew.

"Yes, sir, a thing *malum in se,* as the learned would have it. Not merely *malum prohibitum.*"

"Indeed," said Matthew, as though all this were fresh news.

"And his chamberfellow," Jacob continued in a confidential whisper, "Edward Litchfield, met a similar fate. Cut his wrists, he did. Right down on the Temple Stairs."

"Very curious—both men suicides."

"And there was another."

"You don't say!"

Jacob nodded sagely. Although his matter was gruesome, he seemed delighted to be the bearer of it. "I reckon it thus. If one young gentleman of the House kills himself, then that's a proper tragedy. If his chamberfellow does the same, that's passing strange. But if within a fortnight a third turns himself off by gobbling down poison, well, that exceeds the limit, in my way of thinking. That's what I call an enormity."

"Have you no explanation for these enormities, as you call them?" Matthew asked.

"I, sir? Well, no, Master Stock. Far be it from me to offer an explanation. I say the deaths are curious and a fit and proper enormity and disgrace to the House and the families and the whole lawyerly race. But as far as opinions go, I leave those to the learned."

Jacob asked if Matthew wanted anything else.

"No, Jacob, God rest you."

"And you, sir, and you. It's a cruel night without, sir. God save us all from evil thoughts and the Devil's works."

Jacob glanced quickly at the ceiling, then back at Matthew. He grinned a toothless grin, but Matthew saw a glimmer of fear in the old man's eyes and he knew what Jacob was thinking. He was thinking about Litchfield and Monk, about the corpses of young men who had laid violent hands upon themselves in wanton violation of God's holy ordinance. And perhaps he was suspecting, as did Matthew, that the suicides had been murders.

So earlier. Now Matthew prepared for bed and was on his knees in nightly prayer when a knock came at the door.

It was Keable, his neighbor, bottle in hand, and obviously drunk.

Keable asked if he could come in and talk. "Wilson's sleeping," he said, "and I thought you might like to share a bottle of the grape. It's a bold Spaniard. Very sweet, I assure you."

Matthew said he would not drink but invited Keable in; he was tired, but if Keable wanted to talk that was all the better. He had found out little about the murders from Jacob Flowerdewe; perhaps he would have more luck with Keable.

"I see Jacob has done well by your fire. An amusing fellow, Jacob. He's somewhat of an institution here— senior to some of the bricks and mortar, and a great weaver of barbarous phrases. I suppose he said something about the dead men?"

"He did," Matthew said.

Keable paused, as though inviting Matthew to expand on the theme, but when Matthew made no reply, Keable sat down on the foot of Matthew's bed. He pulled the cork from the bottle with a practiced hand. He had brought two goblets. "You're sure about the wine?"

"Quite sure. Thanks all the same. Go ahead, however, please yourself."

Keable bowed slightly, grinned, and poured himself a full goblet. He sipped it slowly, while Matthew watched.

"Well, then, Master Stock. What think you of this unseemly business?"

"The suicides?"

"Yes, a wicked situation to draw your son into, don't you think?"

"I suppose it is, yet he knows his own mind."

Keable stroked his chin thoughtfully. "You're a clothier by trade, aren't you?"

Matthew said he was, relieved to have something he could speak truly of.

"I thought it was the desire of all fathers that their sons follow them in trade."

"Well, that's true enough," Matthew said. "So was my desire, and so is still. Yet my son shows no love for cloth, and I would not be a father who rules through compulsion."

"Very wise," said Keable, draining his goblet. He poured himself another drink and pledged it to Matthew. "God save all well-meaning fathers, for heaven knows they are a scarce commodity."

Keable's good looks had diminished in his drunken state. His face was flushed and his eyes were bleary.

"Thomas Cooke was saying Litchfield and Monk were involved in some kind of play?" Matthew asked, eager to move conversation off the topic of his mythical son and on to his real interests.

"Ah yes," Keable said. "And so am I. The lot of us had parts, but the play's a wretched piece, as tried and true as a curate's sermon."

Matthew asked which parts the young men played, and Keable answered that both Monk and Litchfield had played woodland nymphs. The youth dissolved in sudden laughter. Tears streamed from his eyes and he slapped his knees. "Some of the men were loath to dress as women. Litchfield had such a part, but was too giddy-headed to object. I suspect he enjoyed it—all that lace and velvet and the stuffed bodice. He was such a fool."

"You speak ill of the dead," Matthew said. "What of Monk, his chamberfellow?"

"Why, he should have hanged himself before." Keable was suddenly serious again.

"Before—?"

"Sooner, rather than later! He was a very knave, you know. More profligate than Litchfield. Monk's grandfather was a great judge of the Court of Chancery. Lawyering was in Litchfield's blood. Speaking of obdurate fathers who overdirect their son's lives, there was a case."

"Who, the grandfather?"

"Nay, sir, his son. Monk's father. Another lawyer, by the way."

"Monk wished to pursue another profession, then, perhaps business or the Church?"

Keable laughed his mirthless laugh again. He let the empty bottle fall to the floor, where he kicked it with his foot. "He followed his father's orders to the letter—a good, dutiful son. Now, me, my own father bade me come here, provided me with furnishings for my chamber, and pays me a comfortable allowance. But I'll tell you the truth, Master Stock, I came here but for one reason and one alone."

"And that was—"

"Why, to do my father's will and therefore to be included in my father's will, for sure as God made little fishes, my father threatened to cut me off without a groat if I disobeyed. While he provides for me generously, I will appear the dutiful offspring, forsaking hawking for the Hall and living well even while I seem to study this lawyerly rubbish. If I need more money to lay in food and wine, I write that I require an even greater sum to buy books. If I would spend on plays and cards, I write that my gown is rent and I must purchase another or be scorned for my poverty. Thus, I play my father like a pipe."

Matthew forced a smile at these words, although they annoyed him. Drunk or sober, he would have never spoken so of his own father. Nor could Matthew respect a man who would. He decided to turn the conversation to Litchfield and Monk again.

"Was there enmity between Litchfield and Monk?"

"Enmity?" Keable smiled, looking at Matthew vaguely. Unsteady, as though he were about ready to topple off the bed. "I think the contrary is true. They were the best of friends—a veritable Damon and Pythias. It was enough to make a body sick to see the two, walking around the grounds arm in arm. It was enough to call into question their very manhoods."

"You mean they were—"

"Nay, they did not approach that vice, though God knows it abounds among our pallid youth. Monk was a whoremasterly rogue, and in that homely liberal art, Litchfield was an earnest disciple. As for Monk, I could name you a certain tavern in the neighborhood of most dissolute character, in which every slattern had taken the measure of his codpiece."

"But you called Monk a zealous student of the law."

"Ah, by day, by day, sir. At night he took his pleasures in the town. You must understand, Master Stock, the two pursuits are not at cross-purposes. Too much work dulls the edge of husbandry."

"What of the other man who killed himself—by poison, I think I heard? What manner of man was he?"

"As opposed to young Litchfield and Monk as night the day," said Keable. "A pure, unadulterated drudge if there ever was one. Lived and breathed the law—and religion. Would you believe it, I never saw the man laugh but once, and that was at some villainously obscure pun in a sermon. Nay, Hugh Giles was an unlikely denizen of these worthy quarters, very pious, I assure you."

"But he remained," Matthew said.

"Hah," replied Keable, his speech slurred more than ever. "He hied off to a better world. Now he's in Heaven—or in Hell, for all his piety, for our ever-quarreling sects do not allow all who pray and preach access to God's throne."

"I take it you liked this Giles no more than Litchfield or Monk," Matthew said.

Keable smiled faintly as though he were remembering something. "In truth, Giles counted me a friend. But you asked for a candid appraisal of his character. I hope you don't think the less of me for giving one. But I'll tell you one thing, Master Stock." Keable paused, breathed deeply, and then bent over with a cautionary finger at his lips as though it were a state secret he was about to disclose. "They formed a close-knit group, those three—Litchfield, Monk, and Giles. A very tight little group."

Matthew looked at the drunken young man, anticipating more in the way of revelation but unsure of the significance of what he had already received. Keable's lips were set. He nodded sleepily, then stood up.

"I must go to bed," he said. "Many thanks for your company."

Matthew assured Keable the pleasure had been his, but felt the assurance stick in his throat. He did not like Keable. He did not like Keable's kind—drunk or sober. And as the young man staggered out, Matthew was not sure whether there had been truth in Keable's wine or an artful deception.

Keable groped his way toward his chambers and was fumbling at the door when he noticed Theophilus Phipps lurking at the end of the corridor. His curiosity, coupled with mild irritation because he despised Phipps, sobered him. "You keep late hours, Master Phipps. About the Treasurer's business, I warrant. Or perhaps the Devil's?"

"The Treasurer's business is happily concluded for the day," Phipps said lightly. "The Devil never sleeps."

"A witty response, Master Phipps. Also true. But I've a bee buzzing in my bonnet and am in no mood for banter. Therefore, if your prowling has some purpose—"

"I assure you it does. A piece of information."

"News of court?" Keable asked impatiently.

"Somewhat closer to home, dear Keable. Yes, somewhat closer to home."

8

B y the time Joan awoke, it was already broad daylight, city bells clamored, and muted voices from distant rooms signaled she was last to arise. After her ordeal of the night before, she had slept like the dead; now her narrow escape from Will Flynch's violence came back to her, along with fresh remembrance of Nan Warren's generous and heroic service. Regretting that a young woman of such qualities dwelt in so loathsome a place, she got out of bed and dressed, thinking all the while how she might help the unfortunate Nan. Then a maid entered to say that the master of the house had left early that day for the Temple and that the mistress lay abed still. Joan was invited to breakfast at her leisure.

In her conversation with the Cookes the night before, Joan had been discreet about her misadventure at the Gull. She had been embarrassed to confess she had been set upon in a common brothel and then forced to don man's clothing to escape with her life—and doubtless with her virtue too. She had resorted to a fiction to save face, and in the version she conveyed to her anxious hosts, she had been assaulted by thieves and had been provided with male attire by an honest stranger who had taken pity on her.

More than plausible, the story had, by all signs she could observe, been accepted at face value. The Cookes had been sympathetic, especially Frances, who, not ungratified at having been proven right by Joan's experience, had repeated her admonishments about the dangers of walking abroad in London when the streets were black as pitch. It had been all Joan could do to keep Thomas Cooke from giving Robert the gate for failing to protect a guest under the master's roof.

"The fault was mine," Joan said. "Robert did his duty. I ran ahead; poor fellow, he could not keep up."

At Joan's insistence, Thomas forgave Robert, and an unusual softening of the groom's normally grim countenance suggested he appreciated Joan's intercession.

Thomas reminded Joan that he was responsible for her safety, especially since Matthew was at the Temple and unable to afford a husband's protection. With a face heavy with concern, Thomas begged her to take greater care in the future.

Unaccustomed to being told where she could go and where she could not, Joan felt like a child. But she promised she would comply, determined nonetheless in her heart not to surrender an inch of free will.

But that had been last night as she stood, quivering and humiliated, by the great roaring fire in the Cookes' parlor, still dressed in the patched doublet and ill-favored, coarse stockings of the adulterous husband of Nan Warren's humorous tale. Now it was morning. Dressed a woman again, she descended to the kitchen, drawn by the aroma of things cooking there and a craving for a full stomach to begin the day upon. She had just finished her breakfast and was beginning to wonder how she might help Nan as well as Matthew under her new restrictions when Robert came in to say that there was a woman asking for her at the door and that she had given her name as Nan Warren.

Joan was delighted at the prospect of seeing her rescuer so soon after the event. She told Robert to show Nan to the parlor, mentioning at the same time that Nan was the helpful stranger who had provided Joan with her disguise the night before.

Joan hardly recognized the Nan Warren whom seconds later she found awaiting her. Dressed in a modest gray gown beneath a cape of sad color, and of a fresh, scrubbed countenance, Nan might have been a shopkeeper's daughter or better—perhaps even a gentleman's wife. She was certainly no longer the siren of the previous evening who had so brazenly flaunted her bosom before the lustful eyes of the Gull's rude patrons and invited them to bid upon her body as though she were a horse at the Smithfield auction.

Joan greeted her guest warmly, then dismissed Robert. When he had gone, Nan said: "I've brought your clothes."

Joan saw the bundle at Nan's feet. She had really not expected to see her gown again, nor Nan either, and she was highly pleased by both.

"You might have kept the gown. It's the least you deserve."

"I thought I might," Nan said. "But then I began to think how fine the gown was. If I was caught wearing it, what would be supposed? That I was a thief. And I am no thief!"

Joan assured Nan that she never thought she was a thief, and offered Nan money in place of the gown, but this too Nan refused with a lift of her soft chin, suggesting that further offers of reward would be similarly declined.

Joan regarded Nan with wonder. What a marvel was here—an honest-hearted whore! "But surely I can do something for you?"

Nan seemed to ponder the question for a moment, then said: "Last night you urged me to consider the life I lead. A very bad and wicked life. And the truth is that I am weary of opening my legs to every drunken sot willing to pay admission thereto. Nor am I so ignorant of true religion to be unaware of my damnable condition. Necessity is as ready a road to sin as greed or avarice, or so the preachers declare."

Joan was gratified to hear such wise confirmation of her own sentiments, and nodded to Nan encouragingly. "Every word you say is true, Nan."

"In brief, then, Mistress Stock, I thought you might help me to reform my life—find a new livelihood. You seem to be a woman of means as well as charitable impulse. You mentioned a husband at the Temple, a prosperous shop in Chelmsford."

"I have both," Joan said. "And friends in London too who may do you good."

"You see, I am in present danger at the Gull."

"How so?" Joan asked.

Nan was not far into the story she now commenced before Joan realized that by strange coincidence her encounter with Nan had led by a circuitous route to her husband's own mortal matter. Nan spoke of her relationship with certain young men of the Inns of Court, young men who regularly patronized the Gull, young men whom she had taken to her bed and from whom she had heard certain things before their recent and lamentable suicides and for which she was now being persecuted by another of the Templars, a man named Theophilus Phipps.

As much as Joan was tempted to reveal she already

knew this same Phipps from her husband's full account of his visit to the Treasurer, she kept silent about her knowledge, waiting to hear what Nan knew.

"He came to visit me the day before yesterday," Nan said, looking worried. "He wanted to know all I knew of the three gentlemen who died, although I knew but two of them, and especially of one named Litchfield, who it is said cut his wrists on the Temple Stairs."

"And what did you know?" Joan asked.

"Less than he hoped, I think. He asked particularly about some money that Litchfield expected to come his way, an inheritance, I suppose. But I knew nothing of that. To tell truth, I hardly remembered Litchfield, one Templar gentleman being so like the other."

"What did this Phipps say to that?"

"He smiled and said he knew I lied. He accused me of knowing more than what I said and declared that if I was not more forthcoming, I would be sorry."

"He threatened to hurt you?"

"To tell the Treasurer I somehow caused the suicides."

"Ridiculous," Joan said. "How could you be accountable for what they did?"

"He said by some witchcraft, for I slept with all of them, sucked out their souls and other such nonsense."

"The villainous rogue—to so threaten a woman," Joan said. "I'll tell my husband. He'll put things right."

"Why, Mistress Stock, does your husband have such authority?" Nan said.

"Well, he is well acquainted with those who do—powerful men."

"Indeed! Then I am more than fortunate to have made your acquaintance, for I am afraid of Phipps."

Nan hid her face in her hands, and Joan reached over and placed a comforting hand on the young woman's shoulder. "You must leave the Gull, that's all there is to it. Then you'll be free from Phipps and his kind."

Nan looked up tearfully. "But how am I to live—by begging?"

"We'll find a way," Joan said. "Never fear. You saved my life—no small matter in my mind. Trust me. Go to the Gull, but only to gather your things. Say nothing to Phipps should you meet him again. Then find decent lodgings, until I can provide for you myself or find someone who can. Here, take this. No, I insist."

Joan held out the coins. It was a goodly sum. Nan looked at them, and after some hesitation, she took the money. "But what about later, Mistress Stock? You are generous, but this won't last forever."

"My dear friend Frances may be able to help," Joan said.

"With employment?"

"Yes."

"But would she find a place for someone like me, a woman—"

"Never you mind," Joan interrupted, forestalling any self-deprecation on Nan's part, "Mistress Cooke shall know nothing of your history beyond your faithful service to me. I told her nothing of the Gull. Only that I was set upon in the streets and a Good Samaritan helped me to a covering for my nakedness. You were that Samaritan. Frances Cooke shall know no more."

"Oh, you are an angel, Mistress Stock," Nan said.

"And so are you, Nan. Call me Joan, please."

The two women embraced, and Joan's eyes filled with tears, for despite Nan Warren's sordid life, there was much in the young woman that reminded Joan of her own daughter, Elizabeth, and she was determined to see her free from the evils of whoredom and the threats of Theophilus Phipps, who, for all Joan knew, was the murderer Matthew sought at the Temple.

Nan Warren left Cooke House, thinking that it was a very fine house and handsomely furnished and remembering with a little pain when she herself lived amid such plenty and had servants at her beck and call and a fine bed of goose feathers to sleep upon and silk next to her skin. But that was another life she had lived—and one she knew she could never resume. Yet she had no regrets. What was done was done. Except for one thing. That was yet to do— the mighty oath she had sworn to the curate in Norwich the day both husband and son were taken from her and an indifferent God kept silent in the face of it.

Under the influence of that bitter memory, her face took on a grim expression as she turned away from Cooke House. Her conversation with Stock's wife had pleased her well. She had confirmed that Joan's husband was investigating the Templar suicides, established an intimacy with the wife whereby the husband's dealings might stand open to her, and implicated the obnoxious Theophilus Phipps. Three birds with one stone, it was; a goodly morning's work, to Nan's mind. But at the same time she realized that her increasing familiarity with the Stocks was not without its risks. Nan's generous patroness had been taken in, but she was no fool. Nan would use the connection for what it was worth, and when it lost its value or became a detriment, she would end it with the same finality as she had ended other connections that had outlived their usefulness.

Nan hoped it would not fall out so, for she rather liked the busy little Chelmsford housewife of such ready tongue and provident purse.

9

The Chelmsford constable learned of his wife's misadventure in the streets of London from Thomas Cooke, who delivered the news hard upon inquiring of Matthew with what cheer he had spent his first night in chambers. Matthew was so alarmed for his wife's safety that he was ready to rush back to Cooke House and let the murderer he sought find himself. But that was before Thomas assured him that Joan was unscathed by her ordeal. Thomas also reported that Joan was strangely undisturbed by the theft of a good gown, and restive under the rules Thomas had imposed on her in her husband's name.

"By God, that sounds like my Joan!" Matthew exclaimed, half-amused, half-relieved, and if there were by order of logic to remain a half to the whole of his response, half-suspicious that something more had transpired the night before than had been reported by her to her host. For although Matthew thought it was very like his wife to be rebellious against husbandly rule, indifference to the loss of a good gown was most contrary to her nature. No, that didn't sound like Joan at all, and he began to wonder what mischief she had really been up to.

But in the foreground of his thoughts was his charge. "To talk to Crispin Braithwaite," Matthew answered when Thomas asked where Matthew was to begin his labors. Matthew had answered confidently—without being entirely sure how he was to approach the only known survivor on Hugh Giles's list.

The two men went to breakfast in the Hall, where Matthew was presented to a score of new faces, all younger men than he, and some positively callow, as though they had been weaned from their mother's milk not the day before. He had asked Thomas if he would find Braithwaite there, and Thomas had assured him it was more than likely, for Braithwaite was a hearty trencherman, as Thomas phrased it.

But Crispin Braithwaite was not at table. Thus, Matthew contented himself with a breakfast of middling quality and a flurry of conversation all about him.

He was gratified that his tablemates did not discourse exclusively on legal matters; instead there was a great buzz of talk about plays, politics, new fashions in dress, theories about the motions of the planets, and talk of voyagers' tales, along with much witty banter among the gentlemen, much of which Matthew thought was somewhat self-serving and belligerent. While Matthew ate, Thomas excused himself to ask after Braithwaite, and returned shortly thereafter to say that Braithwaite was expected to come down later in the morning to rehearse a play.

"And here is the author even now," said Thomas, indicating with a nod of his head a sharp-nosed young man even then approaching their table.

Introductions followed. The author was Samuel Osborne, who seemed too preoccupied with the rehearsal about to take place to do more than nod in Matthew's direction.

"Master Stock would be most pleased to watch your players," Thomas said.

"Oh, he would," said Osborne, suddenly brightening. "Why, then, he positively shall." Osborne reached out to shake Matthew's hand; his palm was moist, and Matthew could see that even though the Hall was hardly warm, sweat glistened on Osborne's face and he breathed deeply as though he had just come on the run from his chambers.

Osborne explained that the rehearsal was to take place in the Hall as soon as the tables had been cleared; then he excused himself to go find several of his players who had not yet appeared at breakfast. Thomas suggested that Matthew might enjoy a stroll in the morning air in the meantime.

"Osborne seems a queer bird," Matthew remarked in the relative privacy of the garden walks.

Thomas laughed. "One of a kind, if you will know the truth. He's completely wrapped up in his playmaking, but a well-meaning gentleman, of good family."

"I suppose he knew all the dead men," Matthew said.

"Of course," said Thomas. "But surely you don't suspect Osborne? I assure you he's as mild as a maid. His violence is all in his pen."

"No one can be beyond suspicion," Matthew said

quickly, before considering that Thomas might think that Matthew suspected *him.*

But Matthew read no expression of offense in his companion's face. Thomas told Matthew about Keable's visit the night before.

"Prompted by neighborliness, do you think? Or suspicion?"

"Suspicion. Keable spoke most openly. Being potted didn't hurt."

"Oh, he was drunk, was he?" Thomas asked, mildly amused. "Keable is a difficult one. Very haughty. He positively despises his chamberfellow, poor Wilson. Keable's father is rich and gives the son whatever he requires and more."

"So he boasted," Matthew said. "He discoursed most uncharitably on the dead men, especially Monk. He said Monk was a profligate—and Litchfield his disciple. He gave me a different impression of Giles than I had from Master Hutton."

"Oh, how so?" Thomas said.

"He agreed that Giles was a religious zealot and good lawyer, but said nothing about debts or melancholy. Surely Keable would have completed the inventory of Giles's sins if indebtedness were a part of it. Tell me, what are Keable's other qualities?"

Thomas thought for a moment, then said: "Well, he's proud of his looks—too proud for extensive friendship, although he has many admirers. Phipps being one, I might add. Keable's ambitious—hot-blooded, too. A classic case of choler. I recall he and another of the utter barristers nearly came to blows at supper one evening. Over spilled salt, would you believe?"

They returned to the Hall. In their absence the tables had been cleared and rearranged. The long table at the head of the cavernous chamber had been pushed back against the carved screen, making of the dais a stage. Here Osborne and about a dozen other men gathered, including Keable and his chamberfellow, Wilson.

"Ah," said Osborne as Matthew and Thomas approached. "Our guest for these solemnities, Matthew Stock of Chelmsford, honorable father of one of our future members."

Matthew bowed self-consciously to acknowledge this introduction while Osborne abruptly turned his attention to his players and continued with his instructions.

"Which is Braithwaite?" Matthew asked after he and Thomas had found a bench to sit upon.

"He's not among them," Thomas said. "I don't know why, for his part is no small one."

Matthew was disappointed. He really didn't care about Osborne's play, but he did want to see what manner of man Braithwaite was. Later, he would determine how he might open up the gentleman who claimed to know so little about what so obviously concerned him.

Collected on the dais, the players took their places as directed. Thomas provided Matthew with a summary of the plot.

"It's a simple piece, as far as the story is concerned. Eve and the serpent warmed over—but with a happier result. The theme is likewise commonplace. The triumph of chastity over lust. The heroine is a shepherdess named Clorinda. In truth she is the offspring of a duke, although this is not made known until the end of the play. She falls in love with another shepherd and thereby excites the envy of a satyr who dwells in the neighborhood."

"Keable's part," said Matthew, his eyes fixed on the players, who were engaged in some sort of dispute with Osborne.

"Yes. The satyr endeavors to seduce the maiden, but

being as virtuous as can be, she will have none of his blandishments."

"Does she marry the shepherd?" Matthew asked.

"How did you guess?" Thomas said, chuckling. "But there's more crinkum-crankum before they marry. Soft, now, the wrangling is finished. The rehearsal begins in earnest."

On the dais Keable and six other men were beginning to dance in a circle around Wilson, who had curled up on the floor pretending to be asleep. Another student played the flute to accompany the dance, and all had removed their gowns and caps for the occasion.

"Very stately, very stately," Osborne cried loudly, directing the dance. "Anon the tempo will advance and there'll be time enough to kick your heels. Steady on, Keable. Keep your eyes upon Wilson. He's doing it right. Watch your feet, man. The maiden lies sleeping before you. Remember your purpose. She should not awake until you have distilled your flatteries into her ears. Speak now."

The dancing slowed and Keable bent over the sleeping Clorinda. He began to speak his lines. Now Matthew was glad Thomas had favored him with a summary, for although Keable's words were in English, the sense was so twisted from the normal patterns of speech that he could not make head nor tail of them. He understood, however, from Keable's gestures and tone, that a seduction was taking place. Keable waved his arms over the sleeping form as though he were a priest performing some rites. He leered and grimaced, while the other satyrs in his crew resumed their dance, slowly circling the maiden, their gestures threatening and seductive.

Osborne said: "Now the poor lady awakes. She recognizes her peril. Advance your step, one and all!"

The flute player outdid himself with trills, and the satyrs quickened their steps as directed. Another student, watching from the opposite wall, picked up a tabor and began to beat it rapidly. The hectic dance went on for several minutes until the dancers were sweating from exertion; and then Osborne clapped his hands, and music and dancing stopped.

Osborne walked over to the center of the dais, his arms akimbo and a disapproving expression on his face. While the dancers caught their breaths, he began to find more fault with their performance, especially Keable's, which Osborne claimed was much too languid. More like a swoon than a galliard, Osborne complained, and he laughed a high-pitched, derisive laugh that even Matthew found offensive, although he had no part in the quarrel brewing.

In response, Keable said it was an easy thing to give directions when one didn't have to do the thing himself, and Osborne said that *he* could dance well enough and he hoped Keable could do half as well. Then Keable called Osborne some kind of name beneath his breath, and Osborne demanded that he repeat what he had said and grew very red in the face.

Thomas left Matthew's side to make peace between the men. "Come, sirs," Thomas said genially. "This is sorry work on both your parts. You, Osborne, are the author of our masque; you, Keable, arguably its chief character since without your enticements there is no plot, but mere virtue unassailed, much to be desired in life but hardly the stuff of drama. So, then, make peace between you that we may proceed in good order."

"God's blood, I'll not be badgered so," declared Keable, apparently unaffected by Thomas's admonishments. "My legs are good enough—and certainly a match for *his*, which are like two sticks with hardly a healthy calf between them."

"I did not badger, as you call it," Osborne protested. "I only suggested you might advance your step a little."

Osborne looked at Thomas as though expecting him to defend his right to be critical, but Thomas said nothing. "The soul of active lust is energy," Osborne went on defensively. "Otherwise, the assault upon the lady's virtue will carry no conviction."

"I have more energy in my little finger than you do in your entire body, Osborne!" Keable declared roundly.

"You mean more impudence in your little finger than brain in your noggin," said Osborne.

"Come, make peace!" Thomas said, raising his voice now, his own face red with irritation. "What is it St. Paul declares? The eye cannot say to the hand, I have no need of thee, nor again the head to the feet, I have no need of you. We are all members of a common body. You, judicious Osborne, the eye; you, hot-blooded Keable, the hand. We must therefore work as one, not aggravate these divisions by oversensitivity to criticism."

"I'll content myself to be the hand," Keable said sourly when Thomas had finished his speech. "If Osborne will be less the ass."

"Shall I shut my eyes, then, while you play the fool?" asked Osborne.

"Neither ass nor fool," said Thomas, dividing a disapproving stare between the men. "Continue in this discord and the play will be ruined. There will be no play, I repeat. There's not an iota of merit in this brainless dispute. Be men, both of you, and not annoying children."

Thomas turned his back on the two men as though his last words had concluded the matter, but Matthew could tell that his friend had achieved only a temporary truce. The hatred between Osborne and Keable had been set; words of another would not placate them.

Suddenly Matthew's attention was drawn to the appearance of a new player on the dais. The newcomer wore a handsome velvet jerkin and cape and a fine broad-brimmed hat with a feather and the other accoutrements of a gallant. Thomas whispered: "This sterling fellow is the Prince of Love. He takes his name from the protagonist of our Christmas revels, the Prince d'Amour, but in Osborne's masque he is another shepherd transformed by love from rustic to gentleman worthy of this much-abused lady's hand."

"It's a handsome suit he wears," Matthew whispered back. "Who is he who plays the part?"

"He whom you have waited for," said Thomas. "Crispin Braithwaite."

Matthew took a harder look at the shepherd hero, now that he knew who he was. Crispin Braithwaite appeared to be in his early twenties. He was of middle height and fair complexion with a long, aristocratic nose and a small mouth above which was a light blond moustache. His voice was strong and well modulated, and as he struck the pose his part required, he lifted his right arm and extended it with the self-assurance of one fully comfortable in his body. Braithwaite spoke of his unrequited love for Clorinda, for her devastating beauty, directing his gaze to the floor, where Wilson, playing still the object of the Prince's affection, reclined as if asleep. Suddenly Braithwaite drew his sword and turned on Keable, who during the former's speech had been standing with a smoldering expression directed at Osborne.

There was an angry exchange now between the prince and the satyr, and in the next minute Braithwaite and Keable had drawn swords and commenced to thrust and parry vigorously.

This part of the performance interested Matthew, for it was action rather than mere words alone, which he only partly followed and whose superfluity he found suspect.

Moreover, it had much the same quality of dance—a dignity and order and grace of movement that appealed to him, especially since it was accompanied by tabor and flute, for all manner of music he dearly loved. Both men were nimble of foot and they handled their weapons expertly, at least in Matthew's judgment, and he could almost imagine that the fight was no mere playing but that it would presently be consummated in the death of one of them.

"Lay on, Keable," shouted Osborne from the sidelines. "Hollow your body more. Note distance and proportion. Thrust, thrust!"

The noisy conflict had drawn a large company of Templars who were not among Osborne's players but who, upon hearing the clanging of swords and Osborne's shouts, had drifted into the Hall to see what was going on. These, knowing the participants well, took sides, and ignorant of the symbolic import of the combat, called out encouragement to whomever of the two they preferred. Keable's partisans took up Osborne's mocking phrase and began to chant, "Lay on, Keable, lay on," while those who favored Braithwaite, the larger group, urged their hero to finish his opponent off.

Either in response to Osborne's goading or because of the appearance of friends to whom he did not wish to appear the weaker of the contestants, Keable now strove more fiercely, and the swordplay began to take on the appearance of real combat. Keable was thrusting and slashing at his opponent desperately, and Braithwaite, his earlier composure gone, responded in kind.

"My God, they're fighting in earnest," Thomas cried, elbowing himself through the spectators. Then, over bobbing heads and waving arms, Matthew saw Keable make a quick thrust and draw blood.

Braithwaite cried out that he had been hit, dropped his

sword, and somehow managed to sidestep a second thrust that, had it been true to Keable's aim, would have found a fatal home in his heart.

The bloodletting proved to be the climax of the duel, and the spectators grew strangely silent where all was commotion before, as though they themselves were responsible for the two gentlemen's loss of control and consequent bloodshed. Breathing heavily and clutching his left shoulder, Braithwaite stared accusingly at his opponent, before sinking to his knees in a faint.

Thomas called for someone to fetch a surgeon and, as a more immediate measure, clean cloths from the kitchen. Several Templars scrambled to comply, although most of the onlookers made no show to move, as though they had never seen a wounded man before or understood how it was possible for a sword to pierce the flesh.

Meanwhile Matthew had come forward to see how he might aid the wounded man.

Braithwaite lay on his back. He had regained consciousness, but his eyes were glassy and his chest still heaved with the vigorous exercise and, perhaps too, fear. From his mouth proceeded a string of appeals for a priest to shrive him, and curses aimed at Keable, who remained standing at a distance, sword in hand, seemingly more astonished than gratified at what he had done.

"Peace, Braithwaite," Osborne said, looking down at the fallen man. "You've no need of a priest. Your wound is only a scratch. Anyone can see that."

Cloths were brought from the kitchen, and Matthew applied them to Braithwaite's shoulder. Matthew could see that Osborne was wrong about the wound. The sword's point had penetrated deeply, and there was a great deal of blood soaked into the velvet sleeve of the doublet and now into the rushes. With the cloth, Matthew bound the wound as well as he could while Braithwaite, as white as chalk, asked in a quaking voice where Keable was.

Keable stepped forward a little but said nothing. Then Braithwaite, getting up on his elbows, declared: "Damn you to Hell, Keable. You struck me on purpose. You came near to killing me and may have yet."

"It was you who first grew heated," Keable charged, his own voice trembling.

"Nay, you, sir," Braithwaite insisted. Someone brought a flagon of wine to give to the wounded man, but Braithwaite would have none of it. He said he would not drink with Keable standing there gloating. "I found you angry when I entered. Because of the quarrel you had with Master Osborne."

"By God, I'll not accept blame for this," Osborne said, looking about him wildly. "It was an accident, as any man could see. What was between Keable and me had nothing to do with the quarrel between you two."

From the sidelines, Wilson spoke up on his chamber-fellow's behalf, declaring the hit to have been a accident, and no one voiced an opinion to the contrary, although Matthew, who had seen the whole of the incident, had grave doubts. Wilson continued, "The men were skirmishing in play, not dueling. It was *per infortunium* and *contra volutatem suam*. A felony must be done *animo felonico*."

Keable told Wilson to keep his lawyerly drivel to himself and called him a learned ass and a piddling knave. Looking around him as though he were still playing a part in Osborne's play, he said he needed no defender of his action, for if it was not an accident, then it was the result of a reasonable provocation and he would say as much to any man.

Thomas told Keable to be silent, for he had done enough mischief for the morning, and he said Keable should look to his standing in the Temple rather than threaten his colleagues, who meant only well by him, and Keable stalked off, shoving some of the spectators aside.

Now Osborne announced in a nervous treble what was painfully obvious to them all, that the rehearsal was done for the morning, and he suggested all stand clear of the Hall, for he had no doubt but that the proper authorities would be looking into the incident and declare it all *per infortunium*, as Master Wilson had earlier proposed. As he spoke, Matthew helped Thomas get Braithwaite to his feet. Thomas wanted to take Braithwaite to the infirmary, but Braithwaite said no. He told them to take him to his chamber instead—anywhere out of the sight of Keable.

While they were leading Braithwaite off, Matthew noticed Jacob Flowerdewe come in. The Hall was quickly being emptied, although not so much in response to Osborne's order as to the lack of any more to see of interest. Jacob approached the spot where Braithwaite had bled, and looking down at the remnant gore, he shook his head disapprovingly and muttered something under his breath. Then he knelt down to scoop the bloody rushes into his arms with the nonchalance he might have shown had a nobleman's horse defecated there.

10

heophilus Phipps grew queasy at the sight of blood. It had always been so with him, since boyhood, when his gruff, overbearing father had dragged him to Tyburn to see a traitor get his deserts. Father and son had stood within the very shadow of the block, pressed in by half of London, it seemed, to Phipps's distant recollection. With seething resentment, Phipps remembered it—resentment not at the traitor, a misguided soul who wept at the prospect of an ignominious end, but at his father, who forced the experience upon him. He remembered his father's mocking jibes, the enmity disguised as paternal counsel.

The father's contempt for the frail, blond son—the spitting image of the sickly mother.

Phipps had stood close enough to smell the hooded executioner's garlicky breath and the traitor's desperate sweat.

Then down had come the ax, and blood spat all over young Phipps's face and jerkin, while the traitor's head had rolled into its trough like a cabbage. His father had laughed and administered a manly thump upon the son's shoulders and said a bloody baptism was good luck and yea, a lesson too for any young gentleman.

But Phipps had been horrified and disgusted. He fled from his father, and since then, he had had no stomach for public executions nor random violence. Nor could he endure cockfights, bearbaitings, dogfights, duels, or the sight of dripping and oozing carcasses in butchers' shops, even though such sights were difficult to avoid in London, a city afflicted with blood lust and blood sport.

Phipps had entered the Hall during the final thrust and parry of the champions of *Lust and Charity* and thereby been an eyewitness to Braithwaite's disaster. Immediately he had felt his stomach churn, his shirt grow moist with sweat, his heart flutter with incipient panic. He prayed none of the onlookers turned their gaze from Braithwaite and his assailant to him, for he was sure he looked quite as undone by the spectacle of Braithwaite's bleeding as was Braithwaite himself.

And Braithwaite did look awful. His eyes were yellow with fear. Even as he cursed, groaned, and pleaded to be shriven of his sins, even as Osborne assured him the wound was but a scratch and that simpleton Wilson cited chapter and verse on law.

Pompous ass, thought Phipps of Osborne. Osborne had not been the one pricked. It was easy enough for him to give assurances, to enjoin the fallen Braithwaite—a better man than he—to endure his pain like a true son of the Middle Temple.

Having had a stomachful of it all, Phipps returned to his office, relieved to find that the Treasurer was still away. Hutton would be fit to be tied when he heard of the duel, or however it was to be construed.

Phipps sat down and looked over the sheaf of letters that had arrived that morning. Most of it was the small business of the Society—rents and accounts of merchants, a letter or two inquiring about membership. There were even several personal letters for Hutton that Phipps discreetly examined, being as he was perfect in the art of epistolary snooping. But he could not concentrate on the contents of the letters, nor was there much there to require his concentration. He kept thinking about Braithwaite's blood and what its shedding might have to do with the Templar murders. For Phipps had spotted Matthew Stock amid the throng in the Hall, bending down over the wounded man as though hanging on any incriminating last words.

Phipps was still pondering the mystery of this connection when the door opened and Keable appeared. Keable was wearing his cap and gown again, but his face was still flushed and sweaty from exercise. He had the look of a fugitive, and Phipps suspected the handsome but irascible young man was being widely blamed for the bloody outcome of the duel.

"They've carried Braithwaite to his chamber," Keable said, without even so much as a good morning as a preface. "A surgeon has been summoned."

"Leyland, is it?" said Phipps.

"I think so."

"God save Braithwaite, then," Phipps said. "He may be

in graver danger from that penurious quicksalver than from your sword."

"You saw it all, then?" Keable asked, not without a hint of pride in the act.

"Your lucky stroke—and the outcome; Wilson's defense of you—for what it was worth."

Keable laughed scornfully. "Not a farthing. A pusillanimous idiot who takes refuge in big words, that's Wilson." Keable didn't wait for an invitation to draw himself up by Phipps's fire. He sat down and stretched out his legs like a hunter home from the hunt. He put his arms behind his head and stared up into the mottled ceiling. "Braithwaite's making much ado about little, if you ask me," Keable went on. "It's a mere scratch."

Keable laughed again, but it was a hollow laugh, with more suppressed terror in it than merriment or ridicule. And suddenly, for the first time in their association, Phipps felt himself to be superior to Keable. He had always admired him before—for his fine air of disdain, his good looks, his full purse. Now his admiration had undergone a serious decline at the spectacle of Keable's apprehension. Was he that fearful of being booted from the Temple? Or was it prison that terrified him? Should Phipps remind him that Templars were forbidden by House rules and tradition from suing one another?

"*He* sent me here," Keable said morosely.

"Who?"

"Hutton."

"What for—disciplining?"

"Undoubtedly. Oh yes, I am also to tell you he will not return for several hours. I met him in the passage. He had word of the duel second- and third-hand from my so-called friends and Templar brethren who have puffed up a misaimed thrust into brazen manslaughter. Such hearsay he lectures against in Hall he now accepts as Gospel, and didn't even bother to ask for my side of it."

Keable got up and began to pace nervously. Phipps told him to rest his feet, that it would not do to wear out the stone, which he would surely do if he continued, but Keable acted as though he had not heard Phipps's words. "In truth, Phipps, I am glad I was sent here. Not because I am eager for chastisement but because I could no longer bear it in the Hall or chambers. Curse them, they shunned me afterward, as though I were a leper. Even those who cheered me on in the fight, which I assure you were the bulk of them."

"Marry, Keable, my friend, you've had greatness thrust upon you," Phipps said ironically. "Don't abuse Fortune. After all, how many of your so-called friends would have delighted in your death who must now bear their disappointment? Think about it. As for Braithwaite, chances are he'll recover. In a week's time you'll be tossing pots at the same table and laughing about the incident."

"But what if it turns out otherwise and Braithwaite dies?"

"Then it will be as God disposes," Phipps said.

Keable thought about this. He ceased pacing as abruptly as he had begun. Then he turned to Phipps and asked him if he had anything to drink. He said the swordplay and its aftermath had instilled in him a powerful thirst.

"I think Hutton may have something in his closet. Excuse me," Phipps said.

Phipps returned quickly with a bottle and two silver goblets of very fine workmanship that the Treasurer kept for special guests. "He'll never miss a drop," Phipps said when Keable looked at the wine and the goblets as though to inquire about the wisdom of using them without their owner's permission.

Smiling his customary smile of disdain, Keable accepted

the cup, which Phipps had generously filled to the brim. The two men toasted friends living and dead, but the toast seemed to strike a melancholy chord in Keable. He was only half-finished with his wine when he said: "You know, Phipps, I've been thinking about what you said the other night. About Stock, I mean."

Phipps settled in his chair and struck a comfortable pose. He leaned forward on the desk to give his friend his full attention. "Yes?"

"What you warned me of, I mean."

"Oh, that. You made light of the intelligence I gave you," Phipps said.

"True, but—"

"As much as said I was a gossip and nothing more."

"A thoughtless slander if the idea ever crossed my mind. But I protest it never did."

"Well . . ." Phipps hesitated uncertainly.

"I was a drunken sot last night, unaware of what I was saying or to whom. God knows what I told Stock in my heedless ramblings."

"God knows indeed," Phipps echoed.

There was a silence. Phipps waited expectantly, trying to read the emotions reflected in Keable's face. He read there caution and uncertainty and yet also an impulse to unburden a secret, and that was what intrigued Phipps the most.

"By which prayer I presume you know more about our dead comrades than you have publicly allowed?"

Keable looked up with a mild surprise, and Phipps made a sympathetic face. Inside, a surge of self-congratulation warmed his heart and increased his confidence. "You may speak freely here. Although I'm no priest, yet you may count me as a friend who prizes discretion above all the world. Remember, too, it was I who warned you about Stock. Perhaps we can exchange information."

"What do you mean by 'exchange'?"

"You know, Keable, tit for tat. *Quid pro quo*. Word it how you will."

Keable looked long and hard at Phipps, as though trying to find the soul of the man behind his offer to bargain. Then, with an expression that suggested the effort was futile, he said: "You know there was found among Giles's things a list of names."

"That's no secret," Phipps said quickly. "It was found in his shoe. An artless concealment."

"Braithwaite was on the list."

"He was—and what if he was? Your wounding of him was an accident, wasn't it?"

"Upon my honor," said Keable earnestly. "Although honesty compels me to admit my damned hot temper had a hand in it."

Phipps dropped his voice to a conspiratorial whisper. "If our minds follow the same path, you fear this list of Giles was a death list."

Keable nodded.

"And what if it is, so our names not be numbered there?" Phipps said, leaning back in his chair and letting his voice rise to its normal pitch. "Come, Keable. I agree Stock's presence gives cause for worry. But do not despair. As I said last night, to be forewarned is to be forearmed. It lies upon us only to keep our heads and guard our tongues. Unless, of course, you know of some more compelling reason for concern—?"

Phipps left the question hanging; there was another long pause as the two men eyed each other, seeming to search among the fragments of their brief relationship for a basis of mutual trust. Phipps could tell that Keable was still doubtful. His eyes had the wary expression of one playing at cards with a suspected cheat. Phipps could tell too that Keable knew something, something he was at great pains to keep hidden. Phipps was determined to have the secret out if he only could before Hutton returned, for the clerk felt the time of revelation was now or never.

Phipps held his breath in anticipation; and when he was beginning to fear all his angling would fetch up nothing, Keable leaned forward and, with an expression of relief and gratitude to have the thing out at last, took the bait.

Matthew found it no easy work getting Braithwaite upstairs. Braithwaite was big-boned, and while they carried him, he complained of his injury and heaped abuse upon Keable, whom he called a besotted mad knave and a disgrace to all lawyers. The little company of Good Samaritans was followed by an even larger contingent, who, having apprised themselves of the incident, tagged along more out of morbid curiosity than concern for Braithwaite.

When they arrived at the injured man's chambers, they were met by his chamberfellow, Adam Foxe, who, although not present during the combat, had already received word of its consequences and appeared genuinely alarmed at Braithwaite's condition. Braithwaite was helped out of his clothes and put to bed. Then the Treasurer came with the surgeon, whose name, Matthew learned presently, was John Leyland. Leyland was a stout, neatly dressed man in his thirties with swarthy complexion, a broad forehead, heavy brows, and a beard with an Italian cut. He carried a black satchel full of implements of his art, and numerous vials and flasks. Hutton ordered the gawkers to their chambers to "let the poor man breathe," as he put it. Matthew and Thomas stayed to watch, as did Osborne, who, despite his protest to the contrary, was now expressing regret for his part in the accident, for he admitted that his own quarrel with Keable had fueled the latter's fire.

Braithwaite, who had ceased complaining since his arrival in his chamber, cried out in agony as the doctor lifted the arm and removed the makeshift bandage to examine the wound. Leyland shook his head, and then pulled out a great wad of clean cloth from his satchel and prepared a new dressing, mumbling all the while about the incompetence of those who thought they could do a skilled physician's work but knew not the art.

When he was finished with the dressing he drew a vial from the satchel, poured some of its contents into a spoon, and fed it to Braithwaite, who did not stint to take it. "What you need, young sir," said Leyland, "is a good night's sleep. There's no substitute for a good night's sleep. That means, sir, no more ranting and raving. You must lie still and be quiet."

Braithwaite seemed to accept this counsel. He leaned back on his pillow and shut his eyes. Hutton turned to Foxe and said: "You must be your chamberfellow's nurse during his convalescence. It will be your duty both as a Templar and as a Christian."

Foxe, a thin, sallow-faced youth, agreed, although he did not appear eager to have the assignment. "But, sir, what of Master Donne's lecture—I would not miss that for the world."

"Braithwaite will spare you the while, Foxe," said Hutton with a placating smile. "I suppose the good doctor's medication will serve to keep this gentleman asleep for several hours."

A few moments later, as Matthew and Thomas descended the stairs with the portly Treasurer, Hutton said: "This Master Donne young Foxe spoke of is a quondam student of the Inns who since became secretary to Sir Thomas Egerton. It is said that in youth, Donne sowed many a wild oat, wrote naughty verses he passed among his friends, and pressed his favors on many ladies of the court. He made a secret and disastrous marriage with Sir Thomas's niece, Ann, as a result of which he was dismissed from his employer's service and deprived of his wife's dowry. He now pecks and scratches amid the ruins of his career for the wherewithal to live, whilst some of his friends urge him to take Holy Orders, so gifted a speaker he is. Tonight he speaks in the Hall by arrangement of one of his good friends, Henry Shadley."

Matthew tried to sound interested in the man Donne, the writer of naughty verses and martyr of love, but he could not so readily dismiss the image of poor Braithwaite on his bed. He deeply regretted he had not contrived to speak to the young man before his wounding in the Hall. Somehow he felt the moment of opportunity had passed, without being sure why. Braithwaite *would* recover, would he not? Was the wound so serious? Leyland the physician had not thought so, and once put to bed, Braithwaite had seemed better—at least in disposition.

Yet Matthew could not shake a sense of foreboding. Hutton did not seem to share Matthew's concern for the wounded man. As the three men continued to walk back to the Hall, Hutton rambled on about the antiquities of the Middle Temple, what person of note had occupied what chamber and in what dimly recalled year. The Middle Temple was indeed peopled with shades of the dead, Matthew thought, and Hutton reveled in their presence, quite forgetting, it seemed, the living but mysteriously imperiled Braithwaite.

11

In the Great Hall, Matthew fed on mutton leg and savory pork pie, salted and peppered to his liking and washed down with a manly black ale, the best he had ever had. Aloft in the gallery, a trio of musicians played sweetly, their delightsome strains raining down but wasted on so small an audience, for many of those who might have enjoyed the music otherwise, Matthew was told, had gone to Westminster to see some ceremony enacted.

After dinner, taking Leyland's word that Braithwaite would sleep many hours, Matthew secured Hutton's permission to examine the records of the Inn, the Minute Book, as it was called.

This was tedious work, Matthew presently discovered, who was no clerk happy to spend a long afternoon of eye-strain and hunched back. Helplessly ignorant in the face of Latin phrases and Law French, he made what he could of fines and exactions, rules and regulations, elections and appointments. He was not sure what he sought, nor were his labors rewarded by any new wisdom regarding the Templar murders. He wanted to pierce the veil that obscured the true connection of the victims, find the common ground between them other than their membership in the Middle Temple. But how?

At six he shut the Minute Book and went to supper, hungry again even though he had done nothing for hours but sit and read. But he was miserable at table. The musicians who had delighted before had been replaced by a half dozen incompetents who Matthew swore had been dragged in off the streets and told to play for their supper, and the Hall was crowded and noisy. The constant talk at table about the ceremony at Westminster bored him, and after no more than a day in chambers, he was passing weary of lawyers and their works.

It was true that his first impression of the Middle Temple had been favorable. Here, he had supposed, was a serious gathering of scholars. Men of intelligence. Men of learning. Men of gravity and probity. But his recent observations had stirred doubts, and the same doubts had quickly grown to conviction. For where before the colorful ritual of Templar life had pleased him, he now found it false and cloying. What a pretense of noble purpose was here. What strutting and posturing and backbiting and knavishness. Behind trapping and traditions lurked what? Greed, ambition, lust, covetousness—all the deadly sins by which man estranged himself from his fellows and offended the Almighty. Why, Matthew asked himself, had these young men—the cream of England—gathered here? To learn Justice and serve Her? Many would be lucky to escape hanging! To cultivate the arts and sciences? Indeed, if such could be cultivated in taverns and leaping houses.

As for those who devoted themselves to the serious study of the law, they too were at fault. Why had they chosen to become lawyers? To see Justice done? To preserve the rights of the downtrodden and disadvantaged? The poor had not the wherewithal to pay the lawyers' fees. How, then, should they be served? Let them go hang! Or starve! Or beg to God in Heaven for redress.

Had these not become lawyers, rather, to seek the advantages of power by which one might exercise unrighteous dominion, marry well, set traps and snares for the unwary, and, ironically, subject their own selves to a higher level of temptation than could ordinary mortals who were not lawyers?

So Matthew believed. For it had ever been so. Of all professions, the lawyer's was the most condemned by the laity. Yet his place was one of the most coveted, for there was never yet a doting parent ashamed to admit his son was a lawyer. Still, Matthew considered, no man was more trusted because he was a lawyer. Or more loved. None fairer of face, straighter of limb, in better health, or in a surer way to Heaven. No man was by legal education made more true of word, compassionate, just, dependable.

So Matthew considered the matter.

Supper done, the long trencher tables cleared of bones, crusts, dirty plates, and wiped clean too, there was no rush to the doors, but the company stayed, and if anything, it grew, enlarged by those who had missed supper or were come from the City as visitors and wore no gown nor cap of the company, but splendid clothes the value of a modest country household. Then Hutton rose from his chair, and where all was talk and laughter before, the whole Hall now fell into a respectful silence. Matthew turned his attention to the man seated to Hutton's right.

Matthew had not been introduced to this personage, but from what he had observed during the evening, he surmised this was the celebrated Master Donne. Donne was a man of about thirty, with a long, thoughtful face, pale complexion, and a wispy moustache that drooped at the corners, giving him a somewhat melancholy expression. Hutton introduced Donne as a former student of Gray's Inn and as a man of considerable learning and wit. He said nothing of the poems, and Matthew supposed Hutton did not think them significant, or perhaps he was embarrassed by their reported contents. When he finished, Donne arose to great applause.

Standing, Donne was not an imposing presence. He was dressed in a dark gray doublet with silver buttons and simple collar, and he was not tall. But he had a well-modulated voice that carried like an actor's, and he spoke with the easy assurance of one used to debate. He pleased his listeners by commencing with a promise. He would not speak at length, he said, for he wished not to keep the young gentlemen from their nocturnal studies (laughter). He said he knew well how attractive were the pleasures of the town—he had been to a tavern or two in his day (more laughter), where he had encountered many a gowned barrister or judge holding court out of session (thunderous laughter and cries of "True, true"). But tonight he wanted to address a somber theme, and saying this, he frowned as though this were the very moment of the theme's conception. It was a paradox, he said, and one by which he hoped to demonstrate that an agile mind could make a silk purse from a sow's ear. His theme was the proposition that women were possessed of souls.

He had no sooner uttered these words than polite silence changed to boisterous laughter, and the applause following was mixed with hooting and catcalls and other vociferous denials of the proposition. Undismayed, and indeed, slightly amused, by the expression of merriment in his face, Donne forged ahead, gathering together such a twisting and turning of reasons and proofs and quoting of old authors, half of whom Matthew had never heard, that Matthew quickly lost interest. For himself, Matthew had no doubt that women had souls, and the whole idea of maintaining the contrary seemed a dubious enterprise at best. But the audience seemed to hang on Donne's every word. At each turn of the argument, he received applause—or more good-humored protests. Matthew had never seen a company of men take such pleasure in an event where there was neither music to delight the ear nor some spectacle to please the eye, but all was words, words, words, many of which, in Latin or Greek with no translation offered, were beyond his ken.

Phipps found a place in the rear of the Hall and considered himself fortunate because of the crowd. He had forgone supper for a late afternoon nap and now felt refreshed, but while those around him gave a ready ear to the speaker's wit, Phipps was thinking about the tale Keable had told earlier.

It had been a sort of meeting, Keable had said. Not a casual gathering, of that Keable had been certain. It had taken place at a late hour in Litchfield's chambers behind closed doors and with a strong interest in privacy, for when Keable had heard a stir within and gone that way looking for someone to drink with, they had treated him like a stray cur come scratching at the door. Litchfield had asked if Keable knew what a late hour it was, Keable went on, mimicking Litchfield's voice, and a good job too, Phipps thought. "I warrant you have wine enough in your own chambers without begging of your neighbors." Keable had referred to the dead man as an insolent bastard for such a scurvy reply.

Keable, according to his account, had pushed himself in, then seen the company. All but one, standing in the corner, in the bad light, the face turned away for shame or secrecy; Keable now suspected the latter. Litchfield, Monk, Braithwaite, Giles, and the unidentified one. Probably he who was called Prideaux—all the names upon the list in some sort of secret convocation. Keable had noticed no cards or dice at play, no filthy drawings being passed around, no hot whore spread-legged upon the bed. What else could it have been but witchcraft or conspiracy? Keable had theorized.

Phipps reckoned there were two reasons men conspired in secret societies, and each the close cousin of the other: power and money. Given the membership of the group, Phipps discounted power. He had known Litchfield and the others well, and there was not the brain or stomach amongst them to strive for power. Had one of them spoken out against the Queen, been of such religious fervor to inspire a rebellion or join its ranks, or had the inkling of an interest in who was in and who was out at Court, Phipps might have suspected otherwise. But each of the dead men—and Braithwaite too—had been true if unheroic sons of the Church, members of the stolid gentry. Even Giles, with his puritanical Bible reading and quoting, seemed reasonably content that the Queen should rule and the bishops preen, although he had often been heard to vilify the latter as usurpers of unwarranted authority.

Which left money as motive, just as Phipps had always suspected, and why he had risked himself at the Gull with Litchfield's mistress. Having lent money to Litchfield, Phipps knew his needs well enough. The raw youth had a natural gift of squandering. Monk too had been a moneygrubber. It had been said that Giles had debts, but Phipps wasn't sure how much faith to put in that rumor. As for Braithwaite, he dressed well, spent freely, and talked of acquiring land in the near countryside.

But in his heart, Phipps knew there must be more that bound the men.

Something in the speaker's words now drew Phipps from his ruminations. He listened a while, without laughing or applauding, taking Donne's theme with a characteristic seriousness. The theme did not please him. Firmly convinced that women had no souls, Phipps could hardly take delight in an argument that subtly presupposed the contrary!

Donne's voice faded in Phipps's mind. He began to think about Braithwaite and what he should say to induce his confidence, for that had been the pact drawn up between Phipps and Keable, that, there being such a mountain of distrust and enmity between Keable and Braithwaite, it must be Phipps who wormed out Braithwaite's secret, securing thereby a greater prospect of money, safety, or, he prayed, both.

The task, Phipps knew, could not be easy. He could not base his appeal on friendship, for there had been none between the men. Phipps knew Braithwaite held him in contempt, scorned him as an effeminate degenerate, made jokes behind his back, mocked his skinny legs, and mimicked his lisping speech. Yet Phipps had not come near to killing Braithwaite as Keable had done! Thanks be to God for that at least.

Would fear move him, then? Phipps could give warning. He could tell Braithwaite about Stock. He could point out, with cogent reasons, that Braithwaite's place on the list of dead men was ominous and that no proffered alliance should be scorned by him under so strange and perilous a circumstance.

Phipps was resolved. He was not sure the strategy would work, but he had no better in his quiver. He looked around him. Donne still held the audience enraptured. Phipps realized that there was no time like the present for his interview with Braithwaite. If the man still slept, Phipps would awaken him. If Braithwaite told him to go to Hell, Phipps would wish him the same fate and so give over the enterprise.

Phipps slipped out of the Hall.

Matthew had seen Phipps enter the Hall and now observed him leaving. Phipps's departure struck him as curious, for no other of the lawyers made a move to adjourn while Donne still orated. So what was Phipps's purpose—a suddenly remembered appointment, a sudden indisposition or need for sleep?

Then Matthew remembered poor Braithwaite. Alone in chambers while his callow bedfellow sat squeezed in amid the present company hanging on Donne's every word. More than eager to follow Phipps, Matthew waited anxiously for Donne to conclude.

And then he did conclude, and as the applause died away and the Treasurer arose to introduce the next entertainment of the evening (if it was another lecture, Matthew wanted no part of it), Matthew made a hurried exit, maneuvering around tables, stools, and their occupants with the desperate expression of one who has overeaten and must find a closestool or lose his supper in some gentleman's lap.

Phipps knocked discreetly, as good manners required, seeing he was alone in the passage and all dark and quiet within the chambers about him. He tried the door and found it unbarred. Pleased, he entered.

The fire on the hearth gave sufficient light to show him his path, that and familiarity with the chamber itself. He said: "Braithwaite? It is I, Theophilus Phipps."

The sound of his own voice in all the silence made him suddenly wary. He approached the bed and found Braithwaite still sleeping—or at least he seemed so, for he made no motion and his eyes were closed, but the bolster upon which his head had rested when he was last seen by Phipps now was at the foot of the bed.

"Wake up, Braithwaite," Phipps whispered, and he touched Braithwaite's hand.

It was warm, the hand, but Braithwaite was so still, and even by the distant firelight, the face was waxy and somehow fixed in expression. Phipps bent over the body to listen for the beating heart or feel the expulsion of breath that might signify life. But there was neither, and Phipps knew that Braithwaite was dead.

Freshly dead, for the hand was still warm to the touch. Perhaps within minutes or seconds. He looked down to the misplaced bolster; the bedclothes too were in disarray, as though there had been a struggle for breath. Surely a wound might kill, but in such a fashion?

The bolster, round and filled with goose feathers—a happy tool of the smotherer.

The idea settled into his mind and then clutched at his heart in a dreadful realization. He began to back away from the bed, trembling all over, drenched with sweat and perceiving by some sixth sense yet another and hostile presence in the chamber but fearful of confirming it by a search. He felt blindly for the door and stepped into the passage, indifferent to discretion, and hurried to the stair head, descending with a clatter. In good time, he saw the glow of a brace of candles coming up, recognized the form and face of Matthew Stock, and concealed himself in the shadows while Cecil's spy passed.

At the stair head Matthew paused to catch his breath and recall which chamber was Braithwaite's. He had fixed his eyes on the proper door when he saw it open and someone come out. The figure advanced upon him quickly and was too cloaked and muffled to be identified.

The personage was abreast of Matthew in the narrow passage before he could inquire who he was and what business had taken him to Braithwaite's room, and in the next second Matthew felt a sudden jab in his thigh, an excruciating penetration.

He let out a sharp cry, forsaking his hold on the candles to grasp the place of such searing pain. Horrified at the feel of warm blood through the cloth, he felt suddenly sick and sank to the floor in a faint before his ears lost the patter of his assailant's escape.

12

oan worried about Nan Warren, as though Nan were her own child and not a total stranger she had known less than a week. Nan had gone back to the Gull, to that nest of swillers and whore-humpers, to fetch what little was hers there. Never to darken its door again, according to her solemn vow. But Joan wondered if Nan would keep her promise. More, would Hodge and the old bawd Mother Franklin suffer it—the loss of their juiciest wench to a clean and godly life?

On Nan's behalf, Joan had inquired about employment in the Cooke household.

"We don't need another maid," Frances Cooke replied

apologetically after Joan had sung Nan's praises as a courageous and loyal woman, beyond worthiness of the place. "Yet this Nan seems a treasure if half of what you say is true. Good servants are jewels. I could say something to Priscilla Holmes. She and her husband have taken a new house on the Strand. They'll require an army of servants. Perhaps this Nan of yours could find a place there. Shall I speak to Priscilla?"

Joan urged her to do so. Priscilla Holmes was Frances's best friend. She, also, was a former Royal Maid. Yes, that would do nicely. Nan was too refined for lesser employment, despite the unsavory past Joan had pledged to conceal.

Later, in her bedchamber, Joan was overcome by a terrible loneliness. She looked at the bed she had shared with Matthew and thought about him where he now was, no more than two or three miles off but a thousand miles away for her purposes, and then she fell deeper into despondency with a presentiment of danger as well.

It sickened her, and she stumbled toward the bed and slumped. For a moment she fell into a kind of trance in which her surroundings dissolved into a clammy darkness. She felt something with her in the chamber, a menacing presence. It had neither form nor name but was like a gaping hole, through which surged a malign despair.

The despair engulfed her. Blindly she thrust her hands out before her face to ward off the terrible influence. Then, in the next instant, before she could think or pray, the feeling passed.

It was a while before she was herself again. She sat there on the edge of the bed gasping for breath as though she had run a long distance or been submerged in water. Her heart beat rapidly and the clothing next to her body was damp with sweat. She did not know what the trance had meant, but she did know what it was, for she had had such experiences all her life. She called them glimmer-ings, and they came unsummoned in the way some others she had known felt a chill in the bone or a tingle at the neck to warn of impending danger.

But now danger to whom? To herself? To Matthew? To Frances and her young husband? Perhaps to Nan War-ren?

Joan was still pondering this question when she heard footsteps outside her door and then a frantic knocking and Frances calling her name. She rushed to open the door and found Frances standing there with a worried look on her face.

"Something has happened to Matthew," Joan said be-fore Frances could open her mouth.

Frances nodded.

"He's dead?"

"Injured, Joan. A messenger is below."

"Oh, God in Heaven." Joan followed Frances down-stairs and saw the bearer of the ill tidings standing with his cap in his hand. He was an old man with white hair. He stood very calmly as though his news were nothing of importance, and Joan could have beaten him for his seem-ing indifference to her grief.

"This is Jacob Flowerdewe," Frances said.

Jacob began to deliver his message a second time, but Frances stopped him. "That's enough, Jacob. I'll tell Mis-tress Stock all about it on our way."

Matthew's wound was not mortal. That was what Frances assured Joan as the Cookes' coach hurried them through the dark streets, although Joan kept fearing the worst. The coincidence of her vision and this woeful news was too perfect to assume otherwise. The dark, overbearing houses seemed to close in around them as they traveled, and the few souls braving the night with raised torches seemed like shades of the dead walking abroad from their graves.

Later she could hardly remember their arrival at the Gate that a day before had seemed to bar her forever from admission. There was no barring now. She was ushered in quickly, across a desolate, moonlit garden, into a long stone building. Thomas met her, and Master Hutton, and there were several other gentlemen bearing torches. Then she was led upstairs and down a corridor and inside a room where she found Matthew in bed and a stout, bearded man standing beside him.

"Your husband is doing well," said the bearded man.

She looked quickly from his face to Matthew's. The bearded man kept talking. "The wound was shallow; it injured no vital organs."

The man, a physician, she presumed, left the room. She rushed to the bed to embrace her husband.

"Thank God you're alive, dear heart," she said, unable to restrain her tears. She wet his face with her tears, and he kissed her too. His lips were warm, but as she looked more closely into his face, she could see the pain he felt. His normally brown complexion was pale; his eyes were heavy-lidded. "Now, tell me what happened," she said.

She was disappointed how little there was to tell, or at least to comprehend—a sudden encounter, a stranger's random violence, a wound that the physician assured him would heal with time and care. And Braithwaite, Matthew's best hope for understanding the connection between the murdered Templars, now gone to join his brethren, carrying everything he might have known with him.

"You followed Phipps from the Hall," she said. "Could he have been Braithwaite's murderer and your assailant?"

Matthew shook his head. "I don't think so. I did see Phipps leave, and followed him, but never saw him until he came with the others in response to my cries. As for the villain who struck me, he had just come from outdoors. I could smell the night and damp about him as he passed, nothing of the smoky Hall."

"But you saw him come from Braithwaite's chamber?"

"Yes."

"And then found the man dead."

"Smothered, I suspect."

"Merciful Heaven," she said. "A fine Temple of the law this is where murders and assaults have become commonplace. What did the physician say about Braithwaite?"

"At first that he would live. Now, that the wound caused his death. He says he has seen stranger outcomes of minor wounds and recited a half dozen cases."

"What does Master Hutton believe?"

"As I—another instance of foul play."

"Oh, Matthew, I do wish we were home again and all well. London is stale—and full of danger. I rue the day I consented to this madness."

He asked her what madness she meant.

"Why, of remaining in London. Of undertaking this dangerous enterprise. Who, even in happy times, is safe in a company of lawyers? Comes a murderer among them and one might as well endure plague time for all the safety he will find."

"Well, I can't abandon my duty now," he said.

"And why not?"

"For one thing, Master Leyland, my physician, has confined me to my bed. More important, I swore to Thomas Cooke and Master Hutton to deliver up the name of the murderer, if not the man himself. Yes, and Sir Robert recommended me in his letter."

Joan pondered the intimidating name of Cecil, the Queen's Principal Secretary, Matthew's great good friend.

Duty, obligation, responsibility. It was useless to debate on these points with the man she married.

"Then I'll stay here with you."

Matthew laughed. "A fine lot of good you'd do me here."

"So how will you perform your duty, as you call it, from a sickbed?" she asked, thinking she might have him there. "Are your suspects to stand without whilst you call them in one by one like naughty schoolboys? And what of the murderer? He spared you once; will he be content to spare you a second time?"

"I shall be well enough off," Matthew said.

"Ridiculous, husband. False courage. Be wise instead."

"I doubt he who struck me believes I saw so much of him as to prove a witness. And would I be in less danger were I up and about?"

"Ah, but what if you're wrong? What if the murderer thinks you recognized him? What if he returns to serve you as he did Braithwaite?"

"Master Hutton has seen to that."

"How so?"

He reached beneath his coverlet and pulled out a pistol. She gasped. "Now I will worry. You'll shoot yourself for sure."

"And he's provided me with a nurse."

"Who?"

"His clerk."

"Phipps. Worse still. It is he whom I most suspect."

"All the better," Matthew said. "I know he is not the murderer, yet if he is otherwise involved—say an accomplice—"

"Or mastermind, yes, what then?"

"Then let him come and serve me. I may yet untangle this skein without moving from my bed."

Joan took a hard look at the man she married—the

strange and perverse creature so different from herself. Or was he *that* different? Then she said, "Matthew, you vex me beyond endurance with your stubbornness. Why don't you listen to reason when she speaks so plainly?"

"I think it is your love that speaks, not reason."

"Can they not speak with one voice?"

"I won't scold you for loving me," he said. "But you are the last person to hoist sail before an enemy. Why commend to me so cowardly a course?"

"But if you are outmanned and outcannoned too, what then?"

He didn't answer her question but shifted the matter. He said Thomas had told him of her own misadventures. Assaulted on the London streets, robbed of her gown. And she recommended to him a course of abject caution!

She told him the blunt truth of what happened, hoping that Nan's account of Phipps's threats would make him think again about remaining at the Middle Temple.

He listened, but without a sign he was prepared to change his mind. "I owe this Nan Warren more thanks than I can give," he said. "Though she may be a whore, yet she has a good heart, and is perhaps more sinned against than sinning. Christ excused the woman taken in adultery; we can do no less."

Matthew's words pleased Joan mightily and she could almost forgive his stubbornness. She was grateful he shared her enthusiasm for her new friend, but dismayed when he continued to argue against Phipps's involvement. "The man lacks the mettle for murder," he said with that annoying way he had of settling an issue with a simple statement.

She asked what was being said about the attack on him. Surely the whole house was now alarmed. A murderer at large. Who would feel himself safe?

"Hutton will give out that gout has driven me to bed.

Only he and I and Thomas will know the truth. Thus, Hutton says, will the House be free from infamy and I from suspicion of being other than I seem. Braithwaite's death will be treated similarly. A consequence of the duel that went awry."

"I think your Master Hutton is more concerned for reputation than for safety."

"Well, to be fair to the man, he may believe his concerns are not at cross-purposes."

They talked a while longer; she examined his wound herself, not content that a stranger should have care of her husband, even if he was a physician. Then she wished him a speedy recovery, kissed and blessed him too, and said it was sheer madness for one to remain in a place he had had so clear an invitation to leave.

He told her to go home—and to stay there. He would do his duty, and she should do hers.

Later, as the coach rattled through the streets and Frances slept on her young husband's shoulder, Joan remained alert, staring out into the night. She felt neither desire nor need for sleep, full as she was of fear for Matthew and concern how she might circumvent his orders that she remain at home.

The damned would freeze in hell before she should be so submissive!

13

I n the privacy of his lodgings, his only companion an ill-tempered brindled cat who
curled beneath his legs and slept, Theophilus
Phipps reflected upon the transparent cun-
ning of old men with power.

Hutton had told him he was to play nurse to the ailing
Matthew Stock. To Phipps's mind, a servant's job. Told
him—with the straight, sober face of a judge instructing the
accused he was to be hanged and when—that, should anyone ask, the Chelmsford clothier was laid up with the gout.
Because Stock had brought no servant to see to his needs,
Hutton said it was imperative that someone share the
man's chamber, to tuck him in and fill his dish and empty

his chamber pot and come when he whistled like a good dog, or so Phipps imagined the loathsome assignment.

But Phipps knew what was up. The business about gout—did Hutton take him for an absolute fool? Stock had been undone by more than gout. Phipps had glimpsed the blood-soaked bandages and had no doubt that beneath the coverlet of his bed, Stock harbored a torment of the flesh inflicted by brutal steel. The nasty work of Braithwaite's murderer, Phipps did not doubt for a minute. And now Phipps was to serve as an unwitting bodyguard—his presence a deterrent to further assaults! He was, in sum, to be exposed to the same danger as Stock!

And yet Phipps had not declined Hutton's order. How could he, under the circumstances? Being so intimate with Cecil's spy was a risk, but also an opportunity. An opportunity to detect where danger lay, and where escape, and where the money young Litchfield had spoken of so indiscreetly.

And thus Phipps had no choice but to accept the assignment, as distasteful and perilous as it was. For he could not refuse to nurse a man he despised (for his social origins) and feared (for his political connections) without revealing to Hutton just how much he knew and by what devious means he had come upon it. He would only have incriminated himself, and Phipps was hardly about to do *that*!

He packed what he would need for his brief sojourn in Stock's chambers, put out fire, candles, and cat, and went to do his assigned duty with a sense of fate and opportunity.

He knocked softly at Stock's door and then entered without waiting for a summons within. He found Stock awake; he was sitting up in bed and holding a pistol aimed at Phipps's chest.

With instincts born of natural cowardice, Phipps threw his hands up before his face and cried out in alarm. Stock lowered the pistol, uncocked it, and put it down beside his pillow. "Very sorry, Phipps. Master Hutton left the pistol with me—as protection."

His heart pounding, Phipps walked over and put his things in a small valise, down on the smaller bed. "Jesus, you gave me a fright," he said.

"I didn't mean it," Stock said. "What hour must it be?"

"Near unto twelve."

"I'm told we are to be chamberfellows for a few days— until I get on my feet again."

"So it would seem."

"Hutton instructed you in your duties?"

"He did."

"Good. Go ahead, unpack. Make yourself at home."

Phipps said thank you but knew very well he would not be making himself at home, not in a chamber where Monk had hanged himself. He was not superstitious, but he wondered that Stock could face a night alone in the chamber so complacently, especially after what he had encountered in the passage, but then perhaps that more than explained the pistol.

Stock shut his eyes, and Phipps undressed; the fire on the hearth had burned down to ashes, and the chamber was taking on that sodden chill that makes slipping beneath the covers on a December night one of life's fundamental pleasures. But Phipps, still uneasy about the pistol and unable to rid himself of the image of the hanged man, despaired of sleep despite the lateness of the hour.

"Too bad about Braithwaite," Stock murmured suddenly, substituting one corpse for another in Phipps's mind.

"Too bad indeed."

"We all thought he would recover—even Leyland, the physician."

"Oh, doctors don't know everything," Phipps remarked casually. He went to the door and bolted it. Stock said that was a good idea. It never hurt to be safe. He wished Phipps good night.

Wearily Phipps climbed into bed. He knew the bed had been Litchfield's, and he found the thought of sleeping in it both depressing and frightening. But it had also been the chamber where, according to Keable, the conspirators had met, and so he was thereby closer to the truth he sought. There was something to be said for that.

Strangely, however, the thought provided him with little consolation.

At the Gull it was past midnight and near closing time. A handful of patrons remained, entertained by a couple of Mother Franklin's scrawny birds who had come down to scratch and preen amid the survivors of the long evening, three gentlemen of Gray's. Ned Hodge, the proprietor, stood behind the bar haranguing one of the drawers. A torrent of epithets drowning the poor fellow in a year's abuse. Hodge stopped as the door to the outside opened and a rush of frigid air blew in to clear away some of the evening's accumulation of stale tobacco smoke.

Hodge waved the offending drawer away with an abrupt motion and turned his wrath upon the visitor. "Close the door behind you, curse you. What do you think, firewood is free?" Squinting, he recognized the newcomer. "Oh, it's you, is it? Come back, have you? Well, close the door then. Where have you been all night? Setting up shop in the Strand, I'll warrant."

Nan Warren made no reply, and Hodge noticed the wench's face was waxy pale and her expression unusually grave for one who was normally as merry as could be. He thought she might be sick, even, and prayed God it wasn't the plague she was afflicted with. Not that he cared about her personally. To him, one slut was like unto another, although he did allow Nan Warren to be better endowed in complexion and form than most.

Curious, he drew her a cup of ale and took it over to where she had taken a stool in the corner. "It's cold out, is it?"

"As your heart," she said, not looking up at him.

"So what were you doing still abroad?"

"Looking for someone, if you must know."

He repeated her words, sneering. "Take care no one's looking for you, mistress, after that trick you pulled the other night."

She looked up at him with sudden anger. "What trick do you mean?"

"Easy, Nan. I mean the trick you pulled with that proud ironmonger's wife or whatever she was who thought herself so grand and dealt a low blow to my good friend. I tell you, I was hard put to make peace after you disappeared with her."

"Were you?" said Nan with a dry laugh. She took the cup and raised it to her lips. "Well, I am heartily sorry for your pains, Master Hodge, but I thought it inconvenient for either of us to be mauled by your good friends, and so we took our leave."

"They were only having a little fun," Hodge said.

"Their idea of fun, not mine."

"I suppose she paid you handsomely for helping her escape."

"If she did, what business is that of yours?"

"Watch your tongue, mistress. If you want to keep those fancy lodgings I provide upstairs."

"I won't be needing them anymore—at least not after tonight."

He laughed. "You've found a friend, then?"

"Maybe."

He laughed again, but less confidently now. Nan Warren had always been more plucky than the other girls who worked for Mother Franklin. Hodge could have twisted her neck off in an instant, so slender it was, and yet there was something about her that made him hesitate, some hidden strength within her that told him she was no woman to be regarded lightly.

The two whores had gone upstairs, and the three gentlemen of Gray's left behind were staring at Nan with quiet interest. She looked over at them and then looked down at the table. A man in a heavy cloak came in.

"Good evening to you, Master Leyland," Hodge called out with sudden cheerfulness. "Been up late bleeding the sick, have you? Well, you'll want a flagon of sack to brace you against that which no physician can cure."

Leyland returned Hodge's greeting, smiling amiably. He said he had been at the Middle Temple, tending wounds.

"Wounds, is it?" returned Hodge, with a hoarse, mocking laugh. "What, the young lawyers have been cutting each other's throats, have they?"

"Two casualties," said Leyland, turning to look at where Nan sat. "One an accident at fence, of which the poor devil died unaccountably later."

"You don't say!" exclaimed Hodge, interested.

"And the other a visitor—a father of a prospective student."

"Died too?" asked Hodge, bringing a glass to Leyland and then putting the doctor's coin into the little pocket in his apron. "Serves the old fellow right for mixing up with men half his age."

"True, it was no accident," Leyland said, glancing over at Nan again. "Someone stabbed him. Got him in the thigh not six inches from his privates. But he'll live to procreate as he pleases."

"A lucky man on both accounts," said Hodge.

Leyland walked over to where Nan was and stood for a

moment looking down at her. Then he said, "Why so hangdog, Nan? You look like death."

She turned her face up to him and regarded him coldly. "And what if I do, is that your concern?"

"Maybe," he said. "Come upstairs with me."

"Not tonight."

"We have business."

"I lack good company," she said.

"I've been known to answer to that description."

Nan finished her drink without replying. Behind the bar, Hodge watched the interchange with interest, straining to hear. He liked Leyland, and although the physician spent his days healing gentlemen, Hodge suspected that beneath, he was an unscrupulous rogue of the same uncouth tribe as himself. Leyland asked Nan if she would have another drink and she said no. He asked Hodge to bring her one anyway. "A good drink will melt the ice in her blood."

"I have no ice in my blood," Nan said.

"Take it from a man of science, Nan," Leyland said. "The blood may chill as much as water since, like water, it is a liquid."

"Spare me your philosophy, sir physician," Nan said bitterly. "I will endure none of your sophistical wooing tonight."

"I, a sophistical wooer?" Leyland asked, turning around to Hodge as though he should judge between them. "Now you do me wrong, Nan, to call my sincerity into question."

It was Nan Warren's turn to laugh, but Hodge heard no merriment in it. Her laugh was rancorous and derisive, and the soft features of her face had been transformed into a mask of harshness and cruelty. But none of this seemed to deter Leyland, for which Hodge admired the man all the more, and he wished him success in taming this willful whore and enjoying her before morning.

Leyland sat down opposite Nan and reached into his

purse. He withdrew some coins; Hodge could hear them tinkling together in the physician's hand. "In faith," said Leyland, "a penny or more in the right palm can do more than alchemy to turn the base metal of refusal into the gold of compliance. Isn't that right, friend Hodge?"

Hodge, who had heard that part of the conversation, agreed readily that it was true. "I know nothing of alchemy or any such hocus-pocus, but the rattle of coins rubbing one another is the prettiest music I know."

Leyland laughed and opened his palm so that Nan could see how many there were and of what worth. Hodge watched Nan's gaze fall to the open hand. For a moment she seemed prepared to utter another rejection, then she looked into Leyland's face and said, loud enough for Hodge to hear this too, "Well, Master Leyland. You have a new patient for the evening after all. Pray, let us see how you can restore me to health."

Leyland laughed again, a deeper, throatier laugh, as large men make when they have had their way about something. He turned and winked at Hodge, whose eyes reflected his own pleasure in witnessing these negotiations.

Hodge continued to watch as Nan and Leyland went upstairs. He smiled to himself and then looked around to bid the last of his customers good night, not realizing until that moment that he was now alone.

"A pretty performance," Leyland said when they were alone in the little chamber that was Nan's. He thought to flatter her out of her melancholy, not about to have so sullen a bedfellow.

"Downstairs, you mean?"

"There—and also at the Middle Temple. Braithwaite will say nothing now, save perhaps to the Devil when he meets him. But tell me, the attack upon this Matthew

Stock, that wasn't in the plan. I suppose that was some sudden whim of yours."

His question caused her to look at him strangely. "Who did you call the man?"

"Matthew Stock—a clothier from Chelmsford. They say his son desires to study the law and he is there to inspect the premises. Bad luck for him, eh? In the wrong place at the wrong time, poor devil."

She repeated the name, and Leyland wondered if she had heard it before, a friend's name perhaps, or, more likely, given her profession, a former client. Then she said: "I didn't know who he was—only that he saw me coming out of Braithwaite's door. I struck only to distract him, to prevent his following. He might have identified me had he had more leisure for observation."

"Why didn't you kill him?"

"I never kill without a purpose, Master Leyland," she said, regarding him with a severity that dampened his ardor a bit. "I tell you I didn't know who it was I struck."

"Well, let's to bed," Leyland said, sorry that the conversation had taken this turn when he fully intended another. "It's very late. The matter is settled at the Middle Temple. We're out of danger now."

"Not yet," Nan said, a worried look on her face that made her seem to the physician suddenly older than she was and of harder mettle. "Stock is no innocent bystander, but a greater danger to our enterprise than ever Braithwaite was. Before we sleep, I'll tell you a story about him that will convince you my fears are no mere woman's fretting. And tomorrow we'll lay plans as to what must be done."

14

With its oval fur cap, freshly scrubbed cheeks, and ruff collar upon which the head rested like a melon on a plate, the face in the mirror might have been a young man's. It was a face upon which age had softly writ, except for webbing radiating from the corner of the eyes. Granted it was a soft, beardless face, but then, so was many a young man's of brown complexion. The least that could be said was that it was a face that would not draw a second look should the body below it be sheathed in doublet, hose, and stocking and carry itself with a resolute, manly air.

It might have been the face of Joan and Matthew Stock's son had such a person ever been born to Joan, whose very reflection now stared back at her with mild surprise from the glass, daring her to the enterprise she contemplated.

No wonder, she thought, the ruffians at the Gull had been fooled. And dour Robert too in thinking she was other than she was indeed. More art would make the disguise perfect.

She would have to do something with her hair—crop it shorter, but not so much. Not lower than her ears, and lank, not curled or rolled, but then, she thought, one saw almost every style on London streets in these days of shame when ancient marks of male and female dress seemed to have converged in an indecent androgyny.

As for her figure, Joan had not been so richly endowed by nature that under wraps her woman's breasts could not be discreetly closeted in loose-fitting doublet and sweeping cape.

In sum, she had convinced herself she could pass for her own son—a young man secured against the cold, quiet out of habit, soft-voiced and reverent like a bishop's clerk. Nothing her husband had conveyed to others about her fictional offspring would be denied by her superficial appearance. Nor did she plan to invite closer scrutiny of her person than a casual inspection.

Besides, she considered further, she had not lived with men for all the years of her life—first father and brothers, then husband, and more recently her young son-in-law— for naught. Did she not know their manner, expressions, voices, and gestures? Had Matthew not complimented her more than once on her ability to counterfeit and mimic this Chelmsford acquaintance or that? Was it not a goodly time to put her talents to a practical end?

For practice, she carried on a short conversation with herself, responding in various voices. She stalked the bedchamber, affecting a masculine swagger. She thrust her hand out boldly as men do to shake another, invisible hand.

Then she set about inventorying her store of clothing.

It was a paltry store, consisting only of the one suit of clothes Matthew had not taken with him to his Temple lodgings. The suit she well knew would not fit at all. The garb she had been given by Nan, however, was so well suited in shank, thigh, girth, and shoulder that indeed all might have been made for her, yet they were threadbare, and she was to be a prosperous merchant's son, no trades- man out at elbows. Would she not be ashamed to be seen so dressed?

Then she thought of Nan. Nan would make an excellent ally. Nan knew London and would not have Frances Cooke's certain reservations about Joan's plan. For Joan did worry about her hostess's response. What would the former Royal Maid think! Her guest running off to the Middle Temple disguised as a man! Would Frances not point out the obvious danger—not to mention the viola- tion of God's ordinance against one sex dressing as an- other?

On this thorny point Joan had some qualms herself. Ac- tors, of course, did it with impunity, since it was unseemly that any natural female strut and fret upon the public stage. For women to garb themselves as men was another matter, although it had been presented as a device in the play *Twelfth Night,* of which Thomas Cooke had spoken with so much admiration. Could therefore art not serve as guide to life, even though Scripture railed against such practices?

Now, Joan's own case, she reasoned, was a valid excep- tion to the prohibition. For she intended not to repudiate her natural sex, but to succor an ailing, vulnerable hus- band, who, having not the good sense—or healthy cow- ardice—to flee from a place of danger, required her to come to his rescue. Must not charity come before a foolish compliance with rules?

Besides, would she not make an even better spy?

But then she wondered, what if the imposture was detected? Would there not be embarrassment beyond enduring? Public disgrace? Perhaps even punishment?

It was well past midnight as she contemplated these things, and finally weariness overtook her. She replaced the masculine dress with feminine bedtime attire, tossed another faggot in the fire, and knelt down beside the bed to pray.

Earnestly she prayed for Matthew, for her daughter and son-in-law, for her grandchild. She prayed for the souls of her stillborn children, one of whom might have grown to be the son she intended to portray, and she prayed even for the success of the child of her brain, the young man John Stock. Then she climbed into bed and blew out the candle.

Sometime before dawn Joan dreamed a strange and disturbing dream. She was in some dark corridor of the Middle Temple, passing chamber doors standing open. Inside of each, young men gowned in burial weeds watched her as she passed, their expressions disapproving, as though they knew she did not belong there. She walked what seemed a very long way, passing open door after open door, and all the men she passed were the same and their expressions were alike and Joan was sorely afraid. Finally she came to a door that was closed, and somehow feeling Matthew was inside, she opened the door and went in.

She found herself face to face with the old man of queer speech who had brought word of Matthew's injury and had accompanied Joan and Frances to the Temple in the coach. He was not disapproving like the others but was smiling broadly with his toothless old man's smile and he motioned for her to enter.

When she asked him where Matthew was, he made no reply but pointed to yet another door. She went the way he had pointed, came to the door, and, without knocking, entered.

She stood in a square room with a single arched window placed high in a stark white wall. There were no furnishings except for a round-backed chair and square table on which many books were heaped. Poring over these moldy volumes and with his back to her sat a person dressed in a flowing gown. She knew it was not Matthew who sat reading these books, but she approached nonetheless and touched the reader on the shoulder.

Strangely, in her dream her fingers seemed to pass through the shoulder as though it had no substance. Then the stranger rose and turned to face her.

The face was indeed a stranger's face, with hollow eye sockets and sharp, pointed chin, and lips so thin there was hardly more than mouth. Joan's eyes fell from the face to the breast, for she saw the gown he wore was open to the small, buttonlike navel, like some old painting of Christ's apostles she had seen. But amazing to her were the two female breasts with swollen nipples as though the hermaphroditic creature had just given suck.

Next morning Joan remembered her dream and puzzled over it. She believed it to be an omen, for like any sensible woman and decent Christian, she believed in the prophetic power of visions of the night, just as she believed in the glimmerings that had so often expanded her awareness beyond ordinary observation.

But an omen of what?

She dressed and went downstairs to find Frances in the parlor, obviously upset about something.

"Why, what is it, Frances?" Joan asked.

"It's my father-in-law. He's been sick all month and now is worse. Thomas and I will be leaving for Suffolk within the hour. They fear for his life, for he is a very old gentleman."

Joan expressed her sympathy and sat down next to her friend. Under these new circumstances, she decided not to propose her plan to Frances, half-glad to lose the opportunity, given her certainty that Frances would think her stark mad and try to talk her out of it. "How long will you be in Suffolk?"

Frances wasn't sure; all depended on God's will, she said. At the age her father-in-law was, one never knew. The old man could go between breaths. She urged Joan, however, to stay as long as she liked. "The house you may treat as your own in our absence. You may rule the servants as you see fit, and I shall tell them so myself."

It was then Joan realized that she need not inform Frances of her plan at all. Frances and Thomas both would be gone. Unsupervised, Joan could now do as she pleased, and there would be no one to tell her otherwise.

Later that morning, as Joan stepped out into the street, she saw that the morning's frost was nearly gone and a pale sun was struggling to penetrate the smoky air. She had left the house with no fanfare, Frances and Thomas having departed in the coach before her. Joan was so dressed to put her disguise to the test and to find Nan and secure both counsel and the clothes she needed to invade the Temple precincts.

She was relieved that, once in the street, her appearance caused no stares of wonder in the faces that she met, which gave her encouragement that her plan was not entirely absurd. As she walked, she practiced her masculine gait, lengthening her stride and swinging her free arm like the pendulum of a clock. She followed the way she knew well, too intent on the strange adventure before her to pay much attention to the passing scene.

The city clocks were striking noon by the time she reached her destination, not the Middle Temple (that would be later) but the Gull. Here she faltered briefly in her resolve as she faced the tavern where she had been a few days earlier so rudely treated, although in the light of day the place did seem far less threatening than when last she saw it. The men who were coming in and going out seemed a more respectable sort than the drunken sailors who had accosted her before.

Inside, she was relieved to find that the ugly proprietor was not at his usual station. In his place was a young man of pleasant and honest-seeming countenance who greeted her courteously and asked what she would have, and most important, gave no sign of observing in her appearance any contradiction between her face and her costume. The tavern itself was half-full, and many of its occupants seemed merchants and small tradesmen doing business over cups of wine or ale. The whores who had descended from above in the night had yet to make their appearance. In a husky voice of uneven pitch, Joan explained to a waiter who inquired that she would have neither food nor drink but wished to see Nan Warren, a former employee of the house. The young man laughed.

"For all I know, sir, Nan is employed here still. I saw her but yesternight. Her room is just up those stairs, although I'll not guarantee she's out of bed as yet, it being only noon and Nan wont to sleep late."

Concerned that Nan had not yet left so loathsome a place, Joan thanked the young man for this information, grateful that he did not regard her with suspicion. Emboldened by these signs of her disguise's success, she went right upstairs and proceeded down the passage to the room where she thought she and Nan had taken refuge the first night of their acquaintance. But when she knocked, an unfamiliar voice answered, and out from the shadowy recesses came a female form so wan and undernourished that Joan was sure this picture of frailty was as near to death as any mortal might be and still breathe.

"Good morning, young sir," the girl said in a velvety voice promising physical delights the unwholesome body before her could not possibly deliver. "You're early abroad. Yet's it's never too early for pleasure, is it? Well, don't stand there, come in."

The invitation was supported by a slender arm that extended, grasped Joan by the shoulder, and drew her in to the little room, where Joan could discern a narrow bed all atumble with dirty bedclothes, a bare floor of planks, and not a stick of furniture else but old, stained wainscoting. The one tiny window was covered with a ragged cloth, permitting only a gray effusion that allowed Joan to see in outline but not in detail. For Joan, the outline was horrid enough, as was the personage clutching at her. She tried to get away, but the girl's appearance belied the strength in her arm.

"My name is Alice," the girl said.

Joan told her she was looking for Nan Warren, an announcement that did not please Alice, for she said: "Nan Warren? Why, the Devil, what has she that I've not? I am as much woman and more."

With this, Alice grasped Joan's hand and pressed it against her emaciated body where Joan could feel the slight swell of the girl's breast. Joan gasped with embarrassment and drew her hand away, her heart racing. She was unsure how to extricate herself from her present situation, how to explain to this pitiful creature before her just why her invitation to illicit passion was so abhorrent. She had fooled the strangers in the street and the young waiter downstairs with her cape and doublet, her hair concealed beneath the cap, but this indeed was the stronger test of her manhood. In the next instant the wanton before her would be removing Joan's clothes, and then how would young John Stock fare?

Behind her, Joan heard another voice. Turning away from Alice, she saw the old woman with the ghastly red wig and wrinkled face whom Nan had called Mother Franklin. The old woman eyed her suspiciously. "What villainy is here, Alice? What, will this maggoty head not pay for his pleasure?"

Joan turned from the old woman to look at Alice. She watched with astonishment as a devious smile of understanding spread over Alice's face. Alice said: "Well now, Mother Franklin. He will not, though I have asked him with much courtesy. Twice he had his way with me and now he claims to have no money about him at all but begs to let him return later."

"Return later, my foot!" retorted the old woman. She flung at Joan a long and vile train of epithets, at the same time clenching her fists and making her wrinkled face more hideous than before. "You miserly rogue, give the girl what you owe here fairly or by all that's holy, I'll have Master Hodge up from below and he'll take it from your hide."

Really alarmed now, Joan tried to explain that she had not used Alice at all, but had only asked after Nan Warren, but the old woman would not be pacified, and Alice made it worse by beginning to shake and blubber most convincingly and swear she had been wronged—an honest working woman deprived of her due and other such nonsense that, in less dangerous circumstances, would have caused Joan to laugh outright at its ridiculousness.

But Alice's professions of injury achieved their purpose. Mother Franklin's outrage intensified, as did the vileness of her abuse. "You whoremasterly spaniel! You son of a three-legged pup! You damned spittle of the lazar house."

Joan was on the verge of disclosing her true identity and suffering the consequences when the more than welcome face of Nan Warren appeared in the doorway. Nan seemed at once to take in the situation—the true nature of the conflict and even Joan's identity, for Joan was dressed in the doublet and hose Nan had given her and of course her face was the same as ever. Nan inquired of the old woman the cause of the turmoil.

"This whoremasterly knave has refused to pay for services rendered."

Alice blubbered that it was all true and glared at Joan reprovingly.

"I never touched the child at all," Joan exclaimed. "I only asked for Nan, here, whom I have come to see on a matter of private business."

"Filthy business, I wager," Alice said.

"What if it be filthy?" Nan responded harshly. "What concern is it of yours, if it is *my* business?"

Joan repeated that she had not touched the girl, much less crawled in bed with her, and Nan said she believed it, for Alice had pulled this same device before with honest gentleman who had not so much as peeked beneath her skirt.

Then Alice called Nan a greasy whore, and Nan called her a lying slut, and in the next instant both women were face to face snarling and grimacing and it was all the old woman could do to keep them from tearing at each other's flesh. Joan watched all this with mute horror, for although she was relieved to have attention shifted from her, she was uncertain as to how this row between Nan and Alice would come out, and she was shocked to see the violence of which her new friend was capable. Nan was the taller and stronger of the two women, and certainly the healthier, with her plump, round arms, full breasts, and sturdy hips, but there was a fiery determination in the pale Alice, who cursed and snarled like a person really wronged and not the fraud she was.

The commotion had wakened the whole house now, and from other rooms women in various stages of undress came sleepy-eyed to know the cause of this noisy dispute. One of these newcomers now supported Nan's story about Alice's former fraudulent claims, and when a third voice was raised in the same cause, Alice began to calm down and after a few further exchanges was forced to admit because of these testimonies that it was in fact "some other gentlemen whom she meant, and not he before her."

Then Nan led Joan from the room and took her to her own chamber and closed the door behind them.

"Mistress Stock! It took me a second before I recognized you. Why are you here?"

"I might ask the same of you," Joan said, trying not to sound censorious. "I thought you intended to gather your belongings and find new lodgings."

"Oh, I do," said Nan. "And I have found new lodgings, but had to return for something I forgot, which having now, I am free to shake the dust from my feet and say farewell to this place forever. But you are at great risk returning to the Gull as you have done."

"You saved my life a second time," Joan said. "I daily grow in your debt. But before telling you my full intent and why I am thus dressed, I must sit down. For that old harridan's oaths and the odor of Alice's chamber have made me want to retch."

Joan went over and sat down on the edge of the bed, which, unlike that of Alice's tiny quarters, was cleanly made. Nan sat down next to her. "Now tell me all," said Nan with an encouraging smile. "Both why you have forsaken your natural sex and why so boldly returned here."

Joan told Nan how Matthew had been attacked, and found, in the process, that she had to reveal more than she intended about his real purpose at the Inns. Yet her confidence in Nan did not now admit the need for caution.

"Well," said Nan when Joan had finished her story. "Thanks be to God your husband was spared a worse fate. You say he was on his way to ask questions of one of the gentlemen of the Inns?"

"Yes, Braithwaite—the most recent victim."

"Ah. I don't remember having heard of him before, but I am sorry to hear that your husband has Theophilus Phipps for a nurse. For my money, he's the murderer your husband seeks."

Joan said Phipps was her choicest suspect, based on what Nan had said and Matthew witnessed.

"Would it not be wiser, seeing your husband is wounded, that he withdraw from these inquiries—and you as well? I fear, Joan, that in close quarters your true sex will become known. Surely your presence will put you into serious danger. Won't you reconsider?"

Joan thought about this, then said. "I'm sorry, Nan. Of course, you're right about the danger. Yet I can't stand the idea of Matthew's being alone there. He's virtually helpless in his present state. Besides, I don't like being excluded just because I am a woman."

Nan commiserated with Joan on that point. Then she said, "Well, Joan, you must do what you must do. I see there's no arguing with you. But why doesn't your husband arrest Phipps for the crimes? Then all would be done and you two could hie home to Chelmsford."

Joan laughed. "You have much to learn about these works of my husband," she said. "Evidence must be gathered, witnesses secured, testimonies presented. It's not as simple as you might suppose."

"Yes," Nan reflected, "I can see it will not be as simple as I supposed."

"Can you find more clothes for me? I can't wear this to the Temple."

Nan said she could. "Why, I know the very place. There's a certain Jew keeps shop in the Old Exchange where poor gentlemen pawn their cloaks and shirts. There's none the Jew can't fit if he's a mind. He loves me well and will give me a good price."

Joan was pleased with this plan and gave Nan money, and Nan said she would be back within the hour, but first, she said, she would take Joan to her new lodgings, where she could wait in greater comfort.

Nan's new lodgings were less than a mile from the Gull, in a better neighborhood, with respectable houses and shops. It was upstairs from an apothecary's and was entered from a side door and some narrow stairs that led up to a landing off which were two doors. Joan's sensitive nose detected an unpleasant odor coming from one of the chambers.

"That chamber opposite is the apothecary's," Nan explained as she inserted the key in the lock of her own. "He is ever distilling his potions. His mother, Mistress Browne, says I will soon grow used to the odor, but I doubt it. Yet the smell is worth what it spares me in rent."

Nan told Joan what she paid, and Joan agreed Nan had struck a good bargain with her landlord. Clean lodgings in respectable houses were difficult to come by in London, unless one was willing and able to pay a great sum. Joan was pleased that Nan had managed her expenses so well and was more than ever convinced that her trust in the woman had not been misplaced, especially when she saw the inside of Nan's apartment.

There were two rooms there, one a kind of parlor and the other a bedchamber. Both were simply furnished, and everything was clean and neat as though Nan had dwelt there a long time. Two windows looked out into the street, and a small fireplace occupied one wall. In the farthest corner of the bedchamber was a hidden recess, which Nan showed Joan with some pride. "A priest's hole," she called it.

Joan commented that it was not much of a concealment, being as it was so shallow, and must therefore hide a priest who was no more than a skeleton. Nan, with a mischievous look, showed her how the boards in the wall gave way to an even deeper and more capacious recess. "Mistress Browne showed me this," Nan explained casually. "She said it was a place to hide in case robbers should break in." Joan said she hoped Nan wouldn't be driven to such an extreme, for the hole was not that large either in height or width, and Nan said that it was very true and that while she was off to the Jew's, Joan should not feel obliged to take refuge there but might enjoy a comfortable chair in the adjoining room.

Joan thanked her friend and sat down to wait.

It was nearer two hours than one before Nan returned, carrying a very large bundle beneath her arm and announcing that what several poor gentlemen had exchanged for a pittance, Nan had rescued in Joan's cause. During which time Joan began to experience her first serious doubts about her undertaking. She had fooled the waiter and lying Alice and old Mother Franklin with her disguise, and even Nan had admitted momentarily being deceived, but would she deceive the clever lawyers at the Temple and especially the treacherous and probably homicidal Theophilus Phipps? By the time Nan made her appearance, Joan had worked herself into a state of considerable anxiety. Yet Nan herself seemed to have cast away her reservations, for she said, when entering, "Now, my good Jack Stock. We'll fit you out as becomes your station as a prosperous merchant's son, with doublet, hose, and codpiece too, shoes with silver buckles, and a cloak neither patched nor threadbare but of good solid stuff."

Joan changed into one of the suits in the bundle while Nan helped her put the final touches on her disguise. Then Nan wished Joan all the success she deserved and the two women embraced warmly as though they had known each other all their lives.

Joan was only a stone's throw from the apothecary's when she was approached by two ragged urchins petitioning her for pennies. The boys, who could not have been past ten, looked up into her face so piteously and asked of her with such earnestness that Joan found it impossible to deny them. She gave each twice what he had asked and blessed them, and they said, "Thank you, Lady," with great politeness.

Joan had moved on a good ten paces when their parting words sank in; she reddened, and considering briefly the compelling logic that if she could not fool a child with her disguise, she could hardly do better with crafty lawyers for whom deception and guile were meat and drink, she gave over her project and returned to Cooke House so profoundly dejected that even Robert's greeting ("Yes, *sir*, who would you see here?") could not remedy it.

Leyland came knocking at Nan's door within a quarter of an hour after Joan's departure and her encounter with the young beggars and reported that Joan's course was set for Cooke House, which meant that she was not bound for the Middle Temple and that he would not have to repeat the performance he had paid the beggars to perform.

"How much did you give them?" she asked.

"A penny each," said Leyland, relaxing in the chair Joan had occupied before and just beginning to enjoy the fire that burned in the grate.

"Then the twain did well for themselves, for my guess is Stock's wife was not ungenerous," Nan said.

"You're going to a good deal of trouble to get rid of Joan Stock," Leyland observed, looking up at her curiously.

"I will not be rid of her yet," Nan said. "Not while her husband plumbs the depths at the Temple. I have her complete confidence now. She will deny me nothing."

"What if Stock learns too much?"

"Then that will prove fatal for him," she said.

"And Stock's wife?"

"What can she learn outside the Temple walls but her husband's surmisings and vague rumor? That, my friend, was the point of hiring the beggars—and of you, too, should their pretended recognition of her true sex fail. She'll avoid the Temple now, except for missions of mercy to her ailing husband, and presently I will persuade her that there is no mystery there at all, for the evidence against Master Phipps is more than conclusive. We will resume our former course, perhaps even more profitably than before."

Leyland smiled and plucked at his thick beard. "Blame could not fall on a more agreeable gentleman than Phipps, for I despise the little effeminate bastard with all my soul."

"Despise him to your heart's content," said Nan with a brittle laugh as she removed the last of her clothing and struck a sensual pose that caused her coconspirator to quite forget their plotting. "Theophilus Phipps will serve our purposes well, and quite without his knowing it. I'll teach him to threaten me."

15

I t was morning, Matthew's ears told him so. In his chamber at the Middle Temple it was black as midnight, but he could hear the city stirring beyond: crow of cock, bark of dog, wheeze and whinny of horse, and the rattle of cart and the shrill cries of men whose work began before light. There was a terrible throbbing in his thigh where the dagger had struck, and his bladder ached for relief. He had slept like a dead man all the night, but in struggling now to get out of bed to ease himself, he felt as weak as a babe. Straining to see in the darkness, he stumbled against a chair, swore, and woke Phipps, who sat bolt upright in his bed and clamored in a hysterical treble for

God to save him from the Devil and bloody murder too until Matthew assured him there was neither Devil nor murderers in the chamber but only Phipps and one gouty clothier of Chelmsford who couldn't see in the dark. Matthew said he was sorry for having made such a commotion.

"I hardly slept a wink," Phipps complained peevishly, falling back onto his pillow.

"A hard bed, is it?" Matthew said, trying to sound sympathetic but hoping that the clerk's discomfort would force his resignation as Matthew's nurse. He did not like Phipps. His presence was more imposition than help—and would have been so even if Matthew had truly had no more to do than survey the premises on his mythical son's behalf. On the other hand, Matthew considered, a notorious gossip such as Phipps was not without his usefulness.

Matthew peed like a rainspout into the chamber pot, and feeling a good deal better, despite the wound, he wished the clerk well for what remained of the night and was climbing back in bed when Phipps remarked out of the darkness, "I had the most awful dream."

"What manner of dream?"

"Horrible. I can't tell it."

"Some dreams are best unspoken. Leave them for the night," Matthew murmured sleepily.

There was no response, and Matthew assumed Phipps had fallen back asleep, for he could hear the clerk snoring softly. Matthew lay awake thinking. He wondered what he was going to do, now that he was a virtual invalid. He had put on a brave face for Joan, pretending the wound was a trifle. Feigning a confidence he didn't feel. Had Joan seen through the pretense? Didn't she know him almost too well?

An hour later, light was penetrating the curtains. The beast was full awake and growling. It was London, all right, not Chelmsford with its rural quiet. Phipps awoke. Now in a happier mood, he was an irrepressible conversationalist. His nocturnal melancholy having fled with the shades of night, Phipps spoke freely of the dream that before had been too awful to speak of. It had been about Braithwaite—Braithwaite dangling from the beam in the chamber, a ghastly corpse, swollen and purple-visaged.

"That was Monk," Matthew reminded him.

"But Braithwaite in my dream," Phipps replied defensively. "It was, after all, *my* dream, not *yours*."

Matthew granted the point. Phipps went on to talk about Braithwaite, about whom he had a great many opinions. "A tragedy indeed," said the clerk. "Poor devil. But such is life. Or death. There he was. One moment in the fullness of manhood. A handsome man by anyone's account, wouldn't you say?"

Matthew agreed.

"Then he is pricked. *Per accidentum,* as his killer would have it, since I cannot believe that Master Keable tells anything but the truth when he declares he meant no mortal mischief. Comes midnight and the man is being measured for his coffin."

Matthew murmured his agreement, staring up at the thick beam from which Monk had dangled. Phipps continued his gruesome theme as he got out of bed and began to dress, taking infinite pains, or so it seemed to Matthew, with his appearance. Matthew watched and listened, hoping that the clerk's chatter would find its way to some closed door that, when opened, would reveal the essential link between the victims.

"Master Leyland was certain the wound was not fatal," Matthew said. "What do you make of that?"

Phipps stopped fussing with his ruff and looked at Matthew blankly, as though the question were quite incomprehensible. "I? Why, marry, I think nothing at all. I am no physician to give opinions," Phipps said.

"I only meant that the death was very strange. Coming as such a surprise, I mean. You must admit that," said Matthew.

"Leyland is a physician, not a fortune-teller," Phipps said, staring into a hand mirror he had pulled from the valise. "Besides, I am of the belief he's not much of a physician. His principal recommendation is that he lives close at hand to the Temple and will willingly come when beckoned. That argues that he has few patients among the rich. He once set the leg of the Treasurer's horse—a great favorite of Hutton or the Treasurer would not have made so much of the achievement. Leyland claims to have a medical degree from Bologna, where there's a famous university, but I don't believe it."

"Bologna—that's in Italy, isn't it?" said Matthew.

"It is," said Phipps into the same mirror as before. "Which to my mind is hardly a commendation. It is said that for an Englishman to travel into Italy guarantees he will come home again debauched—or a Papist. Now, it follows, methinks, that actually to study there—to drink up Italian learning along with the water—is to piss out corruption in every way."

"He might pass for an Italian," Matthew said, thinking of Leyland's swarthy complexion and how much it contrasted with Phipps's, as fair and delicate as a girl's.

"Ha! Were his name Cappello or DiMarco, his denial of Rome or Padua as a birthplace would not be credited by one Englishman in a hundred."

"The physician is corrupt then, according to you?"

Phipps walked over to Matthew's bed and stood looking down at him. He smiled slightly and then bent over as though preparing to share a confidence. "Leyland lives with an aged mother who cooks and cleans and rails at him for being lecherous with his female patients, a charge I can readily believe, for every Italian is a lecher from his birth and would niggle his wet nurse were he equipped by nature at so young age. Leyland seems impervious to his mother's blandishments, however. Were he not a physician, he would make a tolerable lawyer. For he will speak sooner than hear and receive sooner than pay. But for my mind, the real test of his wit is that he chose to practice medicine rather than law."

"How so?" asked Matthew, wondering where all this rambling discourse might lead and eager for some crumb of useful information.

"Why, sir," Phipps laughed, "therein lies the man's fault—the very proof of his folly. For a physician earns but a few pence for casting one's urine or bloodletting, but a busy shrewd lawyer, well versed in his art and dedicated to self-promotion, whilst the same must concern himself with his client's offal and, yea, suck blood too, is well compensated for his labors. Not to mention the higher power his calling may lead to."

At this, Matthew was tempted to ask the clerk why, if he had so low an opinion of lawyers, he dwelt among them, but Phipps prevented it with a question of his own.

"Will you eat, Master Stock? I'll have breakfast sent up."

"Thank you, Master Phipps."

"A small favor—the least I can do."

"Much appreciated," said Matthew.

"Think nothing of it. After breakfast I'll return to see if you need anything else. A great shame your investigation of the Inn is soured by your . . . gout."

Phipps made an odd face—something like a smirk, but not so overtly insolent. Then he went out the door in a hurry, as though he had some pressing appointment and had only just remembered it.

Phipps arrived late for breakfast, but spotted Keable at once at the lower table. Keable was sitting alone, apparently in disgrace. Phipps went over to greet him as though nothing had happened.

"What's the matter? What, bankrupt at last, or a damnable constipation?"

Keable looked up at the clerk with evident hostility. "Spare me your wit, Phipps. Don't tell me you've not heard?"

"Oh, of course, I've heard," Phipps said, sitting down and pretending injury at the very thought he might not have heard. "You mean about Braithwaite. Well, man, so the world goes, doesn't it? We all owe God a death. Braithwaite's account was due, and he paid on demand. It's no great mystery."

"You speak very lightly of these matters, yet it is not you who are regarded as I am. Look how I sit here. Alone. As though I were a leper. Yet the wound I administered was a scratch."

Phipps sat down next to Keable and put a fraternal hand on his shoulder. He made a sympathetic face. "It's that bad, then?" Phipps said, casting his eye around the Hall and noticing, not without a certain secret delight, that he and Keable were being observed by more than one young gentleman still breakfasting.

"They speak of it as manslaughter at least, all the way to Gray's," Keable continued bitterly. "By noon all of London will have heard the tale, wrenched it five ways from perpendicular, and a dozen scurvy balladmongers with garlicky breaths will proclaim a greater massacre here than struck at St. Bartholomew's Day."

Smiling, Phipps whispered, "Why, you *are* in an ugly

mood this morning, Keable. But hark. I have words of consolation."

Keable turned to look at the clerk. He sighed heavily, and for a moment there was a look of hope in his eyes. "I can think of no consolation you could offer, save that the word of Braithwaite's death is a dream from which I will presently awaken. But if you have any, speak. For my poor head beats to a dozen drummers because of lost sleep. All night I dreamed of Braithwaite's hoary corpse tugging at me in my sleep and threatening me with death and dismemberment for my unlucky thrust. I swear before God and angels I never meant to kill the man."

"Don't whine, Keable. It ill becomes you," Phipps said.

"As God is my witness!" Keable protested.

"Spare me more oaths," Phipps said. "*You* never killed him."

"What?"

Phipps put his mouth closer to Keable's ear and shielded his face with his hand. "Braithwaite was mending when we all left him. By rights he should have been up and around this morning, feeding his belly in the Hall. The truth is that he was killed later—smothered with his own pillow by one who had his own reasons for wanting him dead. Not you, Keable, not you."

Keable looked at Phipps suspiciously. "How do you know this?"

Phipps told him what he had seen and done the night before, how he had stolen into Braithwaite's chamber and found him dead, how he had sensed the presence of another in the room—Braithwaite's murderer doubtless—and then, pretending to be unaware, sneaked off before Matthew Stock came to give the alarm and come near death himself.

"But why did you not give alarm yourself?" Keable asked, obviously still not convinced.

"What! Cry murder when no one was around but the dead man and be thought the murderer myself? Do I appear that big a fool?"

"I heard Matthew Stock was bedridden with gout or some such plague."

Phipps laughed softly. "Yes, gout—if that's your word for Spanish steel." Phipps told that story too. And Keable, who before had had nothing but contempt for the Treasurer's clerk, now looked upon the man with something akin to admiration.

Within the hour of Phipps's departure, Jacob Flowerdewe came in with a cold breakfast and gloomy gossip about Braithwaite's death and how no one in the Inn could talk of aught else and how Keable was in Coventry for his crime and Master Hutton in a dither about the reputation of the Middle Temple going all to hell and his chance for advancement at court not worth a turd.

Matthew listened to this news, found it a barren field for his purposes, and was greatly relieved when he was alone again, in which state he remained the rest of the morning and afternoon, Phipps apparently forgetting to order up his dinner.

It was near suppertime when he heard another knocking at his door, and when he said "Who comes?" and the knocker stepped in, he saw it was Joan, a tray of hot food in her hand. A more welcome sight he could not imagine, as hungry and bored as he was and on the point of talking to himself for company.

"Joan! Thank God you've come. Phipps has deserted me and I am left to tedious starvation too. Not to mention the great waste of time it is to be flat on my back."

Joan asked how he did and fussed over his bedclothes as he gobbled down the food, she having assured him that she ate earlier and well. Robert the groom had escorted her from Cooke House, where she reigned as mistress in the absence of the Cookes. Master Hutton had granted her permission to visit Matthew as frequently as she wished. Joan was also full of news about Nan, how she, as good as her word, had fled the Gull and taken up new lodgings in an apothecary's shop.

"Good for her," Matthew commented between mouthfuls.

Matthew listened while Joan confessed what she had planned and how Nan had endeavored to dissuade her from her folly but to no avail, Joan being so strong-willed, she admitted, and then how her guise had been penetrated by two simple urchins, whereupon she had been convinced her womanhood would triumph over male clothes and gave her project over.

They both laughed at the folly of Joan's attempted impersonation, and then Matthew chided her for even trying it, with many goodly admonitions about women's proper place, which she for her part endured with unusual patience.

"I met your nurse whilst coming up the stairs," she said, shifting the matter.

"Phipps?"

"The same."

"A dainty gentleman of ready tongue," Matthew said dryly.

"I can well understand why Nan so hates him. His womanish manner is most offensive. Sincerity oozes from him, yet every smile's as false as hell."

"This morning he was full of talk about Braithwaite but nothing to my purpose except to confirm his own reputation as a gossipmonger and backbiter of the first order.

Then, when he left me, he looked at me most strangely and seems not to credit my reason for being bedridden."

"He knows you are wounded! See, more evidence of guilty knowledge if not outright complicity," Joan exclaimed excitedly. "Your observations and Nan's experience of him point the finger of suspicion even more firmly in his direction."

"I grant it, and yet he may be something less than conspirator," Matthew said. "But at the least we can be sure he knows more than he tells. The thing is to worm it from him, which I will make my project when he returns."

"You are fortunate to have your quarry practically in your bosom," Joan said. "I pray he's not dangerous—he doesn't look so. Oh, Matthew, I wish I were here with you at all hours and not an occasional visitor. You are in the very forest here while I must be content on the verge."

"Where you are safest, Joan, and I most content to have you, given the circumstances. Go home, now, pass your time with your new pet, Nan. Be content to do the work of charity in redeeming her from her fallen condition, and do leave this man's work to me. This is my one and only day in bed. I have put my leg to the test several times this afternoon and I'm convinced that Master Leyland, as a good physician will, makes too much of my disability. Come tomorrow I am up and about, my throbbing leg notwithstanding."

Returning later to Cooke House, Joan went directly to her chamber and prepared for bed. While talking to Matthew, she had been put at ease by her husband's confidence. Her brief encounter with Phipps on the stairs had also diminished her sense of Matthew's danger. For as a chief suspect in the murders, he seemed so harmless and effeminate a creature. But now, alone, she found her old fears come creeping back like a stray dog sent packing, and that night she had another dream. She dreamed she was in Nan's lodgings again, above the apothecary's. She was alone there and waiting, but not for Nan. In due time a knocking came. When she answered she saw it was a blackamoor with stern visage standing before her. He had drawn his sword and brandished it above his head, and behind him crouched two lions with tawny manes and savage jaws.

She asked the blackamoor what he wanted of her, but the ferocious man gave no answer and the crouching lions glared at her with cruel eyes and savage jaws, dripping with blood.

16

hipps did not return to Matthew's chamber until nearly midnight, and then in an oddly sullen mood. He would not be engaged in conversation but to say that he had briefly encountered Matthew's wife on the stairs earlier and so good night.

Perplexed by this sea change in the normally loquacious clerk, but dog-tired from waiting up, Matthew snuffed out the light and went to sleep.

The next morning, true to his threat to Joan, Matthew got out of bed and dressed, determined to keep his promises despite his affliction. Jacob Flowerdewe had brought him an oak staff, and with its help he was able to hobble around with a minimum of pain, although using the staff made him feel like an old man. He went to breakfast with Phipps, whose stony silence a night's sleep had done nothing to relieve. Dressing, Phipps had not said much more than to return Matthew's good morning. Something had happened the evening before. Something compelling enough to staunch the usual flow of words proceeding from the clerk's mouth. But Phipps wasn't saying what it was. And when Matthew commented on Phipps's depression, Phipps looked at him as though there were nothing wrong at all and the very idea was an absurdity.

In the Hall, Osborne and some other Templars whom Matthew had remembered as actors in Osborne's play were sitting at one of the tables; Matthew noticed that Keable had been readmitted to the company, at least provisionally, for although he sat a little apart from the others, he had been allowed to participate in the conversation, which dealt with the relative merits of Masters Shakespeare and Jonson.

"And what do you say, Master Stock?" Osborne said, addressing Matthew as soon as he sat down. Matthew had no intention of joining in the debate. He knew next to nothing of plays, or of those who wrote them. He did intend to eat, however, and he found Osborne's question an annoying interruption of these plans. "I see your indisposition has passed, save for a limp. Come, give us your opinion—which man, Shakespeare or Jonson, is the greater writer?"

"Yes," said Phipps, "which?"

Matthew realized to his embarrassment that all eyes at the table were focused on him and everyone had stopped eating, waiting for his reply.

"Do help us, Master Stock," said Keable from his end of the table. "For we are evenly divided on the matter. Half of us prefer Shakespeare and the other half Jonson."

Matthew thought quickly. He had seen one of Shakespeare's plays and heard so much from Thomas Cooke of another that it was almost as though he had seen it himself—a play called *Twelfth Night*. But he had seen no play of Jonson's, tragedy or comedy. Indeed, he had barely heard his name and had no opinion of his art. Yet by the look of anticipation along the benches, an answer was expected of him if he was to avoid appearing to be a country bumpkin with neither wit nor education. He decided to render his verdict in Shakespeare's favor. "Master Shakespeare's *Twelfth Night* is full of much good humor and witty invention."

Matthew had merely quoted Thomas's offhanded remark one night at supper; he was not prepared for the rebuff his simple opinion would provoke, for he had no sooner said this than those of Jonson's party, who seemed to be in the majority at table, protested vigorously.

"Oh, come now, Master Stock," Phipps declared. "*Twelfth Night* is a silly, frivolous piece, full of fantastic improbabilities that a few lines of witty verse cannot rescue from oblivion. In five years' time, no one will have heard of the play—much less its author. Now, you take Jonson's noble works. And most particularly his *Everyman in His Humor*—"

"Indeed," interrupted one of the gentlemen whose name Matthew had forgotten. "Who would believe that a maiden could disguise herself as her own brother and get away with it—much less win the heart of a gentleman?"

"Save he were a fool and a cuckold," said Phipps.

"Or a base sodomite, delighting in womanish boys?" Osborne said archly.

Osborne had addressed this remark to Phipps rather than to Matthew, and Matthew could see that along the table the nasty insinuation had not gone unnoticed nor unappreciated. Several of the men were smirking, and all the table fell silent and looked at the clerk, whose fair complexion had crimsoned, although he pretended to ignore the slur. Phipps said to Matthew in a strained voice: "Surely you concede, Master Stock, that such an impersonation is improbable—and that a device which so grievously flouts the laws of probability can hardly give legitimate pleasure?"

But Osborne prevented Matthew's answer. "No more improbable than Jonson's plays you, Phipps, so much admire. Impersonation is the common device of comedy, and improbability its essence. Consider Plautus."

"*You* consider Plautus," Phipps snapped, glaring at Osborne. "The greatest virtue of that noble Roman is perfection of form, symmetry of scene. Where can one find that in Shakespeare? A notable grab bag of invention or what you will, undisciplined by the classical art. Why, there is utter confusion of times, places, and persons."

"There most certainly is," exclaimed Keable, coming to Phipps's aid. "The unities *are* violated."

"And so is decorum," said Wilson, who had just joined the group and was half listening and half endeavoring to get a server to bring him something to eat.

"Decorum be damned!" shouted Osborne. "The audiences loved the play. Even you, Master Phipps, were observed to laugh."

"I laughed at Malvolio—such a ludicrous caricature in his yellow stockings all cross-gartered. I also laughed because the play was so ridiculous."

"Perhaps," replied Osborne. "But you and he have the same tailor." Osborne smiled broadly and looked around the table for approval from the others. And there was some laughter, primarily from Wilson, who Matthew thought was a very silly young man and probably disposed to laugh at anything. Matthew noticed that Keable, who had been on Phipps's side before, laughed too—and that Phipps had seen this petty treason and had not taken it lightly. Phipps's face, reddened from embarrassment before, now darkened with rage. He got up from the table and, without a word of farewell, marched off.

"Oh, dear," said Osborne with false dismay, "I do hope I have said nothing to offend Master Treasurer's clerk." Then he grumbled something about sore losers, and even those who had shared Phipps's conviction that Jonson was the superior dramatist agreed that Phipps was overly sensitive to criticism, a damp squib, and the Treasurer's catamite. Osborne was expanding upon this last theme in a particularly salacious anecdote when the subject himself came into the Hall and was practically upon them before a timely jab in the ribs from Wilson caused Osborne abruptly to shift topics.

Hutton looked somewhat harried. He nodded briefly to the others and then asked Matthew if he might have a few words with him. Matthew got up from the table and followed Hutton to his office. Inside, Phipps was waiting. Hutton invited Matthew to be seated. The Treasurer took his place behind his desk, folded his hands on his desktop, and with a portentous sigh, said: "Master Phipps has just given me certain information that may help you in your investigation, Master Stock. Yes, I have told him about your real purpose here. I believe he can be trusted, especially in light of the valuable information he has brought us."

Matthew looked at Hutton with astonishment, then over at Phipps. The clerk's face was without expression.

"Theophilus, tell Master Stock what you have just told me."

"With great pleasure, sir," said Phipps, turning slightly in his chair and smiling at Matthew as though they were the best of friends. "Keable told me a tale I only half believed but have now come to think to be fact. Before the deaths of Litchfield, Monk, and Giles, Keable found them one night in close conversation in Litchfield's chamber.

They would not let him join them, but Keable swears Braithwaite was there, as was a fifth person he did not recognize."

"Could he describe this fifth person?" Matthew asked.

"The man's back was turned."

Matthew looked at Hutton. "Prideaux, do you think?"

Hutton nodded. "Very possibly. A conspiracy, by the sound of it. With all now dead by violence, save Prideaux, who may be the murderer of the others."

"If Keable's word can be trusted," Matthew said.

"He told me in strictest confidence," Phipps said.

"And yet you told us," Matthew said dryly. "Why did you not say something to me before? I could hardly get a word out of you this morning, and last night, upon your return, you acted as though your tongue had been cut out. Surely you had this new intelligence by then, for you had no opportunity to speak to Keable this morning."

"Marry, sir," Phipps said. "I would have told you all had I known what you were and whose great interests you serve. Please believe I shall be more forthcoming henceforth. And as for the betrayal of trust you imply, I thought I owed a higher duty to the Templar brethren and to Master Hutton here than to Keable, whom I hardly count a friend, as you observed yourself at breakfast."

"You did your duty, Theophilus," Hutton said. "Spoken like a true son of the Temple. Now, Master Stock, Theophilus has done yeoman service in providing you with this clue. Keable has always been a troublemaker. This incident with Braithwaite is quite in character. I suspect he's more involved himself in the deaths of Litchfield, Monk, and Giles than he reports. Perhaps also in that of Braithwaite, whose grieving parents I must confront within the hour. I suggest you turn your attention now to him. Determine what else he may know about this secret gathering he discovered. You may take Theophilus here into your confidence. Use him wisely in your secret inquiry even as he has served you as a nurse these past two days."

Matthew sighed heavily and glanced over at Phipps, whose face showed a blank expression, but he sensed the secret triumph beneath the soft, delicate features, and it infuriated him.

"I shall treat Theophilus with no less respect than he deserves," Matthew said coolly with a polite nod in the clerk's direction. "But before I ferret out what Keable has concealed, I would like to meet Braithwaite's parents."

"And so you shall," said Hutton, rising. "Theophilus, go see if they do not already wait outside. If not, find them and bring them here."

"Now I see my disclosing your purpose to Phipps does not please you, Master Stock," Hutton said when Phipps had gone.

"Generally, the fewer who know a secret, the less likely it is to be compromised."

"I heartily agree," said Hutton in a conciliatory tone. "But your recent injury, I thought, called for desperate measures. Concede that you need help. Grant that Phipps has been helpful. Has he not proved his faithfulness in bringing us this information?"

"Perhaps . . . if it's true," said Matthew.

"If it's true! Why, do you believe he would make up such stuff?"

Matthew was about to answer in the affirmative when Phipps returned with word that Sir Henry Braithwaite and his lady had arrived. Hutton rose from behind his desk with a heavy sigh and took Matthew by the elbow. "Come, Master Stock. You asked to be a part of this sad scene. You shall have your wish—and perhaps find out more about this Prideaux."

Sir Henry Braithwaite was a tall, solid-looking man of about sixty, very elegantly dressed, but all in black and dark gray as befit his grief, which was as evident in his sad countenance as it was in the colors he had chosen. By his side was his wife, a small, delicately boned woman who seemed her husband's junior by about twenty years. Her face was pale and drawn and partially concealed by a hood. She walked haltingly, timorously, like a person on foreign ground, braced up by her husband. With them was Leyland, the physician, looking morose and perhaps a bit nervous, his hat off and his lank black hair all blown, although there had been no wind. Leyland was carrying his little satchel, and behind him came another gentleman, much better dressed than Leyland but similarly equipped. Matthew recognized him as Thomas Millcock. Matthew had met Millcock briefly at summer's end when the illustrious physician had been summoned to give his verdict on the cause of death of a man whose mortal remains had consisted of no more than an ankle and foot. It had all happened amidst the stink and confusion of Bartholomew Fair. Matthew surmised that Millcock's presence now had a similar purpose. So Sir Henry disputed the cause of death. As well he might, thought Matthew.

Matthew was relieved when his eyes met Millcock and there was no sign of recognition in the physician's face. Millcock should have remembered. Matthew had made somewhat of a name for himself then—at least among those privy to the circumstances of the case, as Millcock was. And yet Matthew didn't need *that* now—exposure as one who by trade had become a ferreter of mysteries as well as a simple clothier with a shop in Chelmsford.

Introductions now followed words of consolation from Hutton, who spoke a very long time about the inevitability of death and the glorious resurrection. Then Hutton led the way to the end of a passage where they descended to chambers below the great Hall. They went inside one room that was small and cold. Matthew realized at once that it was used as a mortuary, for there were no furnishings but a single bed without a mattress but only planks, and on this, covered with a sheet, lay Braithwaite's body.

"I'll need more light than this," Millcock said softly to Hutton and Phipps, who had tagged along after Matthew was dispatched to find more candles. In a moment he was back with a brace of six, all burning now, and these, along with those that were lighted before, gave ample light to see the waxy whiteness of the dead man's face and the sweat glistening upon the brow of Leyland, for whom, Matthew realized, Millcock's examination was a trial of his competency. Braithwaite's mother wept softly, but the father stood calmly by, somewhat detached, like a general watching his troops from a great distance. Matthew heard Sir Henry ask her if she wanted to go upstairs, but he did not hear the lady's reply. She remained. Leyland joined Millcock by the body. Millcock looked up at Hutton, and Hutton nodded. Millcock rummaged through his satchel for instruments, then pulled back the sheet slowly. Matthew heard the mother gasp and then there was silence as Millcock began his work.

An hour later, they were all gathered in Hutton's office again. Millcock said to Sir Henry: "I must agree with my colleague, Master Leyland. The wound is clean of any infection, nor would I have expected it so hard upon the stroke itself. It has been competently cleaned and bound. The internal organs of your son seem without noticeable disease. They give no evidence that he was sick at the time of his death with any undiscovered ailment. He might have lived to be eighty with luck and God's blessing."

"Yet he is dead," said Sir Henry. "If it was not the rapier that killed him, then what?"

Millcock shook his head. "The question is perhaps better put to a doctor of the Church. I inspected your son's body from the crown of his head to his toes. Other than the wound in his shoulder, there is no mark of violence upon him. All his organs were in perfect condition. Master Leyland did his work well. He cannot be blamed for your son's death."

The learned physicians said their good-byes and departed. Matthew asked Sir Henry and his lady if he might speak to them privately. Hutton said Matthew could use his office. He had some business to see about, he said. "My clerk can stay."

"That won't be necessary," Matthew said firmly, determined that Phipps should not be present while he spoke to the Braithwaites, and prepared to make an issue of it. But Hutton said, "Have it as you will."

Matthew ushered Braithwaite's parents into the Treasurer's office and closed the door in Phipps's face.

"Master Hutton tells me you yourself have a son in the Temple," said Sir Henry when they were alone. He spoke in a quiet voice. His mind was obviously still on the grim mortuary and the mystery of his healthy son's death. "And that you were the one who found my son's body."

"That's true, sir," said Matthew. "I had come to your son's room to ask him some questions."

"Questions?" interjected Lady Braithwaite suspiciously. "What manner of questions?"

Matthew decided to tell the truth. There was no point in dissembling with these grieving parents. Ensconced in Surrey, they could have had no part in the murders. "Your son's name was one of five on a piece of paper found in another gentleman's chamber the same day the latter poisoned himself."

"Giles, you mean," Sir Henry said with a frown. "We heard he took poison. Richard told us the story on his last visit home. But he said nothing about a list."

"Its discovery is not generally known, and I pray you

keep its existence and what else I shall relate to you privy between us."

Sir Henry and his wife said that they would.

"The names were Litchfield, Monk, Braithwaite, Giles, and Prideaux."

"Three of those you name are suicides," Lady Braithwaite said. "We are not so remote in Surrey as not to have heard that grim report. But I hope you are not suggesting that my son took his own life."

"No, madam. But the other deaths are now suspected by Master Hutton and myself to be murders, devilishly disguised. On my way to ask your son why his name should have been found among the others, I was attacked—very likely by him who had just taken your son's life."

"But how?" exclaimed Sir Henry. "You heard what Master Millcock said. There were no marks upon the body."

"I'm not sure," Matthew said. "Perhaps he was smothered—a pillow placed over his face while he slept. He was in a weakened condition. Leyland had given him something to sleep. Whatever it was, your son is dead—the fourth upon Giles's list to die. And I know I limp and walk with a staff where before I was whole. Believe me, the figure I saw emerge from your son's chamber the night of his death was no child of my fancy—he has left his mark upon me."

The Braithwaites were silent for a moment, staring at Matthew with drawn, confused expressions. He had given them much to take in; he knew that they needed time to absorb it all, to come to trust him. Then Sir Henry said: "But who would want to kill my son—or, for that matter, the other men? Does a monster walk the Temple? Why hasn't the truth been proclaimed and the murderer openly sought?"

"Yes," added Lady Braithwaite. "Had it been so, perhaps my son would be alive at this moment to speak for himself."

"Master Hutton wanted the murders to be investigated quietly, for the sake of the Inn's good name. I was chosen."

"By Master Hutton?" asked Sir Henry.

"And by Sir Robert Cecil."

The well-known name had the effect Matthew intended. The Braithwaites regarded him with more respect than before. With the quiet authority he might have used with one of his own house, he asked them to sit down.

"Did your son ever speak of some secret society—one he might have been a member of?"

"What nonsense is this?" Sir Henry said gruffly. "Secret societies? No, he never mentioned one. Nor can I believe he would make himself a member of such a group."

Lady Braithwaite agreed with her husband and said she trusted Matthew was not imputing any scandal or treason to her son. "It's true, Crispin was occasionally unruly. But we put that down to the wildness of youth. He was," she said with a sob, "only twenty."

"We provided him with what money he needed," Sir Henry said. "He spent his money on books. Of course, he required additional sums—for clothing . . . entertainment. There's no purpose living in London if one must live like a monk."

The unconscious play on the name of one of the victims reminded Matthew of Keable's irreverent remarks about his father and his provident purse. All the young men were well provided for—a great pool of money if put to some common purpose. No, the four dead men had not denied themselves much, except perhaps for Giles, the bencher. His father dead, he had not been well off like the others. Was that important?

Matthew said: "Had you noticed any strange new manner in your son since he took up residence in the Middle Temple?"

It was the mother who wanted to know what Matthew meant by *that*. Like her husband, she was still on edge, defensive of the dead son, not entirely trusting of this modestly dressed, unassuming inquisitor who claimed to be Cecil's agent.

"I meant a change in habit—or attitude—toward yourselves—or the servants, perhaps."

Lady Braithwaite said: "Only that when he came home last he seemed to linger abed of mornings longer than he was wont before. I thought he might be unwell. He said he only needed rest. Sometimes I'd come into his chamber and find him fallen into a kind of trance betwixt sleep and waking. Sometimes he was difficult to arouse from his lethargy. I thought to call Master Millcock, but Richard told me not to. He made light of a mother's fears, insisting that he was as fit as ever, that he slept more because of long hours of study, although I never saw him read at home."

"Did he ever mention Litchfield, Monk, or Giles to you?"

"Oh yes," replied Sir Henry, to whom the question had been directed. "And why shouldn't he? He knew all three well. As for Giles, I was acquainted with the man myself. His father, Edmund, and I were chamberfellows in our youth, having both been Templar brethren. The family was from Norfolk."

"Did he ever mention someone named Prideaux?"

"I don't think so," Sir Henry said. He looked inquiringly at his wife. She shook her head. Then Sir Henry said, "While my son said nothing of Prideaux, I knew one of that name. Or heard him spoken of. There was a Christopher Prideaux who was a figure of scandal in Norfolk a half dozen years ago, I believe. Master Millcock told me the story, and I do believe my old friend Edmund Giles was victimized by this man."

Interested, Matthew asked what this Prideaux had done.

"He was a false physician and apothecary, who made indecent use of his medicines, for which he was brought to speedy justice for his crimes and rightly hanged, I think. There is also a Prideaux in the City—a great practitioner in the Exchequer and an expert in the law common and civil. I can think of no other by that name."

"Well," said Matthew, "at least one of these persons is connected with the law, and there may be something in that. As for this Norwich apothecary, he seems too far removed to have an interest in these matters. Besides which, the man is dead."

It was now nearly noon, and in the passage outside the Treasurer's office, footsteps and muffled voices could be heard. Through the leaded windowpanes Matthew could see a flock of Templars advancing across the quadrangle. Their mood was cheerful—and why should it not be, Christmas being so close and all the Hall decorated accordingly? The weather too had warmed, and apparently the memory of their dead brother was no longer fresh enough to cause a stay in their own headlong rush to ultimate dissolution. He thanked the Braithwaites for the information they had given and promised to let them know if he discovered anything. "Bring my son justice," Lady Braithwaite said, her pale face streaked with tears. "Find his murderer."

Matthew solemnly promised them he would.

He showed the Braithwaites to the door and said goodbye again.

When they were gone, Phipps stuck his head around the corner. "The doddering pater held up well under the circumstances, like the old campaigner he is," Phipps said, grinning. "But the mother is the wonder."

Matthew made no reply. He was still watching the Braithwaites move slowly down the passage and through the doors, as though practicing for the funeral procession to come. He was weighed down by their grief and the burden of this new promise and was in no mood for the clerk's flippant comments. But his silence did nothing to deter Phipps.

"Could you believe the woman? Such winter blood! Imagine, to insist upon remaining while your own son is cut open and his innards fingered promiscuously by an unfeeling surgeon. Jesus God, I have seen more emotion displayed over a dead spaniel."

"She contained her grief admirably, I thought," Matthew said sternly, much resenting the clerk's cynical tone and the relationship Hutton had forced upon him. He almost regretted that Phipps had betrayed Keable's confidence. It had almost given him pleasure before to think of Phipps as the murderer, or at least an accomplice. But Matthew supposed that solution was now out of the question. Phipps was in Hutton's good graces, and Matthew was obliged to wring from Keable whatever he may not have told to Phipps. Matthew didn't like Keable either, but his instincts told him that whatever else the proud young man was guilty of, it wasn't murder.

"Your wife, sir. She's at the gate and sent me to fetch you."

"Thank you, Flowerdewe," said Matthew. He had been on his way to dinner, hoping to talk to Keable. Keable would have to wait. Joan would come first.

They found a quiet place to talk in the garden. A little stone bench, shaped like a bow. Then he suffered her chastisements. He was up and abroad prematurely, in open defiance of his physician's instructions. This was what came of her lack of supervision. Matthew smiled and offered no defense, waiting for Joan's mothering to spend itself.

When it did, he told her about Phipps's new revelation;

how Hutton had practically appointed the man Matthew's assistant.

"What Keable told him in confidence, he betrays to Hutton—a fine confederate indeed," Joan said. "The smooth-faced villain."

"A truly contemptible man," Matthew agreed. "But I shall tell him nothing I wouldn't broadcast from the housetops, despite Hutton's orders."

"Phipps said nothing as to the purpose of this secret meeting Keable observed."

"No."

"Or the identity of the fifth man."

"Probably Prideaux."

"Ah, him. He sits at the center of this mystery and mocks," she said. "While we run around in confusion and doubt."

He told her what he had learned from the Braithwaites too.

"A northern man, this apothecary," Joan said. "Tell me, whence came the other gentlemen?"

Matthew tried to remember. Since his arrival at the Middle Temple, so many facts had passed over his head, through his brain. Which was significant, which not? He rattled off the answer to her question as though by rote memory. "Braithwaite is from Knoll's Cross, Surrey. Litchfield and Monk were sons of London merchants. Giles from Norfolk."

"Then there's a link," she said, brightening.

"A weak link. The apothecary was hanged five years ago."

"But you assume, husband, that Sir Henry gave you the whole story. Say, however, this apothecary wasn't hanged, but escaped. Did you not say he had this information from

Master Millcock? You know how these tales are twisted in the telling."

"But, Joan, say Prideaux the apothecary is he upon Giles's list; what sense does that make? At least the London Prideaux is allied to the Inns by profession."

"Giles was from Norwich, this apothecary from the same. I grant that may be a mere coincidence."

"Coincidence indeed. Norwich is a goodly town of at least fifteen thousand souls. A man must be from somewhere."

"Well, you visit your lawyer and I—"

"Now, I hope you don't intend to travel to Norwich," he said, suddenly fearful that that was just what his wife might be intending to do.

She laughed pleasantly, kissed him on the cheek. "Don't worry, good goose. It's much too cold and wearisome a journey. Why, I would not do it were it high summer and the roads as firm as iron. But I do intend to find out more about this apothecary of whom Sir Henry spoke, and I will not need to make my way to Norwich or to ask the haughty Millcock, who thinks the world and all of himself."

"Well, I for my part will better spend my time talking to the lawyer, but first I must find Keable. The man is clever and cautious and I doubt he'll yield much unless it serves his purpose, but if I fail to speak to him, there will be the devil to pay with Hutton. Phipps has persuaded him that Keable is knee-deep in all these murders."

"Go your way, Matthew, and I'll go mine," Joan said. "Let's meet here when Paul's strikes two. Between us both we may find some stronger thread to unravel all this mystery."

17

After she said good-bye to Matthew, Joan had second thoughts about Prideaux, the apothecary of Norwich. It was, as her dear husband had pronounced with masculine certitude and the annoying implication that an alternative view was airy female silliness, a tenuous thread that might lead nowhere at all. And yet she knew how to confirm the story of Prideaux's malpractice, and since in doing so she could at the same time determine Nan Warren's progress, she thought the pursuit of the thread was no waste of time. After all, she had to do something while Matthew was pursuing his own threads at the Middle Temple.

She collected Robert where she had left him waiting her

at Temple Gate and steered them both toward Bishops-gate Street, telling him only that she had to see an apothecary there. It was Joan's thinking that if apothecaries were anything like clothiers, they kept abreast of each other's business and that certainly a scandal of the proportions suggested by Sir Henry's story would make the name Prideaux a hiss and byword among his brethren in the trade.

It took her a while to find the house she remembered, and since there were several apothecaries in the neighborhood, Robert inquired of her whether the first they passed would not do as well as the next. He was tired of walking, he complained. His feet were sore, the air unhealthy and smoky, and the crowds in the street displeased him. But since Joan hoped to see Nan as well, she insisted they continue, and at last she saw the house she remembered.

Robert waited outside while Joan entered the shop, which was small, with a low ceiling and a counter running the length of the back wall, lined with bottles and vials and powders. A cross-looking woman of about fifty stood behind the counter, her ruddy, fleshy arms folded upon large, drooping breasts.

"What will you have, mistress?" said the woman, whom Joan took to be Nan's landlady, Mistress Browne. "A clyster or unguent, perhaps? An emetic or soothing ointment useful for burns or the scab? A tonic for the dropsy or palsy or gout?"

"I'm looking for an ointment for my father," Joan said confidently, having concocted this fiction as she walked in the door. "But I forget its name. Father used it with much success."

"You've forgotten its name, you say?" said Mistress Browne disapprovingly. "What is your father's affliction?"

"Gout."

"A curse, a pure curse." The woman turned and began searching the vials and bottles on the wall behind her. She took down a small green vial and examined it briefly. "Here it is. Just the thing. It won't take me a minute to mix up a batch. Sixpence it is."

"Oh, I don't think that will do," Joan said, meaning the concoction offered her and not its price. "The vial was much different in appearance."

"Vials often differ in appearance," Mistress Browne responded indulgently. "It's what's in the vial that matters."

"But my father would take no other."

Mistress Browne scowled. "I assure you that this remedy is most effective for its purpose. Many the customer has come in, aggrieved by gout, constipation, rank cancers, and boils, and has taken health's road thereby. Its price is not so dear as you might suppose. Did I say sixpence before? By the Mass, I meant but four."

Joan shook her head. "I suppose I must go elsewhere."

"Elsewhere you'll find nothing but what I have in store," Mistress Browne insisted.

"My father lived in Norwich many years and there had a good physician and apothecary in whom he placed his confidence. It was this same person who prescribed and sold him the cure, a rare medication he had learned from a Turk, I think."

"Oh, those Turks know less about the virtues of herbs and plants than is commonly supposed," replied the woman with an air of quiet superiority.

"I think the apothecary's name was Prideaux," Joan said.

At the mention of Prideaux's name, the expression on Mistress Browne's face suddenly altered. Her eyes narrowed suspiciously. "What did you say the man's name was?"

"Prideaux."

"You speak foolishly, good woman," Mistress Browne said coldly. "There never was such an apothecary of Norwich that I can remember, and my husband and I used to live in those parts. Now, if you will have the remedy I offered you, well and good. Otherwise, my time is as valuable as yours, I'm sure. Good day to you."

With these words, Mistress Browne turned abruptly and disappeared through a curtain that led into the back of the shop.

Displeased with the woman's rudeness, but satisfied that Mistress Browne had indeed heard of Prideaux and for some reason was concealing the fact, Joan went out into the street and told Robert that he must accompany her to still another apothecary, for this shop did not have what she wanted. Robert sighed, and again complained that he was very tired from walking and standing, but when Joan offered to send him home alone so that she could continue on her way unescorted, he said he wasn't that tired.

They started back the way they had come but had only gone a few yards when Joan saw Nan walking toward her on the opposite side of the street. Joan was about to call out a greeting to her friend when she noticed that Nan was not alone. With her and engaged in conversation with her was the physician who had attended Matthew at the Middle Temple, Master Leyland.

She was so taken aback by seeing Nan with Leyland that she turned a corner quickly to avoid being seen by them, although, having done so, she was not sure why. When they had passed and she had answered Robert's peevish query as to what new destination she had chosen, she went out into Bishopsgate Street and looked after Nan and her companion. She watched while they went into the side door of the Brownes' shop before continuing on her way again.

But not so exuberantly as before. The chance encounter with Nan and Leyland had undermined her confidence in Nan. Yet Joan was not sure why it should. Joan had always understood that Nan knew many Templar gentlemen. It was not unreasonable therefore that she might also be acquainted with a physician who regularly met their medical needs. The other possibility, however, was that Leyland was one of Nan's customers and that even now they were in Nan's upstairs chamber, doing what Nan did for money.

Joan's sense of fairness bade her suspend so harsh a judgment. There were, after all, other explanations for Nan's being with Leyland other than a precipitous fall from newfound grace. One of which was that Nan was ill and required Leyland's care. But Nan had not looked sick a moment before, but her buxom self, energetic and winsome. On the other hand, Nan might have met Leyland by chance in the street. He might have sought directions to the apothecary shop, and Nan, being the good soul she was, had offered freely to be his guide since she lived upstairs. Or Nan may have known Leyland honestly, as a customer of the Gull, and encountering him in the street, she naturally commenced to walk with him.

Deciding to suspend judgment for reason and charity's sake, she put these disturbing speculations out of her mind as she approached an apothecary shop she and Robert had passed earlier. This establishment was larger and finer than Mistress Browne's and boasted a handsome bow window in which the apothecary's goods were on display. The inside of the shop made the same positive impression, with neatly stocked shelves and the apothecary and two of his apprentices behind the counter waiting on a half dozen customers in the shop.

Joan waited her turn, and when the apothecary asked her how he might serve her, she told him the same story she had told Mistress Browne, convinced that an indirect approach would be more likely to obtain the information she sought and arouse less suspicion of her motives.

"You must mean Christopher Prideaux," the apothecary said. He was a short, thick man with a bulbous nose and close-set eyes that regarded Joan with quiet curiosity. "Your father, if he was one of Prideaux's patients, was well rid of him, for he was a disgrace to our calling, if you must know the truth. He was a zealous student of him they call Paracelsus, but was corrupted by greed and lust."

"Why, what was it he did?" Joan asked.

The apothecary frowned disapprovingly. "Prideaux applied quicksilver to the bodies of young women that came to him, causing them to stand stark naked for him to feast his eyes upon them, and then in the guise of relieving what ailed them, he prepared certain compounds that induced trances."

"Trances?" Joan asked, fascinated.

"Prideaux said he wanted to ease their pain, and of course, they believed him."

"And did he ease their pain?"

"Why, he relieved them of pain—and then their virtue! Afterwards some of the women came for more of his devilish compound. Came and came again, wanting more and paying whatever he asked for it."

"I have heard Prideaux was hanged for his crime," Joan said, trying to sound casual.

"Yes, he was hanged—as he deserved. He got with child a daughter of a gentleman of the county, and when her condition was known, there was a great uproar. He married and impregnated still another gentlewoman. Then the father of the first had Prideaux taken, and the false apothecary was tried for witchcraft, for so it was believed he practiced, so strong was the hold he had upon his gullible patients."

"You're sure he was hanged?" Joan said.

"As I hope for Heaven," said the apothecary. "His death was reported in a broadside that I bought from a bookseller's at Paul's and read twice over. My wife's uncle has a neighbor who knew one of the women Prideaux treated."

Joan thanked the man for the information and gave him tuppence for a vial of medicine she didn't need. Then she went out into the street where Robert was waiting.

"Did you find what you were looking for, Mistress Stock?" Robert asked.

"I believe I did, Robert," Joan said.

"May we go home now?" Robert said hopefully.

"First we must stop at the Temple again. Afterwards I promise there will be no more errands."

Robert looked grateful for small favors.

It was now midafternoon, and Joan waited by the Temple Gate for Matthew. She searched every face that passed, for she was eager to tell him how she had used her time. It had been an intriguing tale the apothecary had told—and even more intriguing because of Mistress Browne's denial of having heard of so infamous a character as Prideaux. And yet she claimed that she and her husband were from that part of the kingdom. The question in Joan's mind was whether the story had anything to do with the Templar murders, or was the similarity of names just a coincidence. She wondered, too, whether she was merely fascinated by a story of chicanery and seduction or endowed with one of her glimmerings.

She looked up the street and down. There was still no sign of Matthew. Where was he?

If it was a glimmering, she hoped Matthew would take it well. With respect to his acceptance of her sudden intuitions, Joan had to admit that Matthew was far in advance of most men. Never did he scoff or belittle her, tell her to mind her house or forswear the devil's work—much less threaten to beat her if she even so much as mentioned whatever would not immediately submit to cold, rational proof. As did some husbands she could name, a pox upon them. On the contrary, Matthew had respected her glimmerings and had at times been schooled by them. The worst that she could say of him was that he was frequently overcareful, especially when her safety was concerned, thus subjecting her to odious restraints upon her will, which restraints she was of no natural temperament to endure.

Then, suddenly, Matthew appeared. He was moving along slowly, staff in hand, as though he carried a burden upon his back. She waved and called out his name; he looked up and waved back. He looked very tired and dejected, and she felt sorry for him because of the responsibility he shouldered.

Sending Robert off to a nearby tavern for something to eat—he was near to starving, he complained, and dead tired from all the walking he had done and to which, as a household servant, he was woefully unaccustomed—they went inside the Temple Gate and found the bow-shaped bench where they had sat before.

"What fortune, Matthew, with Keable and the lawyer Prideaux?" she asked when they were comfortably situated and sure that their conversation would not be overheard by passersby.

"Keable wasn't at dinner. Someone said he had gone into the City. I went to visit the lawyer."

"And learned?"

"The man lives in a great house, in one spacious chamber of which he practices his lawyering and confers with his clients. At first I was made very welcome and invited to sit in a kind of waiting room. There were at least a half dozen gentlemen and one woman before me, all looking very anxious and keeping to themselves. A servant in livery brought dainties on a plate and a refreshing punch. The servant thought I was a potential client, you see. After a good hour I was let in to see Prideaux himself. I told him I was servant to Sir Robert Cecil and had come to inquire about his knowledge of certain persons at the Middle Temple. But when he found out I wanted only information and had no suit to bring to line his coffers withal, he roundly declared that he was no balladmonger, and that if I wanted news, I should go into the streets and not trouble him. He said he was a Lincoln's Inn man and that the Middle Temple was a sinkhole of vice and ignorance into which he never yet set foot nor would. He spoke viciously of Master Hutton and called him ambitious and unscrupulous. When I protested his rude treatment of one who had come to him with good intentions, he called his servant, a mad fellow about seven feet tall if he was an inch, to show me the door."

"He sounds like a most disagreeable character," Joan said. "No wonder he prospers in his litigious art. Poor Matthew," she said, patting his shoulder affectionately. "This haughty man needs to learn manners as well as charity. Anyway, I doubt he is the person we seek."

Then she told him of her own adventure in Bishopsgate Street, Mistress Browne's denial of having ever heard of Prideaux, and the full account she had received from the honest apothecary.

To all this Matthew listened without comment, but when she had finished he said: "I don't know, Joan. This mountebank of Norwich was undoubtedly as great a devil as the apothecary said—and surely his account agrees with that Sir Henry told me he had from Master Millcock. But perhaps this Mistress Browne lied because she was ashamed to acknowledge him as one of her husband's calling. A rotten apple spoils the lot, you know. If she denies the rotten fruit, she may thereby preserve the reputation of the rest."

"That may be," Joan said doubtfully. "How, then, do you explain the second apothecary's forthrightness? Marry, is he to be blamed for failing to defend his brethren because he spoke so candidly of Prideaux's sins?"

"The important fact is that the man is dead," Matthew said firmly. "The fifth man in Litchfield's chamber was alive, no Norwich ghost. The names are coincidental. Besides, what can a false apothecary have to do with the murders of lawyers?"

She had no answer to this question, yet she was still convinced she was right. She said: "I wonder if Giles knew Prideaux. Giles was from Norwich. Sir Henry said Giles's father was a victim of the scoundrel. A gentleman's daughter was one of the women seduced. She had a child by Prideaux. Surely, Matthew, this all adds up to something."

"I think a powerful collection of coincidences," he said wearily.

"Will you do me a favor?" she asked.

"Speak it."

"You have access to Temple records. You can confirm what I suspect. First, that Giles was in Norwich five or six years past when Prideaux was about his mischief."

"And if he was, what then?" he asked skeptically.

"Why, then it proves he knew Prideaux."

"Which proves what?"

"*Please*, Matthew."

"Oh, very well. Trust me, I'll look at the records. You said 'first.' What comes after?"

"Find out if Giles had a sister."

"That's no crime."

"What if Giles had a sister who was seduced—by Prideaux?"

"Then it is passing strange he should make merry with his ghost in Litchfield's chamber."

He smiled at her as if that was the last word on the subject. She said calmly, "You have given me your word that you will search these questions out. I expect that you will keep it."

"Oh, I will keep my word," Matthew said. "But because you ask it, not because I have much faith in this Norwich connection you hold so dear. But what if the Templar records tell me nothing?"

"Then ask old Flowerdewe, who claims to know so much of Templar history. And don't forget Sir Robert. His agents will supply you with facts soon enough, even if he has to send all the way to Norwich to do it."

Grudgingly Matthew agreed to do what she had asked. "I wonder what hour it is."

"Why?"

"Supper. I missed dinner entirely waiting to see Prideaux the lawyer. Damn the man, when I think of him I want to curse him with blindness, palsy, and impotence, all in the same instant."

"I suspect supper is still a few hours off," Joan said. "Time sufficient for you to do what you have promised. But I must go. I have uncharitably abused poor Robert in dragging him from one end of the town to the other this day so that I could keep my promise to Frances Cooke not to go abroad alone."

They rose to go when Joan spotted Jacob Flowerdewe coming toward the Gate. "There's Flowerdewe. Ask him now about Prideaux."

"He has been asked—and answered that he never heard of the name, save for the London lawyer."

"Ask him rather about Giles, then," she urged.

Matthew intercepted Jacob and drew him back to the bench where he and Joan had talked. The old man appeared pleased to be asked for his opinion and betrayed no curiosity as to why Matthew and Joan should want to know more about Giles.

"Poor lad," Jacob said, shaking his head. "I knew him as well as any man here. He was a thoughtful, sober sort, with an open hand and his nose always in a case or in that Bible of his. He was a bencher, you know."

"He came from Norwich, I believe," said Matthew.

"Ay, sir, he did. He and his father before him, and his father too. Three generations in the law they made together, the Gileses of Giles Hall. And now their name is done."

"Giles's father had but one son, then?" Joan asked.

"A son and a daughter, now both dead."

"A great pity," said Matthew.

"The whole line is done." Jacob looked very sad at the thought.

"Did you ever hear Giles speak of one named Prideaux?" Joan asked.

"I don't remember that he did," Jacob said. "It's a French name, isn't it? There's a great lawyer in the City by that name. Is it the same you mean?"

"I don't think so," Matthew said, wincing at the memory of his ill treatment.

"You said Giles had a sister," Joan said. "You said she was dead. How did she die?"

"Oh, there's the saddest tale of all," Jacob said, nonetheless looking rather pleased to be invited to relate it. "Master Giles told me the story once. Said he had a sister that was his twin. It was some years ago he told me—"

"How many years?" Joan asked.

"Four, five, six, I don't recall exactly, but it was about

then, before Master Hutton was Treasurer. He and this
sister were two birds on a single branch, being that they
were twins. She had fallen into the hands of a man
learned in all manner of pills, salves, and infusions, and
these he administered to her recklessly. He also com-
mitted abominations upon her body, got her with child.
Then she died.''

Joan said: "Tell us, Jacob. What was the man's name,
the one who had wronged Giles's sister?"

The old man scratched his head and rolled his eyes.
"Why, Master Giles never mentioned the man's name. He
never did. Yet he spoke most evilly of him and called him
the Devil incarnate, a gross lecher, and a fiend and said
that if the law hadn't hanged him for a witch, he would
have torn his heart out from his throat—and this from a
man who was the soul of kindness otherwise."

"This fiend, as Master Giles called him, had a wife. Did
he ever say anything about her?"

"Not that I remember."

"Thank you, Jacob. You've been very helpful."

Jacob doffed his cap and moved away toward the Gate.
Joan looked at Matthew and said: "Deny now, husband,
that Giles knew Prideaux of Norwich. Why, the man violated his sister, his twin!"

"*If* Jacob's memory serves," Matthew said.

"Do you doubt it, Matthew? Come now, let's have no
fiddle-faddle about this. Have Sir Robert confirm the facts
if you can put no trust in an old man's memory. For me,
the gathered parts are too much in accord with the whole
to deny them. The ancient, honest doorkeeper is perfect in
his tale."

"All save the name," Matthew reminded her. "He could
not remember that."

"Because Giles had never told him what it was," Joan
said. "Compare his story with what I heard the apothecary

tell. They agree on all principal points. The apothecary said that Prideaux was brought to justice by an outraged father, whose daughter the villain had undone with his medications and vile practices. Giles's father was the very gentleman! His sister the victim!"

"Granted all you say is true," Matthew said. "Now explain to me why the name of a man who for five years has been food for worms should have been included on Giles's list of living Templars. That's the question that still wants answering."

18

K eable had been listening to the learned doctor of the law lecture on wills, testaments, and conveyances for nearly an hour but had given over any attempt to follow so arid a subject, although as his father's presumptive heir, he had on other occasions found these matters worthy of his attention. Free of condemnation for the death of Braithwaite by the Treasurer's sudden and most strange but welcome pronouncement that Keable's unlucky thrust and Braithwaite's death were unconnected, Keable accepted the verdict without questioning Hutton's motive. Like most inherently selfish young men, he believed he richly deserved whatever good came his way, and freedom from the threat of imminent arrest for manslaughter was definitely a good.

As was his new freedom from the importunities of Theophilus Phipps. His fear and isolation immediately following Braithwaite's mysterious death had caused him to forge a disgraceful alliance with the effeminate clerk—an alliance that had climaxed in the latter's outright proposition of the evening before that the two become lovers.

Not that the apparent settling of the Braithwaite matter had completely eased Keable's fears. Quite the contrary. Cecil's spy still lurked about the premises, crutched but still dangerous. Who knew what bitter fruit Matthew Stock would pluck from all his snooping. Phipps—that petty intriguer and shuttlecock of gossip—had been right about that at least.

Phipps, whose indecent proposition, again remembered, stuck in Keable's craw, gagging him with its recollection. Keable had pushed Phipps away, disgusted and enraged. Called him a degenerate knave, and laid upon the clerk a dozen other names no less insulting. Phipps's face had turned as red as a radish. The jaw had set like a trap. Phipps had grated: "You'll rue those words. There's no wall about you, Keable. You think you'll live forever. But look what befell Litchfield. And the others. You're contaminated by the very association. I'd look to my life if I were you."

Later Phipps's warning had sunk deep into Keable's heart and would give him no rest. His mockery of the clerk at breakfast—that stupid wrangle over plays and their makers—had been a petty revenge. In the clear light of day Keable had reconsidered his situation. The victims had all been members of Osborne's company of players. So was Keable. All had been present in Monk's chamber when he had inadvertently stumbled upon their covert meeting. Here, thought Keable, pausing in a methodical, lawyerly way, a distinction might be drawn. *He* had been no fellow of that conspiracy. An innocent bystander, rather. On the other hand, as Phipps had so trenchantly implied, Keable had slipped into peril by happenstance, and a slip certainly could prove as fatal as a deliberate step.

Contemplating these matters now, Keable felt a mighty stirring of his old fear. Meanwhile, in the background of his thoughts, the learned doctor of the laws droned on. Some of his audience had slipped out of the room; the lecturer seemed hardly to notice. He spoke in a deep, resonant voice, weighing his words, savoring the heavy phrases of his sullen art, proposing death as a legal problem, even as Keable sat sweating out Phipps's warning again.

He looked anxiously about him for a familiar face in the Hall. He knew them all, but none was his friend. He could not trust his chamberfellow, Wilson. Wilson was an idiot. All others had turned against him over the Braithwaite affair, save for Phipps.

A sprinkling of applause terminated the lecture. Several of the audience went forward to speak to the learned doctor of the laws, but Keable remained where he sat, even after the Hall had emptied and the servants entered to prepare the table for the evening meal.

"What, meditating the muse or the supper to come?"

Keable looked up at the familiar voice, so distasteful with its nasal sneer.

But Phipps's expression was not unfriendly, despite Keable's rebuff of the previous night, the condemning phrase, and the mockery at the breakfast table.

"Oh, it's you, Phipps."

"*Theophilus*, please. No hard feelings—at least on my part. Intemperate words are small matters; a wise man forgets and forgives them. But why are you sitting here all alone?"

· "Thinking."

"Ah, a dangerous pastime. Another wise man has said that he who devotes an hour to honest thought will determine presently that life is not worth the trouble."

"A truly depressing view," replied Keable, rising. He wanted to get away from Phipps. This reconciliation was somehow unnatural, but Phipps took Keable's arm and steered him toward the door, keeping close to him like a jailer escorting his prisoner to his cell.

"Sir Henry Braithwaite and his lady, both full of grief, came this morning along with their surgeon, the illustrious Millcock, he who is prince of physicians both in skill and fee."

"With what result?" asked Keable, resigning himself to Phipps's company and in fact pleased to learn any new information regarding his status in the Inn.

"Millcock pronounced Braithwaite's death the result of natural causes, clearing Leyland of blame and, of more interest to you, sir, your honorable self."

"Old news, Theophilus," Keable said. "Hutton told me before noon."

"Of course, Millcock's diagnosis is false," Phipps continued undisconcertedly, "as I told you. All of which serves to demonstrate that human mischief is always a step or two ahead of learning."

They found a quiet alcove in which to continue the conversation.

"Well, then, I have saved the best for last," Phipps said.

"And that is—?"

"After the body was looked into, the Braithwaites went up to Hutton's office, where they conferred a good half hour with Matthew Stock. Naturally, I listened at the door."

"Naturally," Keable said dryly.

"Stock asked a great many questions about young Braithwaite, most particularly about what he knew of any secret combination among the students."

Keable looked quickly at Phipps. "My God, how did Stock find out about *that*?"

Phipps smiled and started to put a comforting hand on Keable's arm, but Keable had seen the overture in time to prevent it. He shrank a little, and Phipps withdrew his hand. "Easy, man," Phipps said. "I told him, that's how. But not from whom the information came. That remains our little secret. I tore a page from your own book, you see. To secure a confidence, one must be forthcoming himself. You now see before you Master Stock's assistant—by Hutton's appointment."

"I suppose that is why you had to listen at the door," Keable said, smirking.

"Oh, that, well, that was for the Braithwaites. I swear to you everything I overheard by stealth, Stock confided to me openly later."

"What did Sir Henry say in response to Stock's question?"

"He knew nothing at all—scoffed at the very notion. His good lady said she knew nothing of secret combinations, found the suggestion an offense to her son's memory. She said her son was a healthy young man who in recent times had slept a good deal more than before and had trances or some such blather, but nothing more."

"What's this of trances?"

"The very word she used. I made nothing of it—a mother's fussing about her son's habits. As common as dung. Much learning dulls the edge of husbandry, say I. Not that Braithwaite could be faulted on that score, but the habits learned in the Temple are not easily practiced at home. What the woman did not know was how late

Braithwaite was probably staying up carousing, although God knows what he found of interest to do of nights in Surrey."

Keable asked if there was more, engrossed now, his curiosity having overpowered his repugnance.

"Only that Stock was curiously candid. He told them he was Cecil's agent. Named Cecil outright! I wonder that the Principal Secretary cannot find agents of more discretion. Now, there's a post you'd fill with distinction, dear Edward, should you grow weary of jurisprudence."

Keable said nothing in reply. Mention of Cecil's name had started him to worry again about his own precarious position. Maybe Braithwaite had died of natural causes and Phipps had trumped up the story of the skulking murderer. Maybe the suicides were all just that and the gathering in Monk's chamber no more than young men telling dirty stories after dark. But Matthew Stock was real enough—and Cecil was no man to take lightly. There was indeed something to worry about.

"Stock also asked the Braithwaites about Prideaux."

"Yes, and—"

"Sir Henry mentioned a noted lawyer of the City. You have heard of him."

"Yes."

"Sir Henry also mentioned a Norwich apothecary of the same name. No relation, evidently. Someone who was hanged five years ago."

"Then Stock learned little from his interview," said Keable, relieved.

"In late morning he and his wife had a long conversation in the garden. I watched from a distance. Unfortunately I couldn't get close enough to hear anything. After a quarter of an hour they went separate ways. I tracked Stock."

"Where did he go?"

"To the house of Prideaux the advocate, where he stayed a good hour and a half before emerging again."

"I wonder what he found out."

"Ha, you will praise my ingenuity, Edward, when I tell you that after he left, I, surmising he was about to return to the Temple, went into the same laywer's house—a very elegant establishment, I assure you—and representing myself as a client *in potentia*, wheedled out of Prideaux's man the whole story of Stock's visit."

"And—?"

"He was given the boot."

"What?"

"You heard what I said. I had it from the lawyer's man-servant himself. Evidently Prideaux was gracious enough to the little clothier until he found out he was not a paying client but had come only for information."

"So the visit came to nothing," said Keable.

"Nothing for Stock. But something for us, Edward. For we have learned, my friend, that if anything, Stock is more fogbound than we. He gropes in the dark, for all his grand connections to the high-and-mighty Sir Robert Cecil. His long walk to Prideaux's house for such small reward sounds the depth of Stock's confusion. After all, the name Prideaux on the list—despite the fifth man you observed in Monk's room—may only be the doodling of an idle mind."

"I wouldn't call Giles's list doodling," Keable said. "I knew Giles well. So did you. His mind was never idle. His very sobriety was a fault in him. As for scrupulousness—"

"I agree Giles was scrupulous," Phipps replied sharply. "But if he had few friends, it was because he cared more for his scruples than for his friends."

"You're bitter on that point, Theophilus, because he once scolded you for wearing your rapier in the House."

"And like a busybody, reported the same to Hutton,"

Phipps said. "But I won't speak ill of the dead. He that violates the memory of a dead man is like a swine that roots up graves."

"Well, you will never be guilty of so grave a sin, Theophilus," Keable said. "I am going to my chamber. I've no stomach for supper. I just hope to God that with Braithwaite's death, all's done and past, and that Matthew Stock will discern no more than he now knows."

Phipps looked at Keable with hard eyes. "You may pray all you want, Edward, yet you and I both know it will fall out otherwise. Unless we first discover what Monk and the others were about in that chamber when you saw what you should not have seen."

"And how are we to do *that*?" Keable asked.

"Follow Stock," said Phipps. "For even a blind man will sooner or later find what he seeks—if he doesn't fall into a pit and break his neck first. As for your worthy self, avoid Stock like the plague. If your paths should cross, deny everything. Meanwhile I'll follow our Chelmsford constable for whatever crumbs may drop from his table."

Having said good-bye to Matthew the second time that day, Joan remembered what she had not told him about her earlier excursion—that she had seen Nan and Leyland walking together and going into the Brownes' house. Why had she forgotten to say something about that? It had disturbed her so at the time, and she did not feel much better about it now. Was she trying to protect Nan from Matthew's ill opinion of her? Did she fear Matthew's suspicions might confirm her own and undermine her loyalty to the young woman who had been so loyal to her?

She gathered up poor, dutiful Robert, who was a little wobbly now after a good hour in the tavern, but what he had lost in sobriety he had gained in tractability. She was two streets from the Temple Gate when by chance she saw Jacob Flowerdewe coming back from whatever errand had taken him forth, his eyes fixed on the cobbles, inured to the way like a blind man who needs no cane. She stopped him and asked what she thought it wouldn't hurt to ask, about Leyland, where he lived. It was a natural question, she thought, coming from the wife who might reasonably need to consult with the physician about her husband's condition. Yes, Jacob knew the house. Had he not fetched Master Leyland from thence a hundred times to minister to the sick and injured of the Middle Temple? Master Leyland occupied a house on Bishopsgate Street. He lived with his old mother, a widow, who kept an apothecary shop.

"The mother's name wouldn't be Browne, would it?"

Oh yes, that was the name. Then Joan knew where Leyland lived after all. Jacob smiled. Yes, that was the place. He wished Joan good day.

Joan thanked him, shook his trembling old man's hand firmly, and wished him the same. So Nan and Leyland occupied the same house! Why shouldn't they be walking together in the street—and into the door?

Now she was glad she had not disclosed her fear to Matthew and undermined his own confidence in Nan. In a second the mystery had been solved.

Or had it? Suddenly it struck Joan as curious that Nan had said nothing about having the physician for a neighbor, particularly one who frequently practiced at the Inns of Court.

The curious thing made her feel all prickly. Doubt again, someone walking on her grave. Weary from her ramblings, she had planned to go home, keep her promise to foot-weary Robert, sick of trudging after her. But she needed to settle her doubt. That must come before the comfortable parlor, warm fire, clean sheets, and the repose of earnest merit.

It was late in the afternoon now and already darkening; lights were being lit along the street, the crowds were thinning out. She turned to Robert, whose expression had taken on the long-suffering droop of a martyr, and told him they would make one last stop along the way. She assured him she would be only a minute. The apothecary shop on Bishopsgate Street. This time to confer with her husband's physician. Robert regarded her blankly and said nothing. Joan set out.

She had no trouble finding the house this time. She told Robert to while away the time in a tavern across the street, a proposition to which he agreed with great alacrity. The apothecary shop downstairs was closed already for the day, but the door to the upstairs was unlocked and Joan went up, thinking she would find someone at home, either Nan or Leyland.

She climbed the narrow stairs to the landing and inhaled again the acrid exhalations of the apothecary's art. She knocked at the door opposite Nan's and waited. She could hear footfalls within, then the bar being lifted.

"Ah, it's you again, is it?" Mistress Browne said sternly, peering out from a half-opened door. "Still looking for a potion for your father? I suppose you have remembered its name now, but the shop is closed for the day. You'll have to return tomorrow."

Joan said she was looking for Master Leyland.

"Oh, *him*. Well, he isn't here," Mistress Browne said, looking rather pleased to be the bearer of these tidings. Then she declared with a pride too obvious to be feigned, "He's my son, you see."

All this while, Mistress Browne had spoken from inside the partially opened door. Joan could see only the woman's face; a little light showed through the crack.

There was the noxious odor of chemicals. A gurgle of something aboil. An image of gross witchcraft enhanced by the old woman's cranky expression floated in and out of Joan's mind, causing temporary confusion. Why was Joan really here? What did she expect to confirm or refute?

"When will he return, your son?"

"How should I know? I'm not his keeper, only his mother." She said this bitterly. Joan sensed a domestic broil lurking beneath the old woman's comment. But wasn't it natural for sons to go their own ways?

"My husband is a patient of his—at the Middle Temple," Joan said, thinking that honest information would make the old woman more forthcoming. Now she felt an even stronger need to settle her doubts. Joan smelled a rat. Perhaps it had nothing to do with the Templar murders, but it had something to do with Nan Warren.

"Strange you did not mention the fact this morning when you came on your father's behalf," said Mistress Browne, closing the door a little more so that now only her eyes and forehead could be seen. "What's your game? You weren't come for medication today, or you would have taken what was offered you. Now you come asking for my son. A likely story, too, since his practice is very small. You don't look like a lawyer's wife to me—you don't talk like a lawyer's wife. And all that are there in the Middle Temple are lawyers, so says my son. As thick as fleas on a dog. Tell me why you are really here asking all these questions or you'll be sorry."

Mistress Browne stepped out from behind the door and glowered at Joan threateningly. The woman was a good fifteen to twenty years older than Joan but a head taller and much broader, and her intimidating stance caused Joan's heart to leap into her throat with alarm.

"I warrant you're a thief or burglar, snooping around to

see what breaking and entering may profit you. Confess that it's so, or I swear I'll call the watch, I will, but first I'll beat you roundly."

The angry woman seized Joan by the collar, then hurled her against the wall. "Why, you're a puny thing, you are," snarled Mistress Browne.

"I've come to consult your son," Joan managed to say, trembling with fear of another attack by the sturdy old woman, and racked with pain from where her shoulder had struck the wall. "I am no thief, nor burglar, but an honest Christian soul. My husband has a wounded thigh, which your son healed with his art. My husband resides at the Middle Temple. He's a guest there, no lawyer. About the Queen's business. Earlier when I was here, I had no idea Master Leyland was your son. I'd have come to consult him about my husband's condition."

"And pray, fish-face, who told you he lived here?"

"It was the old porter at the Middle Temple, Jacob Flowerdewe."

The mention of the familiar name seemed to calm the angry woman. She assumed a less threatening posture. "Well, old Jacob I know. If what you say is true, then all well and good. My son isn't here, and I don't know when he'll be back. He goes his own way now, now that that woman has come to live in the house." She nodded toward the door opposite.

"You mean Nan Warren?" Joan said.

"So you know her too," the old woman asked suspiciously.

"Yes." Joan thought it better not to reveal to the mother that Nan was a friend. She was beginning to sense the grounds of dispute between son and mother, jealous of a rival in the house, a young woman in her prime.

The old woman made a snorting noise and opened the door enough for Joan to see inside. It was not a bedchamber, for there was no bed to be seen, but more of a scholar's study or alchemist's den. In the center of the chamber was a long table laden with jars and vials, alembics and other glass vessels. There was also a furnace all smoking and stinking. Joan glimpsed a yellowing death's-head like the ones grave scholars used to contemplate their mortality. It was being used as a paperweight beneath which were a sheaf of papers, and everywhere, upon the table where the vials and other vessels were not, were books and manuscripts.

Mistress Browne noticed Joan's stare and grew suspicious again, but she didn't close the door or obstruct Joan's view. "You're a curious sort, aren't you? This is my son's study, that's what it is, and he makes his medications here. Come in."

Wary but too curious to refuse, Joan accepted the invitation. Mistress Browne led Joan over to the table with all the vials, the stinking furnace. The woman pointed to the skull. "See that? You'll notice a hole in the death's-head. Now, here was one overly curious as to matters none of his concern. And see what befell him. See that vial over there?"

Joan saw the vial—at least she saw a vial that she thought was the one she was being directed to look at. It was pear-shaped and stopped with a cork. Inside was a pale, yellow liquid the color of urine.

"There's a pretty little sublimate for you," said Mistress Browne with a cackle that conjured up another vision of witchcraft in Joan's head. The woman made a move toward the vial, made as though to pick it up, then stopped and smiled grimly.

Joan did not stand on ceremony in her leaving. She turned and rushed for the door and was down the stairs and into the street within seconds, gasping for breath and looking about for Robert. Where was the man when she needed him? From upstairs came peals of hoarse laughter.

The street was dark now except for the little alehouse. Music came from it, men's loud voices, and Robert's, she thought. She crossed the street and peered in the window. Robert was leaning on the bar, grinning foolishly at the man next to him. He was disheveled, slobbering, another tosspot out on the town. If Frances Cooke could only see her husband's dour groom now, Joan thought with wry amusement. A fine guardian he was in his present condition, but then, was she not in some way responsible?

She would have to go inside and drag him home—in some ways a more onerous chore than her encounter with the awful Mistress Browne. She turned to look back at the apothecary's and noticed Mistress Browne leaving, in a great hurry to get off somewhere. Upstairs, there remained a light in the window of Leyland's study. An intriguing place, all those books and papers. The mysterious vials. Something told Joan the room was important, Leyland was important—beyond his connection with Nan, whatever it was.

She peered again into the window. Robert was lifting another glass. It was hopeless now. She might as well go home alone—or back to Leyland's study.

She contemplated the wisdom of this—or the insanity. Curiosity had ever been one of her demons, and without Matthew's solid masculine judgment to restrain her, she felt unable to resist its call. She knew she would have no second chance to inspect Leyland's premises. Whispering a prayer for her safety and the old woman's leisurely return, Joan crossed the street.

The door was unlocked, or perhaps the lock was broken, since there was a keyhole, and she went in, leaving the door slightly ajar so that she could hear footsteps on the stairs if anyone came. On the table the furnace still gave off heat, but the gurgling alembic had been removed. She lighted a candle and looked around. She examined the books on the table. They were about medicines and astrology, secrets of the ancients, and the enigma of numbers. She suspected Leyland of being an alchemist. One book, heavily annotated, was by Paracelsus. Her heart leaped with excitement. Paracelsus—he of whom the apothecary Prideaux was a disciple.

Now she was sure she was on the right track. Eagerly she began to rummage through the drawers of a desk occupying one corner of the room. In the bottom drawer she found an old ledger. Its leather cover was battered and dirty, and inside there was a long list of names, and next to these, notations of money received, all written in a delicate script so tiny that she could hardly discern the characters. She noticed the dates next to the entries. They were from five years earlier. She flipped through the pages again, stopping on the flyleaf to notice something she had unaccountably missed before. But, of course, it was obvious. The book's owner, whom she had assumed to be Leyland, had not been secretive about his ownership. He had had, then, no reason to be. He had inscribed his name there in the same minuscule hand as the entries, and although tiny and faint, the name was unmistakable.

Christopher Prideaux, it said. She uttered the name, and then again. No, it was not her imagination. There could be no question.

Her heart thumping with excitement at this discovery, she concealed her precious find within her cloak and was about to leave when she heard footsteps on the stairs. She quickly extinguished the candle and hid herself behind the door, fearful of shutting it. She waited; the footsteps ascended. Then there was a pause. She heard a key turning in a lock and realized it must be Nan, returning home. She held her breath, heard the door open and then shut again. She waited another few minutes, not daring to move. The coals in the little furnace gave off light, and her eye caught the vial with the amber liquid. Carefully she crossed to the table and snatched it up. It, too, was evidence, if only of Leyland's malign nature. Then she tiptoed down the stairs, feeling like a sneak thief despite all her good intentions, and a betrayer of Nan Warren, without being sure why.

In the alehouse, Robert was slumped across the bar unconscious. Joan decided to let him find his own way home.

19

Theophilus Phipps was considering whether his vigil was worth the boredom and discomfort, so damp and cold it was. He had been standing in Bishopsgate Street for a solid hour by his reckoning and the testimony of church bells, and he longed for the warmth of his own chamber at the Inn. He would have obeyed his better judgment and hied homeward had he not witnessed the graceless exit of Stock's wife from the apothecary's upstairs, been intrigued to know its cause, and had his curiosity piqued to a second pitch by the sight of the same wife sneaking back in again. He was at least happy to have had a wild guess rewarded. Inquiring earlier of the garrulous

Jacob Flowerdewe as to whether he had seen Matthew Stock, Phipps had been treated to the old porter's account of how he had provided directions to the wife of the same. It had seemed incredible to Phipps that a man would use his wife to do his own work, but then, stranger things had been observed. After all, didn't a woman rule the royal roost? Besides, he laughed to himself, a crutched, hobbling, and questionably competent Matthew Stock needed all the help he could get.

So Phipps had pursued the wife rather than the husband because he had no idea where the husband was, but the wife, he knew, had her nose to Leyland's traces.

Then, hell-bent for somewhere and mumbling curses as she went, Leyland's old mother had passed Phipps in the dark, too intent on her immediate business to notice him lurking there. Phipps knew that something had happened within the shop to raise the old harridan's hackles and trigger Joan Stock's unceremonious leave-taking and most abrupt and surreptitious return. But what?

Phipps wanted badly to know, and when a few minutes later he saw Nan Warren go into the house and then Joan Stock come out again, he knew he could not forsake his vigil without an answer. Was the house a brothel as well as an apothecary's? Was Leyland's mother the bawd? More to the point, under what circumstances did Joan Stock know Nan Warren?

Phipps had not spoken to Nan in a while. She had been a closemouthed piece before; would she open to him now? He thought it was worth the effort.

He entered the house, and when he got to the top of the landing and was confronted by the two doors, he noticed that one was ajar; a weak light shone within. He assumed Nan was inside and entered boldly, being no respecter of common trulls or their privacy.

He realized his mistake at once, for he smelled the odor

of chemicals before he made out the room's contents. He was on the threshold and about to cross to the other side of the landing when he saw Leyland's mother coming up the stairs.

"Who in the devil are you?" growled Mistress Browne as she gasped for air from her climb. "Another thief—the accomplice of her who was here before?"

Phipps had no time to rectify the old woman's confusion before she reached the top of the stairs and seized him by his loose sleeve with one hand and, with the other, shook a fist in his face. "Thief, burglar, whoreson dog, what have you taken?"

Surprised by the old woman's strength and ferocity, Phipps gaped idiotically. She repeated her question. What was he doing there? she demanded to know. He started to explain, but in his confusion it all came out overly complicated, garbled, and false-seeming, and then she began to thump him on the chest with her index finger and then whack him, and growing more heated and suspicious, she spun him around and shoved him toward the edge of the stairs. He lost his balance, and it was all he could do to keep from breaking his neck in the fall, while his assailant clattered down in hot pursuit, still screaming "Stop, thief!" By the time he was at the bottom of the stairs, Mistress Browne had fallen upon him with a vengeance, beating him about the head and shoulders, laying upon him even more vile names, and swearing to call the constable and his watch and the high sheriff too.

Then, above Mistress Browne's fury, Phipps could hear Nan Warren's voice from atop the stairs inquiring what the commotion was and who was being murdered and why. The old woman gave over her railing and beating and twisted her head round to answer. "This scum is confederate of her who was here before—a sniveling, lying sort come to spy out the house and doubtless intent on murdering us all in our beds. I am giving this sot no less than he deserves."

In his pain and confusion, Phipps heard another voice. It was Leyland's. He looked up and saw the man himself blocking the doorway, his legs braced like a seaman's on a ship's rolling deck.

"Mother, what is this broil?" Leyland demanded.

"Why, I saved the constable the trouble of dragging the miscreant to the prison, where he richly deserves to lie till he rots," gasped the mother.

"It's Master Phipps of the Temple," Leyland said.

Nan came downstairs to confirm Phipps's identity.

"So claimed the woman to be, from the Middle Temple, that is, and she said something about her husband being a patient of yours," said the mother to her son.

"I think you have made a mistake, Mother," Leyland said. "I can't believe Master Phipps is a thief."

"Mistake! I think not!" She glared at Phipps where he sprawled, his hands shielding his head and neck from further blows, and his hat with the high crown smashed beneath him. "I saw the villain coming out of your study with my own eyes. A sly woman came round earlier asking questions, pretending to want medication and asking about a certain person of Norwich."

"Who was this woman?" Nan interjected from behind, but she got no answer from Leyland's mother, who flung a look of scorn at her and continued to address her son. "I knew she was lying, just as this craven villain is lying now. I don't care what Temple he claims he's from."

"I hardly think Master Phipps would steal. As for the woman you mention who was here—"

"Not a thief! Well, God be blessed and the Devil cursed; if you go upstairs, you will find it even as I have said. Something will be missing. Else why would he have entered a door closed against him and come out so stealth-fully? Good God in Heaven, just look at him! Guilt is writ as plain as day upon his scurvy-white face, I warrant you."

In a dry, fearful voice Phipps protested the charges against him. Hot tears of pain and humiliation were streaming down his face and he was glad of the darkness of the staircase to hide his shame. "I am no thief, nor a spy, nor any of the things you accuse me of," he whined. "You know me, Master Leyland. And you too, Nan. You remember me when I came to visit you more than once at the Gull. I came here following the woman you mention. You know her, Master Leyland. It's Stock's wife—he whom you attended only a few days ago in the Middle Temple."

Leyland exchanged glances with Nan. Then he looked down at Phipps again and said sternly: "If what you say is true, Master Phipps, you will not object to accompanying me upstairs to put my mother's accusations to the proof."

Phipps struggled to his feet, plagued by a dozen aches from the old woman's blows and his tumble down the stairs. He brushed the dirt from his cloak in an effort to regain his dignity, looking from one suspicious face to another. "I am satisfied you'll find it all as you left it—the study, I mean—which I entered by mistake, thinking it was Nan's. I was there but a few seconds, saw nothing I remember. Left as soon as I realized my error. I am injured, as you see, bruised mightily. Slandered and battered, for which I might be moved to contemplate a suit at law."

"Let us not speak of suits before we determine that no forced entry or other larceny has taken place for which you may be criminally liable," said Leyland with frigid dignity. He nudged Phipps up the stairs, and seeing no ready alternative, Phipps complied, his fear growing, for although he knew in his heart he had taken nothing, he somehow felt evidence would presently be found to the contrary, and he was terrified at the thought of arrest and imprisonment.

As they proceeded upstairs, Mistress Browne resumed her role as keeper, clutching at his arm in case, she said, he should make another effort to escape. In the study, Leyland lighted candles the better to see and began to look around on the table.

"I told you to have the locksmith repair that door," Leyland said to his mother.

"And so I did, but he has yet not come," said the mother.

Leyland probed among the books and papers on the table, then went to the desk and began to search through the clutter there. "I kept a ledger in the bottom drawer," he said, looking up suddenly at Nan, who had come into the room as well, and then accusingly at Phipps.

"Not the one I am thinking of?" said Nan.

Leyland nodded. Nan cursed beneath her breath. "Search Phipps," she said. "If he has it on him, get it back."

Leyland came over and began to search Phipps roughly. Terrified, Phipps made no effort to resist. "I never took anything. I was only here a moment before realizing I had entered the wrong room. But Mistress Stock may have been here—for at least ten minutes or so. I saw her leave before you did, Mistress Browne, then return immediately thereafter."

"She came back again, you say?" said Mistress Browne, less cantankerously than before.

"Oh yes," Phipps said. "I swear it. I saw it all from across the street. She went in, then came out. Then you came out, Mistress Browne, and walked away in a great hurry. Then the Stock woman went in again, then Nan here, then Stock came out."

"A busy coming and going," said Leyland dryly, looking at Nan. "He doesn't have the ledger on him."

"If something has been stolen," Phipps offered desperately, "then Stock's wife must have taken it. Why else would she have sneaked back in after Mistress Browne sent her packing?"

"And left without talking to me," Nan said, looking at Leyland. "According to Phipps here, Mistress Stock left after I had returned. She must have heard me coming up the stairs. Yet no greeting."

"A vial is missing too," Mistress Browne interrupted suddenly. "It was right here by the alembic. I remember because I pointed it out to the woman when she came in, told her it was deadly poison to be administered to those who were too curious for their own good. I gave her a scare, I did."

"And no doubt suggested in doing so that the vial was worth taking along with my ledger," Nan said pointedly.

"This is not your house," Leyland's mother replied sharply, "but mine."

"Be silent, the both of you," Leyland said.

"If you will only let me go, I will pay for whatever was taken," Phipps said.

Leyland stared at Phipps without replying, as though he was seriously considering the offer. Nan and Leyland's mother looked on without comment. "We don't want to make Master Phipps more anxious than he already is," Leyland said at length. "It is true he has nothing on him save what is his. The breaking and entering is another matter!"

"What! But I broke nothing—my entry was a trespass at worst. Besides, I gave evidence against the thief."

"True, but you trespassed, by your own admission. And you have virtually confessed yourself to be Mistress

Stock's accomplice in offering to pay for what she stole. For what honest man would pay for what he never took, without protest?"

"But I most strenuously *do* protest!" cried Phipps. "If you will only let me go, Master Leyland, I promise that henceforth you may make what use of me you will. I am not without influence in the city. I have the ready ear of Master Hutton, and my name is common at Westminster. I could increase the number of your patients, weed out those who cannot or will not pay your fees, and put you on to any number of wealthy widows seeking husbands among professional men."

"Now you belittle me by suggesting I would accept your bribes," said Leyland.

Phipps quaked in his boots. This was the worst night of his life, and if he survived it, he resolved to turn again to religion, forswear usury, and even give up boys, if only God would help him to escape. "What will you do with me?" he asked faintly.

Leyland took his time answering, stroking his lower lip with his thumb and forefinger thoughtfully. "How much do you have in your purse this instant?"

"I don't know. Perhaps three shillings, odd silver. I am not a rich man, Master Leyland."

"On the contrary, I have heard you do well by yourself, Phipps," said Leyland. "Would you, by the way, be interested in doing even better?"

"How do you mean, 'better'?"

"I am thinking of a more lucrative practice than usury."

Phipps blanched. So Leyland knew about that too. But whatever did the man mean by "better"? Was he about to receive an offer?

"Let me see your purse."

Phipps handed it to him and watched while Leyland poured the contents out into his palm.

"A decent estimate, Theophilus, if I may be so bold as to call you by your Christian name."

"Please do," Phipps said, desperate for favors no matter how small.

"This, then, in my hand, in return for what was stolen: the ledger and the vial."

Phipps started to protest. Now that Leyland's apparent softening allowed the clerk to consider the matter, the contents of his purse was an exorbitant sum for a ledger and a vial full of some stinking ointment. But he restrained himself. He saw how the bargaining had eased the dangerous situation. Mistress Browne was watchful still but quiet, and Nan Warren regarded him less contemptuously than before. "Have it as you will, sir."

"And so I shall, Theophilus, so I shall," said Leyland. "Let's say, then, that we even the score. Your money for my ledger and vial—all an adequate compensation for invading the privacy of my cell. That's worth something, you know."

"And for assaulting me," put in Mistress Browne. "For he did with willful and deliberate malice aforethought kick my shin—and very painful it was too."

Phipps opened his mouth to protest this new charge, but shut it again. He realized now that the less he said, the better.

"Cheer up, Theophilus," said Leyland in a sudden burst of good humor. "My good mother in her zeal to catch a thief has caught you in her net. Count it as an honest mistake on our parts. But now peace is made between us. The bruises on your person will keep you watchful tonight, for the which I will give you something to ease the pain and bring dreams of such sweetness that you will thank your stars you suffered this abuse. At a later time, I'll give you some more, but in return you must do something for me."

"What, sir?"

"Keep this evening's little misadventure to yourself. And we for our part will do the same. This agreement kept on all sides will be earnest money for another kind of transaction that will provide you with pleasure and great profit."

Phipps wanted to know what manner of transaction Leyland spoke of, but Leyland wouldn't say, nor would Nan, who smiled at Phipps encouragingly as Leyland selected a vial from the table and poured from it a generous spoonful of the contents.

"The hour is late," Nan Warren said. "You may want to spend the night in my room after you have taken what Master Leyland has offered you."

"In your room?"

"Yes. The night is cold and it's a dreary walk and dangerous to the Middle Temple at this hour."

Leyland held out the spoon. It crossed Phipps's mind it might be poison he drank, but he was almost too weary to care. He sipped the liquid. It was bitter and tasted a little like almonds.

He felt Nan Warren take his arm gently. She whispered seductively, "Come, Theophilus."

She led him to her own room and invited him to lie in her bed. She said nothing of what he must pay for the privilege. He felt his eyes close; heard the ringing of the hour from St. Paul's. He did not sleep at once but lay thinking of all that had happened and what it meant and what Leyland had meant by his hint of a more lucrative transaction in which he might become involved. Was this, then, what Litchfield had alluded to in his promise of future wealth or some covert enterprise reserved for a choice few? He was still contemplating these possibilities when a delicious warmth stole over him, and his physical pain and dreams of wealth vanished in a wondrous transport of happiness.

* * *

Leyland sent his mother to bed downstairs at the same time Nan escorted Phipps to her room. Then she returned, closed the door, and the two talked.

"What on earth did you have in mind when you hinted to Phipps that he might be one with us?" Nan asked sharply.

"You'll see, my dear," Leyland said nonchalantly. "What were you thinking when you invited that sniveling miscreant to share your bed?" Leyland was sitting in a chair by the desk with his legs thrust out before him.

"I invited him to sleep in my bed, not with me, for I shall sleep here with you, my love," she answered coldly. "Answer my question. What is your plan?"

"He knows everyone, and his usury has made him rich, I think—he does not have to wheedle money from a scrupulous parent. That has been our trouble all along."

"Our trouble has been a lack of discretion," she said seriously. "That was Litchfield's trouble—and Giles's. Now you would take in Phipps, by your own description a miscreant for whom the word secrecy has no meaning whatsoever. You must be stark mad."

"Mad like a fox," said Leyland.

"We are the foxes indeed," Nan said. "And the Stocks are the hounds. You heard what Phipps said. It was Joan Stock who probed your desk and found my husband's ledger."

"And what will she find there—old moldy records of treatments and fees? A lot of good that will do her or that husband of hers."

"My husband's name is written in the flyleaf," Nan said. "What if she takes notice of that and connects him with the Prideaux on Giles's list?"

"Oh, what if she does?" said Leyland impatiently. "She doesn't know who you are but a fallen woman turned virtuous. Besides, they are looking for a man, not a woman. If Giles hadn't recognized you from your husband's trial and put you down as Prideaux, the only name he knew you by, you would never have been connected with the others."

"He paid the price for that treason," she said. "But what if Joan Stock sees the name inscribed in the ledger— and finds out what stuff the vial contains? Will she not think you are Prideaux, since ledger and vial were found in your desk?"

Waiting for his answer, Nan studied the hairy face of her accomplice. Leyland was slow but he was sure, and her quicker wit and his physical strength made an excellent match, to her way of thinking. He grinned confidently and said: "I think there's little chance of that."

She said, "I think what I have said is more than probable. Yet I wish it were otherwise. If my words prove true, Joan Stock and her husband will have to go."

"Home to Chelmsford?"

"To Heaven or the Devil," she said matter-of-factly. "I've come too far to lose all now. Who knows? They may by some chance put the puzzle together. See how industrious Stock's wife is in collecting the pieces. We must serve up one last piece—our friend Phipps, perhaps—and then good night to them all."

"You're not doing this for the money, are you, but for vengeance?" Leyland said, regarding her curiously.

She tossed her head and laughed. "Greed is a petty motive, worthy only of base scoundrels. An honest revenge is another matter entirely, and I have cause, good Doctor Leyland, believe me. Besides," she said, looking at him directly and growing solemn again so that her face took on a masculine hardness, "what does it matter to you? You provide the dreams for our fat lawyerly calves and milk 'em good. Therefore never ask why, but only who next and how much."

20

"aster Leyland *is* Prideaux," Joan declared, too certain to mince words.

This was the first news from her mouth the next morning when she arrived at Matthew's chamber and had determined that Phipps was not lurking there to eavesdrop. "I found proof."

"What proof?" he asked.

She disregarded the defensive tone of the question, the silent assertion of male logicality that always irked her. Knowing the ledger was irrefutable proof, she could afford to be patient, even generously so. Matthew was already dressed and fed, looked his old self, and had forsaken the crutch, although he still walked with a slight limp, like an old soldier.

Joan showed him the ledger, opening it to the flyleaf and thrusting it in his face as though the book spoke for itself. "This I found in the desk in Leyland's study." She sat on the edge of the bed opposite him and began to tell all that she had done after leaving him the previous afternoon.

He listened, but did not soften. He seemed harder, more critical. "I can't believe you did all *that*," he said when she had concluded her tale. "Surely this was some dream you had and have confused with waking."

"No dream, husband," she said, offended at the suggestion. "Before you is the proof of that too. And this," she said, handing him the vial.

He looked at the vial. It was ordinary, he said. He noted the maker's mark on its bottom—a little cross and base. Then he began to scold her for her recklessness, reciting her crimes: trespassing, breaking and entering, theft. Not to speak of the danger—prowling the city by night, with only a drunken groom as a companion.

She shrugged at all the husbandly admonishments and brought him back to the point. "But, Matthew, what do you make of the ledger, with Prideaux's name written therein? Is it not proof positive of what I have long suspected?"

Sighing with exasperation, he examined the signature and then turned the leaves of the ledger. "The name is Christopher Prideaux," he conceded. "The same of Norwich, unless there are two apothecaries by that name."

"Reason staggers at such a thought!" she said.

"Ah, but why would Giles have written the name of a dead man on his list? Leyland *cannot* be our Prideaux. This ledger proves only that he was in possession of the man's book. Present possession isn't proof, Joan. If I acquire my neighbor's horse with his mark upon its bridle, I do not become my neighbor. I do not become his horse. But remain myself."

"Oh, Matthew," Joan groaned.

"See, Joan, I haven't been entirely idle since we last talked. I found this treasure. Here, read for yourself."

Joan took the sheet of heavy paper offered her. It was rumpled and torn around the edges and smudged with dirt as though it had traveled through many hands. Printed in large block letters at the top of the sheet was the title *A True and Faithful Account of the Wicked Apothecary of Norwich.*

With mounting excitement and persuaded that whatever she was to learn from the broadside would only make a stronger case, she began to read. After a summary of Prideaux's career was a graphic account of his victims, including the daughter of one leading citizen of the town who died from Prideaux's ministrations. It mentioned as well that he had seduced another well-bred young woman and impregnated her, but she too was presumed dead. The apothecary's wife, it said this same woman was. The broadside purported to give the last words of the miscreant, a garbled confession full of such sentences that Joan had many times before seen attributed to repentant criminals for the moral edification of the public. There was also a picture, crudely drawn, of Prideaux. It showed a thin man in his twenties with sharp, hawklike features, a receding hairline, and a little scraggly pointed beard like that the Devil was said to grow. Joan wondered if the artist had drawn from life or only from his imagination, imputing to a man he never met an appearance compatible with his reputation.

"Well," she said when she had read the text twice over. "Prideaux as represented here looks no more like Leyland than you do. Leyland is stocky and broad-shouldered with a square head." She asked Matthew where he had found the broadside, and he said he had found it among Giles's books, some of which had remained in his old chamber.

Joan slumped, suddenly disappointed in her find. She realized that Matthew was right—just because she had come upon the ledger among Leyland's things did not mean it was his or that he was really Prideaux. On the other hand, Matthew's discovery of the broadside in Giles's book did prove that Giles was mindful of his sister's murderer even after his sister and Prideaux had been dead five years. These were not matters a man could readily forget or forgive. Yet desperate to justify the value of her dangerous expedition to Bishopsgate Street, she tried another interpretation:

"Could Prideaux have been Mistress Browne's husband, the one that is dead?"

"Too old," Matthew said, shaking his head, his brow creased with thought. "Prideaux was a young man, younger than Leyland, and Leyland is Mistress Browne's son, you said. Besides, other explanations offer themselves. Say this Mistress Browne's husband or perhaps Leyland himself purchased Prideaux's books from some bookseller. This ledger may have been among a lot of them."

"What value to him an old ledger of another man?" she said, her turn to be skeptical. "And what of the other things I saw—this vial and the alembic? Mistress Browne threatened me with its contents, said it was a deadly poison to snuff out the overcurious."

"As for the alembic, flasks, and vials," he said, "these may be the stock of the alchemist indeed, yet they are the tools of the apothecary as well. But even if Leyland is an alchemist, that's no crime. The Queen has her Doctor Dee to cast her horoscope. His alchemical experiments are well known. I hesitate to think that Master Leyland is other than he seems, an honest physician. Did he not attend me in good order? See how I can move about now. I have cast off that wretched crutch. Why, the pain is almost gone. Leyland's mother may be a shrew, but that does not taint the son, who must stand or fall on his own account."

She thought about this and felt her conviction weaken even further. She had taken a desperate chance in venturing back into the laboratory and removing the ledger and vial. Was it really all for naught? She looked at the vial again and said: "The ledger I will keep for what it yet may be worth. As for this vial, I am curious to know its contents. The friendly apothecary who first informed me of Prideaux of Norwich may be able to determine what this little vessel contains that invited Mistress Browne to use it as a threat."

"From what you tell me of her character, the terrible woman could have used plain water for the purpose."

"Oh, I doubt this is plain water," Joan said. "I saw the manner of its concoction."

"Well, it might be poison and still be nothing to our purpose."

"What, Matthew, how so?"

"It does not follow that because Mistress Browne said the vial was poison that it was; nor that if it be poison, she ever used it; nor that if she did, she also killed the lawyers."

She paused to take her husband's reasoning in, thinking at the same time that it was an intolerably smug expression etched upon his face and determined not to betray her intuition. "Each day you sound more and more like a lawyer, Matthew. Pray God you finish this business with dispatch and hie home to your own true self to Chelmsford."

The smugness was replaced with a familiar grin, and she liked him again. He said, "Very well, Joan. By all means, go ask this helpful apothecary of yours. Satisfy your curiosity. Nothing ventured, nothing gained, I say. You will either find out something to the purpose or his knowledge will put your mind to rest about Leyland. I am not so much of Hutton's opinion that Keable is our man to deter you."

"I shall go," she said with as much dignity as she could muster. "By the way, where is Phipps? He's early risen and gone abroad."

"I wouldn't know," Matthew said. "He never came home last night, nor have I seen him this morning."

"Now, that's very strange," Joan said.

Matthew shrugged. "I can't say I miss him."

"And how will you spend your time?"

"At Master Osborne's rehearsal. Tonight is the performance itself. I have yet to talk to Keable. He was nowhere to be found yesterday afternoon or evening. His chamberfellow, Wilson, didn't know where he was."

"Keable gone? Phipps gone? What does it mean, Matthew?"

She was gratified that he who thought he knew so much had no answer to her question.

When Matthew came to the Hall, Osborne and company were already in the midst of their rehearsal. Matthew quickly spotted Keable. He had not shared with Joan his fear that Keable's disappearance and Phipps's might mean the two men had become the latest victims of the Templar murderer. Keable was in his satyr costume, a coarse, tightly fitting suit faced with shaggy fur, and slippers resembling goat's feet. His face had been stained dark to give him a menacing expression. Wilson, as the lovely Clorinda, was almost beyond recognition. Wigged in blond tresses, powdered, and painted, he had been transformed into a vision of conventional feminine pulchritude.

Though attired in a splendid gown of green and gold, and generously bosomed, he still moved about with the awkwardness of the boy he was. Since the rehearsal was proceeding without interruptions from Osborne, Matthew could hardly do more than wait its conclusion. When, after an hour or more, Osborne congratulated the players and announced, to a chorus of groans, that they should do all the play over a second time, Matthew was too weary of sitting to endure it again and decided to leave.

He made an inconspicuous exit through a side door, thinking it might give him access to the garden, and found himself instead in a kind of cloakroom or, as it was called in the theaters, a tiring house. Here evidently Osborne's players had changed from their caps and gowns into their costumes, for clothing was strewn all about, draped on stools and chairs and hung on hooks along the walls, and everything scattered and disorderly as though the players had all changed in haste. There was a little table in the corner and a row of stools beneath, and beside the table was an open chest the size of a carpenter's toolbox. Matthew looked inside and saw no hammers or saws but jars of dyes, washes, and paints, and several good bristle brushes and a little mirror with a hinge on its back and powders in boxes and an assortment of jewelry—brooches, medallions, and rings, all of which, on closer inspection, proved to be made of glass or paste. Fascinated by this paraphernalia and aware that Keable must return to this room in order to divest himself of his costume, Matthew decided to bide his time by exploring the contents further with no more serious intent than to satisfy his curiosity as how players managed to remake their appearance—to lighten or darken their natural complexions, make great their eyes, or turn pale lips ruddy. In the midst of this casual inspection he saw that several of the little vessels in the box were like the vial Joan had taken from Leyland's study. They were pear-shaped and corked, but filled with fucus and other stains, not the amber liquid Joan had fetched home and thought was poison. Then, at the very bottom of the box, he saw another of the vials—this one empty except for a moist residue. Pulling out the cork, he raised the vial to his nose and detected the same odor that had sprung from Joan's vial, while he saw etched into the glass the tiny cross and base that was the manufacturer's mark.

A noise behind him caused him to jump and instinctively thrust the vial into his pocket. He turned and saw that it was Keable.

"Master Stock. I thought you had gone."

Matthew got to his feet. "Evidently. I have been looking for you since yesterday noon."

"I had pressing business—in the City," Keable explained, not very convincingly. "What did you want of me?"

"Master Hutton suggested you might help me with some information."

Keable reached down into the open box and drew out the mirror. He sat it up on the table and then picked up a coarse cloth and began slowly wiping the stain from his face. "Could your questions not wait until later in the day? You see how busy I am now. I had to take my leave of my fellow players—a pressing appointment in the City, for which I dare not be late."

"I will be brief," said Matthew in a peremptory tone. "Besides, it's best that we speak privately."

Keable stopped wiping his face with the cloth and looked up at Matthew.

"I understand you observed a secret meeting of Litchfield, Monk, and Osborne too. In Monk's chambers."

Keable shrugged. "That's news to me, sir. I never saw

any such thing. Besides, why should such a matter interest you even if it were true?"

"I ask on my son's behalf," Matthew said. "It's of interest to me if there are conspiracies in motion here. Naturally I want no son of mine keeping company with traitors."

Keable laughed nervously. "You have been deceived by loose talk, Master Stock. There was never such a conspiracy, and if there was, I never heard tell of it."

"Master Phipps says otherwise."

Keable laughed again, even less convincingly. "Theophilus Phipps is a very inventive gentleman—and a notorious gossip. He will tell any story to make himself the center of attention, but a wise man will take half of what he says as pure falsehood and the other with the proverbial grain of salt."

"Yet it seems a probable tale," Matthew said, not content to allow Keable such an easy retreat. "All those reported to have been present are dead—save one, perhaps—and that argues some subtle connection not inconsistent with treasonous confederacy."

"A ringing phrase, Master Stock," Keable said easily, having now completely cleaned his face. "And likely food for conspiracy mongers. There are those never happy but they explain all associations—no matter how innocent—as subversion. It's the humor of our time."

"I think you dissemble, Master Keable," said Matthew sternly.

Keable ignored the direct accusation. He seemed now to ignore Matthew. He stripped off his satyr costume and replaced it with hose, doublet, and hat. He did not have his gown or cap, Matthew noticed. Perhaps he really did have an appointment in the City—or perhaps he only wanted an excuse to avoid further questioning.

"Oh, by the way, Master Keable," Matthew said. "I was admiring your paint box here—truly a rich variety of false colors to sail under."

Keable paused on his way to the door. The expression on his face suggested that Matthew's change of subject had taken him by surprise. Evidently less threatened, he said: "That box of trash? That's none of mine. It belonged to Monk. We of Master Osborne's play were joint heirs to it when he died."

"I wonder where he came by so many paints and powders."

"That I *can* answer," laughed Keable, regaining some of his old nonchalance. "He had them from the whores at the Gull, but died before he could get aught else from them, if you catch my drift."

With that, Keable walked out the door.

Joan had come alone to the Temple that morning. After his debauch, Robert had staggered home sometime during the night and was still in bed, sick unto death, he said, but since Joan knew the cause of his trouble, she did not offer to fetch a surgeon, but was content to be a solitary voyager, feeling relieved of the responsibility of adhering to her promise to Frances now that her guardian had disabled himself.

She was happy to find that the pleasant apothecary was in his shop and without a customer at the moment, so she went directly to him with her question. He remembered her from the previous day's visit but was surprised when she said she wanted not medication but merely to know what a vial she had in her possession was.

She was thankful he didn't ask why she wanted to know; he seemed to take her request as a test of his skill, and he made a great to-do of it, by examining first the vial—pronouncing it as a very common sort—and then removing the stopper and sniffing it. He alarmed her by pouring out a few drops in a spoon and starting to taste them. She told him she feared the substance might be poison, for so she had been led to believe by one who gave it to her.

"And who would that be?" he asked, interested.

She thought it would be better not to tell him Mistress Browne's name or Leyland's, so she just said she got it from another shop on the street and she wanted its identity confirmed before she administered it to her husband.

"It's far from any poison, I can tell you that," said the apothecary, smiling. "At least not in moderate doses." Then, as though to prove his words, he tasted it himself, screwed up his face, and said, "Yes, as I thought. Your husband may take the medication without worry. Is he in pain? If so, this will ease it, bring him sleep—and, if what I have heard is true, remarkable dreams."

"But what is it called?" Joan asked.

"It is laudanum," said the apothecary. "A marvelous discovery of the great Paracelsus and made from the white exude of the unripe *papaver somniferum*, mixed with gold and pearls that it may have the greater virtue thereby."

"It must be no common stuff then," Joan said.

"As yet little known in this country," said the apothecary. "I have tasted it once before. The taste is bitter to the tongue, but the distillation is potent and beyond the skill of most apothecaries. Oddly enough, it was probably this very substance that that Prideaux you inquired of yesterday used in his practice, for Prideaux was a great student of Paracelsus."

"It must cost a great deal."

"I think it does," the apothecary said, handing the vial back to Joan. "Of course, that depends on who sells it and who buys."

"What do you mean?"

"Gold and pearls ground into a fine dust will increase the cost, of course. The other elements are not dear, and these, doubtless, are more effectual in producing sleep and visions. A man could become used to the substance, and then, like a wine-bibber, pay anything for another draft. Such is the power of habit, creating a need where none was before."

Joan thrust the vial deep into a pocket of her cloak and offered to pay the apothecary for his information, but he refused to take anything. He wished her good day, and Joan went into the street and started back to the Middle Temple.

Her conviction that there was some relationship between the Norwich apothecary and the Prideaux on Giles's list had now been confirmed. But what exactly was the connection? Christopher Prideaux was dead; she no longer questioned that. It all seemed to have something to do with this marvelous elixir laudanum—laudanum that eased pain, induced pleasant sleep, and in larger doses transported him who partook thereof into an ecstasy. Giles had known Prideaux of Norwich and hated him; Leyland's possession of Prideaux's ledger suggested strongly that he may have known him too. Perhaps it was Leyland in the room that night of the secret conclave, but why would Giles have written Prideaux and not Leyland?

As she hurried, she remembered it was Leyland who had pronounced Giles dead, named its cause, an unknown poison, self-administered. The friendly apothecary had implied laudanum could be dangerous if taken in too large a dose. Did he mean it could be fatal?

She was pondering these things and crossing to the opposite side of the street at the same time when the sudden appearance of a large wagon being driven in her direction caused her to jump aside out of harm's way and at the same time glance behind her. As she did, her sharp eyes picked out of a crowd of strangers a familiar face. It was a young man, slovenly dressed. His close-set eyes were fixed upon her, as a soaring hawk might target a scampering mouse. He looked away and then seemed to dissolve into the crowd. Suddenly Joan felt a gnawing of dread. She hurried on, trying to remember where she had seen the man before. She knew it was no one from Chelmsford. She knew everyone in her own town and his name. It was London then, someone she had taken in, with a casual glance perhaps. And yet she felt the contact had been of longer and more significant duration. But not at the Middle Temple. He was no lawyer, whatever else he might have been, not in those clothes.

She stopped and turned quickly. Behind her she glimpsed him again, in steady pursuit. By accident or design? She racked her brain. Where, where?

The crowds in the streets and the constant passing of wagons, carts, and horsemen left little room for maneuvering and less for a quickened pace. She thought she might dodge in a shop to let her pursuer pass. But what if he came in after her?

She decided to put her fear to the test. Ahead she saw the sign of a tailor's shop. When seconds later she drew abreast, she ducked indoors.

The shop was no bigger than a small closet, and her head almost scraped the ceiling, but there was a small, irregularly shaped window from which she could see the street. She watched through the dirty panes, smelling the leather, her heart fluttering like a bird's. She did not see her pursuer pass, but then she thought perhaps she had missed him. There was such a throng in the street. He might have slipped past. She prayed to God he had.

The tailor, a crookbacked little man in a leather apron, came out from behind a curtain and asked her what she needed. She told him she had changed her mind and stepped back out into the street, proceeding in the same direction as before. It was a while before she had the nerve to look behind her. Her glance confirmed her worst fears. Now her pursuer was not alone. There was another man with him, a barrel-chested, moon-faced man in seaman's dress whom she recognized instantly and whose identification now enabled her to remember his companion. It was Flynch, the wretch who assaulted her at the Gull and whom she had served according to his deserts by jabbing him in the groin. And his younger companion had been one of the friends who had stood by laughing.

But surely they did not intend to attack her in the street and in broad daylight. Surely they would not be so bold.

Joan looked back again. She did not see Flynch or his friend. They were gone—for good or temporarily? She knew she had not misidentified the pair, but she prayed she had misconstrued their purpose. There was a possibility that they had not seen her at all, but only happened to be traveling in the same direction. She was considering this happy possibility and was not more than a quarter mile from the Temple Gate and refuge when someone grabbed her wrist and she was dragged into a narrow, filth-strewn alley before she knew who had her. In the next instant she was staring into Flynch's craggy face and feeling his hot breath on her own.

"Don't hurt me," she gasped, struggling to free herself from the sailor's grip. It was apparent now what had happened. Surmising her destination, they had gotten ahead of her. She was about to cry out for help when she felt a rough hand cover her mouth and nose. Someone behind her, strong, like Flynch, rank with the smell of sweat and fish. The younger man probably, an accomplice. The men drew her deeper into the alley. She could still hear the voices in the street, possessed now only of a vanishing memory of her freedom, too occupied in fighting for breath to strike out at her abductors.

She bit down hard on the hand that smothered her, winning a momentary release before his fist struck her cheek and sent her hard against the wall and then on her knees in the filth of the alley. She screamed for help, tasted the young man's blood, looked up to see the flash of a dagger drawn from Flynch's belt and held high over her. "Damn bitch, I'll fix you," Flynch bellowed. At the same moment she rolled over and shielded her head with her hands, thinking of the terrible dagger, and heard a din of new cries and alarms from somewhere outside the alley. "Get the vial, William," she heard Flynch say. "It's in her purse."

Blinded by terror, she felt her purse ripped from her belt, and then heard a clatter of boots, Flynch's and those of the man he had called William, fleeing like the craven cowards they were, and the cry of "Stop, thief, stop!" from a dozen new voices, approaching.

She was lifted off the cobbles by strong arms. Voices asked if she was hurt and how badly and what did the robbers steal and what a shame it was that decent folk couldn't walk the street safely in broad light of day. She looked around into the blurred faces of strangers and thanked them one and all as best she could. One of her rescuers, a butcher by his bloody apron, asked her if she wanted him to fetch the constable's man, but she said no. She said she knew a constable that would make things right, and the sooner she could get herself to where he was, the better.

Bruised but undaunted, Joan found a carter to carry her the rest of the way to the Middle Temple, not because she was unable to walk but because she feared a second attack from Flynch and his companion. When she arrived at the Gate she saw Jacob, who made no comment on the condition of her cloak, which was covered with the alley's filth, but escorted her to Matthew's door. It was now late in the afternoon; supper was still a good two hours off. She was gratified to find Matthew where she hoped he would be.

Of course, taking one look at her bruised face and filthy cloak, he wanted to know what had happened and where she was hurt. And telling her tale of woe, she began to cry despite her determination that she would not. Matthew drew her close, kissed the bruised cheek. He helped her off with the cloak and assured her all would be well, despite the loss of her purse—a trivial thing after all, thank God she was not murdered by the ruffians.

"They did not get the vial," Joan said, retrieving it from the pocket of her cloak.

"Which reminds me that I have found one identical to yours in shape and mark," he said. "In an actor's chest our friend Keable says belonged to Monk. Keable also claims Monk had the paints and other items from the whores at the Gull."

"A story easily put to the test. We must go to the Gull," she said. "The laudanum is the key. Monk may have used it; Giles may have been poisoned by too great a quantity of it. His including Prideaux's name among the others on his list meant something—but something to do with laudanum, I think. The parts are coming together, Matthew. We want only a few more pieces and the picture will be complete."

"Tonight is as good a time as any," Matthew said. "All our friends will be at Osborne's play—an excellent opportunity to investigate matters at the Gull. And with luck we shall find those devils who attacked you there and see them get what they deserve."

Matthew said this with grim determination, and she looked at him with alarm. Did he realize what a bully Flynch was, and his friend, the one called William, no better?

But he sensed her concern without her telling it. "Don't

worry, Joan. We won't go to the Gull alone. Master Hutton is, among other things, a magistrate. He'll issue a warrant for the arrest of Flynch and his accomplice for assault, theft, and attempted murder, and we'll take the malefactors by force."

"We and what others?" she asked dubiously, not at all calmed by his assurances.

"A half dozen of the sheriff's stoutest men if need be. Hutton will see to it. I'll go find him this instant and have our warrant in hand by supper. In the meantime, you rest. You look as pale as death."

"Oh, I'm well enough," she said. "But I would fain lie down for a while. Yes, and perhaps sleep too."

"The bed is yours, Joan. Sleep well. I'll be back before supper."

"I won't eat a morsel in that Hall," she said. "You men may have it for yourselves."

"We'll feast in the town, where there are better cooks," he said, "and afterwards to the Gull, to search the business of these laudanum vials out and, if fortune smiles, apprehend Flynch and his friend."

Matthew gone, Joan tried to sleep, but she was too bone-weary, and her bruised cheek kept her awake. She remembered what the apothecary had said about laudanum—dangerous in excess, but in moderate amounts, a provoker of nothing more sinister than restful sleep and vivid dreams. Curiosity tempted her. She rose, found the vial, and removed the cork. She took a small sip, then a second larger. Bitter, yes, but she was more used to it now. She lay back down on the bed and shut her eyes, waiting for something to happen.

Nothing did, and she felt cheated by the substance that the apothecary had spoken of with such respect. But presently she realized she no longer felt her aching bones, the throbbing cheek. She felt, rather, a wondrous ease, as though her body floated in something yet more refined than air. She felt a pleasing warmth, and then she dreamed. Summer. Insects chirped, and a soft, warm breeze, delicious to feel. At twilight, two sleek cats with yellow eyes glided through tall spears of grass. A round moon hovered above them, a great shiny disk larger than any mortal moon she had ever seen waking. The cats came to the bank of a stream and, without fear or hesitation, lowered their heads to drink. Then, much to Joan's surprise, they entered the water and began to swim. The water was a blue she had never seen in any earthly stream, and smooth as glass. The cats made no ripple or wake as they swam; their fixed expressions showed no fear. Joan looked up at the looming moon and was amazed to see that there were two moons now and then a third where there had been but one before, all the same size, and as she looked, they seemed to grow larger and larger until she thought she could see mountains and valleys on their craggy faces.

She looked for the cats again, saw that they had been transformed into lions and were emerging from the water with dripping coats. They moved toward her stealthily, their heads lowered almost to their immense paws.

Her dream was not so pleasant as before, and when Matthew returned some time later, she was glad to be awakened and sorry she had experimented with the laudanum.

21

They had proceeded to the Gull without an arrest warrant, and with only Osborne's solemn promise that he would deliver to Hutton, immediately upon the Treasurer's return, the message requesting both warrant and officers to enforce the same. Joan agreed with Matthew that they were going off half-cocked, but that time was of the essence. She had an overwhelming sense that the case was hard upon its conclusion; that if they didn't act now, they might well never.

Standing outside the tavern, Matthew shook his head and commented disparagingly on its dilapidation, the shabby neighborhood, the grubby clientele stumbling in and out. Joan knew her husband's opinion of the Gull would not improve upon venturing indoors. *There* was the problem, she thought. Neither officers nor warrant had appeared. Had Hutton got the message? "You should have left word with someone other than Osborne," she chided. "He will have his mind on one thing and one thing alone—his play. Believe me, your message is safe in his pocket. He'll recall it at his leisure."

But it was bitter cold standing in the street. Her sense of urgency would not leave her, and it was far more powerful than her sense of caution. Matthew said he would go in, look things over. Flynch and William wouldn't know him from Adam, wouldn't expect the husband, even if they were on watch for the wife. There was always the chance that, identified by their would-be victim, they had fled London, put to sea in some vessel. And if that was the case, there was no need for the warrant or the officers.

She had no trouble describing Flynch to Matthew: the man was ill favored and repulsive every inch, so disgusting as to be beyond honest villification. She took a pleasure in the attempt, remembering his evil face, his fishy smell. He was also a well-known "character" of the place; half the clientele were his friends, no doubt the other half his enemies. More important, he was an old acquaintance of Ned Hodge and hail-fellow-well-met of the drawers and waiters, bawds and whores. Nan Warren had said as much. If necessary, Matthew could inquire of Hodge or one of the drawers or waiters. Matthew said, "If he's there and his friend, we'll have to wait for the warrant and officers, that's all there is to it."

She was tempted again to bring him to account for entrusting a message to that scatterbrain Osborne. An ill-conceived move. But what else could he have done? she thought. Phipps wasn't there—and could hardly have been trusted if he had been. It was Hutton's fault for being such a gadabout.

Within a few minutes Matthew was back with his report. "A sinkhole of villainy and vice, but I didn't see your man Flynch. A drawer I cornered and bribed said he hadn't been seen all day and he was usually about by this hour."

"What about William, his accomplice?"

"The same from the drawer. He had been at work since five o'clock, and neither had been in. He knew William well, he said. William Simmons is his full name."

"What color did you give to your interest in them?" she asked.

"That I was an old friend from the country, wanting to surprise them both. I told him I would be back, told him there were certain other residents of the house I wanted to see for old times' sake. He laughed."

Inside, Joan saw that Ned Hodge was doing a good business. Hodge was arm-wrestling with a burly sailor, and the contest had so captivated the attention of those present that it was no difficult matter for Joan and Matthew to slip up the stairs unobserved.

On the landing Mother Franklin materialized out of some obscure alcove, and with a proprietary air asked what they would have. On their way to the Gull, Joan had told Matthew about her confrontation with Alice, assuring him that if anything more dishonest than bawdry was afoot at the Gull, Alice would be up to the neck in it. Accordingly, in response to the hideous old bawd's query, Matthew asked for Alice, an excellent wench, he had heard, a very good lay, at reasonable rates. He smiled lasciviously, almost enjoying this permissible descent into feigned degeneracy. Mother Franklin acknowledged that Matthew was a stranger, but accounted him honest and no rioter or bully, she said. She kept a clean, honest house, she said. The authorities left her alone. Most of her clients kept coming back, and she hoped Matthew and his female companion would do the same. She gave Joan a curious stare, and for a moment Joan feared the old woman would recognize her from her earlier escapade. But no danger of that. Mother Franklin apparently thought it nothing strange that a man and woman together should want to see one of her girls.

But Alice was sick, she said. Wouldn't they want another, maybe Beth or Mary or Corinna—all plump, saucy wenches? Clean too, she said, each as hot as red pepper and as pliant as the other.

"It *must* be Alice," Matthew said with conviction. He asked how much that would be, a visit with Alice. Mother Franklin stroked her chin and named a sum. Matthew countered with a lower, and a bargain was struck in between that seemed to satisfy the old woman. She pointed down the passage and said, "Third door on your right. Knock with a will, the wench is probably asleep."

A softer knock than Mistress Franklin recommended brought results. A wan face appeared from the shadowy interior, along with the stench of foul linen and something worse. A dead rat, stale urine, rotting garbage? Joan didn't know how the girl could stand it, the odor, the sweaty closeness of the little room, the ragged smock, the rat's-nest hair. Alice was worse than before—skin and bones, sick if not dying. A single nub of candle was her only light, and it illuminated a room bare but for a narrow bed with stained sheets, and coverlet all twisted and torn, and a pile of rags in one corner.

Like her aged supervisor, Alice did not seem amazed that a man and woman should simultaneously require her services. She beckoned them come in, and went and sat down on the bed and coughed deeply.

Matthew shut the door, told Alice he had a few questions. Information was all he wanted, he said, speaking gently, quietly, like a kind father addressing a beloved child.

While her husband talked to Alice, Joan watched the pitiful figure on the bed, not so pitiful or sick, however, not to want something in return. Alice looked upward, her jaw fixed, her eyes narrowing with suspicion. More raucous coughing. Joan waited and watched. Then Matthew showed her the vial, and Joan could tell by the expression she had seen it before, or one like it. Alice began to reach for the vial, a longing in her eyes. "Please," she said, her voice dry from coughing and desperation.

Matthew pulled the vial away. His tone changed. "You've seen this before." It was an accusation, no question. The truth was self-evident. Joan wanted Matthew to hurry. They weren't in a private place, despite the door, which had neither lock nor bar. Privacy was an illusion here. At any moment anyone might walk in. Unspeakable acts of licentiousness could be discovered within and cause no suspicion, but information gathering was a dangerous business.

Alice said maybe she had seen it, or one like it. Maybe she hadn't. It was hard to tell about vials. All looked alike, she said. She really wasn't sure.

"Think hard," Matthew said. "It's important—and worth something to you."

Alice hesitated, considering the implied offer. She looked at Matthew, then at Joan, and then back at Matthew.

Matthew reached into his purse and pulled out a shilling. He started to hand it to her, hesitated. Alice licked her lips. She said: "What do you want to know?"

"Where you got the vial like this one."

"The old bawd—Mother Franklin."

"She gave it to you?" Joan put in.

"Not the vial. A few drops from it. Is that vial empty?"

"Who else did she give it to?" Matthew asked, ignoring her question and the implied suggestion he should give her some of its contents.

Alice said she didn't know. "I had a cough. It wouldn't go away. Mother Franklin got the medicine for me. It had a great virtue, she said. After I took it a while I got used to it. It eased my pain. Life here wasn't so bad as before."

"She gave it to you at no cost?" Matthew asked, incredulous that the wicked harridan should do anything for free.

"At first," Alice said. "Then she kept a little from my wage for the elixir, as she called it. Then a moiety. At last all. She said I was greatly in her debt for it and if I wanted more, I should do whatever she bid me and not complain or I would never have any more of it and die."

"Did she give it to anyone else—drops, I mean?"

Alice shook her head negatively.

"To any of the patrons—the lawyers from the Inns, for example?"

"I don't think so."

"What about her other customers? The men who come whoring?"

She didn't know about them either. But she said if she had some of the elixir, she wouldn't have shared it. If the other girls did, he should ask them.

Joan watched the girl's face during the questioning. She knew Alice was a practiced liar. But she seemed to be telling the truth now.

Then Alice hid her face in her hands and began to weep piteously and shudder like a frightened animal, and Joan thought what an abject creature the girl was and felt sorry for her. She seemed more sinned against than sinning, and Joan would have gone to comfort her had she not been increasingly eager to be gone from this place.

She said to Matthew: "Come, we've heard enough from her—she confirms what Keable said. Monk got the vials from here. If not from this poor girl, then from some other. This place is the center, the womb of corruption and no other. Now we must wait for the officers and Hutton's warrant."

The word officers brought Alice out of her lethargy. She sat up erect and shot a questioning look at Joan, then at Matthew. "What is this about officers?" she asked. "I did nothing wrong. Oh, please." Alice began to wail and tug at her hair. Joan tried to calm her, regretting the unsettling word she had used, but sickness and fear had combined to produce a growing hysteria in Alice. She whimpered and gulped great gulps of air and would not be pacified by Joan's or Matthew's assurances that she would not be arrested if she told the truth.

Joan heard heavy footfalls in the passageway, men's voices; in the next instant the door burst open and Mother Franklin rushed in, followed by Ned Hodge and Flynch. All looked very angry.

"That's them," said Mother Franklin, pointing first at Matthew, then at Joan, with an accusatory finger. "They said they wanted Alice, but see what fraud is here. They're all still dressed—even Alice. Now, there's proof if proof be wanting. And *her, her*," the old bawd went on, singling out Joan, "I recognize from before, when she falsely pretended to be a man and wrought havoc in the house betwixt Alice here and Nan Warren."

"Easy on," said Hodge to Mother Franklin. "We know who they be and why they've come and have had proper instructions as to what to do with them." He walked over and wrenched the vial from Matthew's hand, held it to his nose and, smiling grimly, put it in his pocket.

"He stole it from the doctor," said Mother Franklin.

"Peace, old woman," Hodge snarled. "The less said, the better."

As yet neither Matthew nor Joan had said anything, being too surprised by the sudden invasion of the room to answer, and unsure as to what could be said, under the circumstances. Alice was on her feet now, glaring at Joan. It was obvious that now that Mother Franklin had spoken, Alice remembered too. But the girl seemed more frightened of Hodge and Flynch than hostile toward Matthew or Joan.

Hodge seemed to enjoy his role as bully and captain of Flynch, who stood slightly behind him with his hand on the pommel of his dagger. His eyes were fixed on Joan, and Joan was very much afraid. "We paid our fee to have commerce with this wench and now we're done and will be on our way," Matthew said, his voice tense.

Behind Hodge, Flynch laughed. Hodge told him to shut up. The men didn't move; they blocked the door. Hodge was bigger than Matthew, and Flynch bigger than Hodge. Joan noticed Flynch had a pistol in his belt. Hodge looked down at Alice, who was cringing like a dog expecting to be beaten, and said: "Speak, pasty-face. What's this man been telling you?"

"Aye," said Mother Franklin. "What's *she* been telling *him,* that's what I would fain know."

"They made me answer questions," Alice whimpered, drawing back from the innkeeper fearfully.

"What questions?"

"About the vial they had and who gave one to me and for what reason."

"And I suppose you told all?" Hodge said with contempt.

Mother Franklin asked Hodge what he was going to do with the interlopers, as she called them, but he just told her to mind her business and get out. He would take care of things as he had been instructed, and the less she knew of it, the better.

Mother Franklin glowered at Joan and Matthew and did what she had been told.

"Don't think you're going anywhere," Hodge said to Matthew, who had made a little motion as though to follow Mother Franklin. He turned and signaled to Flynch with a raised eyebrow. Flynch pulled the pistol from his belt, cocked it, and leveled the barrel at Matthew's chest.

"You can't keep us here," Matthew said in a trembling voice unfamiliar to Joan. Her sense of his fear made her sick inside. Gladly would she have the day to begin again to do things differently.

"Think again, Stock," said Hodge. "You're trespassing in my house. I have some rights, as any of your lawyer friends will tell you. Flynch and I will just escort you two to the door. And don't make any sudden moves. Flynch here is a more than tolerable marksman. His pistol's cocked and upon my command will belch forth a ball that will put a hole in your cockscomb the size of my thumb."

Flynch accepted the compliment with a nod of his great moon-face, keeping his eyes on Joan, much to her terror. If he had occasion to fire, she had no doubt who would be his first target.

"What will we do with the girl?" Flynch asked, waving the barrel of the pistol at the quaking figure on the bed.

"Bring the tattletale along," said Hodge with a little laugh. "Her flapping tongue is a mighty inconvenience to our efforts, and in her condition a man would rather go to bed with a skeleton. God, how it reeks in here."

Hodge went to the door and, opening it, looked out into the passage. "Coast is clear," he said in a loud whisper.

He told Alice to come, and Joan and Matthew too, and they all went out into the passage, but instead of turning toward the stairs, they headed in the other direction, coming after about twenty paces to a door looking very much like the others but, when opened, revealing a narrow descending staircase. Behind them, Flynch asked Hodge if he should fetch a lamp or taper, and Hodge sent him back to Alice's room for her candle. Then they descended the stairs, Hodge leading the way, Flynch and his pistol bringing up the rear, and Matthew, Joan, and Alice in the middle, and God only knew who was the more fearful of what was to happen next.

The stairs were creaky and steep, and there being no banister but only the walls on each side, Joan descended with her shoulder to the wall and one of her hands on the back of her husband, who was walking in front of her. It was, Joan surmised, a stairway not for normal use, but rather an escape route, constructed years before, by its looks. The impression was strengthened as they continued to descend beneath the main floor of the tavern, a passing she detected by the sound of muffled music and voices coming from the other side of one wall. Then the staircase turned at a sudden angle and came out in a kind of cellar with low ceiling and rough timber walls. With the candle, Hodge set a torch in the wall to burning, and now she could see all there was to see. She looked upon a very spacious room with a dirt floor and a row of wine casks on one side. The cellar appeared to be unused for its original purpose, however, for Joan breathed no winy sweetness but an earthy stench, as in tombs or caves; there was a layer of dirt over the casks and a world of spiderwebbery in between and a sense of no one having entered the cellar in a long time.

Hodge ordered them to keep moving and led them away from the stairs and deeper into the cellar, and now Joan's sensitive nose detected something new and fouler still, the distinctive stench of the Thames at low water, when all the muck and rottenness floated up, and she became more apprehensive than ever and clutched to Matthew's hand as though any moment he would be snatched from her by some unseen presence and vanish into the darkness beyond the torchlight.

They came at last to the end of the cellar, and Hodge stopped before a small door. He fumbled for the keys at his belt and, finding one, inserted it in an old-looking lock. The lock opened; the door creaked on its hinges and opened into a seeming nothingness. Hodge knelt down and took from the outer side of the door a ship's rope ladder and hung it over into the darkness. Then he ordered them to descend, one by one, threatening them with instant death if they tried any trickery.

During their subterranean journey, Alice had been sobbing and whimpering and occasionally coughing; otherwise there had been a stony silence on all sides. Now Hodge told Alice he was tired of her whimpering and that he would have no more of it or she should die first. While waiting her turn to climb down—Matthew and Hodge were the first to go—Joan went over and put her arm about the girl's frail shoulders and whispered to her that she should do what she was told since there was no help, and this had the effect of silencing her.

Then Joan climbed down, fearful of the ladder's rungs and the darkness below, and having come to the bottom of the pit, as she supposed it to be, found herself six or seven feet from the level of the doorway and standing on a rocky shelf only a little distance from black water.

They were in a vault, but of what kind or purpose, she could not discern. On both sides were walls of rough stone, as in a fortress, but at the opposite end was no wall at all but an iron grillwork or portcullis, through which she could see the river. Above them, she supposed, were houses and even streets, all built at the river's edge while this vault was beneath, a secret, hideous dungeon.

"Don't even think of escaping by water," Hodge said, seeming to sense the direction of Joan's thoughts. "The water yonder is the very vomit of the city. The foulest of sewers. One gulp and you're a dead man with twenty pestilences in your belly. It's also deeper than it looks."

Joan was taking in the measure of this threat when she detected a sudden movement in the corner of her eye. Searching the darkness beyond Hodge's torch, she saw a rat, as large as a terrier, creeping from the shadows. The creature began to gnaw at something at the water's edge. He was joined by several other rats, who seemed to have no fear of the human intruders in their domain. Joan uttered a little cry of disgust, and even the terrified Alice screamed, but Hodge and Flynch only laughed and said they should be grateful for the company and not complain. There were worse ways of dying, Hodge said, than this. He enumerated several in grisly detail, but the invidious comparisons did nothing to allay Joan's fears or her loathing of her captors.

"Shall we leave them light?" asked Flynch, implying by his tone that to do so would waste a good candle, even if it was only a nub.

"Oh, they shall have light," Hodge said with a mirthless laugh. "And company. Yet both shall be short-lived. This is what comes of snooping in other people's business. It's a shame it must be your last lesson."

"Don't try calling out either," Flynch added, his mocking voice floating down from above them. "For none shall hear but the rats. This cellar is old as Abraham's uncle and long forgotten. You're as safe from discovery and rescue here as you would be in Newgate or the Tower itself."

Hodge used the torch to relight the nub of candle. He

handed it to Joan. "When this night is over, you'll wish my friend Flynch had finished you in the street, Mistress Stock."

Matthew asked Hodge what would happen to them. Were they to die of the cold or starve? And what did he mean about their having company and the night being worse than a dagger in the back? He asked whom Hodge had taken his orders from, and he looked forlornly at Joan and she at him while Hodge laughed and said they should wait upon the event. He doffed his cap, wished them good night, and ascended with a mariner's practiced footing. He pulled the ladder up after him. Then the door was shut with a thud as final as the striking of the last nail in a coffin's lid.

22

They stood in a little island of light waiting for death, as they might have waited for some proud lord to make his will known, reverent and abashed. It was not clear to Matthew how it could be otherwise, virtually entombed as they were and with the tide rising, the dark, swirling water already lapping at their shoes. Matthew held Joan tightly; Alice stood a little farther off. Her plaintive cries had resumed as soon as Hodge and Flynch had shut the door upon them. But now she had fallen still again, overcome with a sense of her fate. They were all subdued now, and the little nub of candle had burned so low that its tenuous flame seemed to grow out of Matthew's fingers.

"How high will the water come?" Joan asked. It was a sensible question, but her voice was strained and distant, despite her nearness.

"Not so high as the door's threshold, but over our heads."

He had already inspected the stone walls for handholds. The old stonemason had done his work too well. Without the ladder, they were at the mercy of pit and tide. They would have to tread water. Or swim to the portcullis and cling all night to the bars. But neither Joan nor he could swim.

It was Joan who suggested that Hodge might have lied about the water's depth. Surely at one time the little inlet might have been dredged out to afford harborage for boat or barge, but these had ever been shallow-draft vessels, not seagoing ships, and wouldn't it have filled in over the years? Besides, she reasoned, how did Hodge know how deep it was? If the water was as pestilential as he claimed, he certainly wasn't wading around in it himself.

"The portcullis is our only chance. Our screams will not bring him back," she said.

"But time may—to see if the tide has done its work."

"And then?"

"We shall see."

"As we are, we're as good as drowned. See, Matthew, the water is already at my knees."

He saw how little there was to lose in the endeavor. If the water proved too deep, they could return to the wall for what little time and light remained beyond that. He told Alice the plan, but she made no response. Frozen in fear, she stood as one already dead, and when he tried to drag her, she let out little shrill cries and clawed at his face and nearly caused him to lose the candle.

Joan told him to let her stay where she was. It was futile and dangerous to force her.

Matthew took Joan's hand and moved into the water toward the portcullis, which he estimated at twenty paces or more from the wall. He held the candle aloft to extend their vision.

The vertical bars of the portcullis reflected the light; beyond was absolute blackness.

They had become accustomed to the water's stench; now they felt the soft yielding and sucking of the channel bottom, the frigid grip of the water as it penetrated their garments and made bold against the warm flesh of their bodies, causing their very frames to tremble, their teeth to rattle, and the air to be sucked out from their lungs. Halfway, the water was to Matthew's belly and rising. His heart was in his throat. He hated deep water, yet how insistently had bitter fortune thrust him in. Once before in London in the swollen Thames. Again in Derbyshire in Challoner's dismal mere. Deep water had become his personal image of death, replacing fire and ice. Sucked down into the blackness, almost overwhelming his hope of Heaven.

Beside him came an anguished cry, a resistance to further progress, and an "Oh merciful Jesus."

He stopped and turned to where Joan was, candle aloft. She had averted her face from him, out of shame or horror. No, he saw it was not from him but from something floating by her, something doubtless that had touched her or she had touched unknowingly, emerging from the unseen depths or floating near her, half-submerged like a rotten log. It was a body, a man. He told her not to look again, as though she needed to be told, and raised the candle over the bloated horror, turning it over and seeing to his own amazement and disgust what it was and who it had been. So this was the company Hodge had meant. Their predecessor in death. Theophilus Phipps. Drowned dead. And by the ravaged face, as smooth in life as a girl's, Matthew saw the Treasurer's clerk was already food for rats.

"It's Phipps," he said. "Come, let's move on. There's no help for him now."

"Oh, curse Hodge and Flynch and Leyland, who did this," she said.

He thought, Amen, yes amen, but was too intent on reaching his goal to utter it, pulling Joan after him, the water swirling around his shoulders. His arm was weary from holding up the candle, and the wax was melting to a warm nothingness in his hand.

He cried, "Reach out, take hold on the bars." He sacrificed the light for the opportunity, unwilling to let Joan go. Their vault dissolved into darkness, he pushed forward and with his free hand seized the rusted iron of the grill and pulled himself to it.

His legs swung free of the river bottom. Beside him he could see Joan's shadow. She had made it too. So they wouldn't drown, although how long could one survive such numbing cold? He turned to look behind them, and might as well have been a blind man for all that he could see. Then Alice's single ungodly cry broke from the awful gloom.

"Oh, Matthew, save her," Joan gasped.

But there was nothing to be done.

Suddenly his foot found a submerged cross brace in the grillwork, and with what seemed the last of his strength, he stood upon it, rising from the turgid stream until his head touched the roof of the vault. He told Joan to do the same. She found the same support and in an instant was beside him.

The question then in his mind was how high the water would still come. They enjoyed several feet of air between the timbered ceiling and the surging water, but that space was rapidly diminishing. He could see enough to tell that the vault extended another dozen feet beyond the portcullis before opening into the river. Surely someone walking upon the bank could hear them if they cried out, but who would be walking there at such an hour, and what could he do to free them if he heard? Would he not think their appeals a ghost's wail, or some brigand's trick to lure him to destruction? They would have to save themselves.

Her teeth chattering so that she could hardly speak, Joan mumbled how cold she was and said, "Let's pray," for they had done what they could and God must do the rest. He agreed to the prayers, but for salvation, not to surrender to what was beyond help. No, he would not give up yet. He must live to avenge them all, yes, even the wretched Phipps, who, whatever his sins had merited, could hardly have deserved so ignominious a death. And he must save Joan. He shook the bars violently, and found no cause for hope there. The grill covered the entrance of the secret harborage, joined bleak stone on each side. But what was beneath?

A little hope reclaimed his courage. Without telling Joan his plan, he stepped off the crossbar and let himself down until his mouth was just above water, exploring with his feet the unseen depths. His effort was rewarded. He pulled himself up again to meet Joan's objection that he had frightened her to death, for she thought the tide had pulled him under or his will to live had failed.

"Not failed, stronger now," he gasped. "I have found a cause of hope. The grillwork has a limit. We can go under. We need only hold our breaths and the bars. We shall come up on the other side, work to the wall."

"But I'm afraid, Matthew."

"Do as I do," he said. He took a deep breath and went under.

It took some effort for him to submerge. The tide worked against his efforts, and his lungs were near bursting when he felt his way beneath the portcullis, finding only a few feet of clearance between it and the river's bottom and then scrambling quickly up the other side. He looked through the bars at Joan, who said, "Oh God, I can't. I can't."

He screamed to her she must, screamed to her again

how he would save her. How he would go down again on his side and under to bring her round if he must, but she said no to that. "Don't let Leyland have his way, Joan. Breathe deep and give me your hand. Trust me."

He almost laughed with joy when he saw her take a deep breath and go down. He went down too, groping for her in the water, feeling her slide more readily beneath the portcullis than he had done, and the next moment she was in his arms, shooting upward to the surface and gasping for air. "Now to the bank," he cried. They floundered in the water; beyond them now was the open river and farther yet the lights of Southwark like little dim stars, low in the sky, and beautiful to see.

He found a ready purchase in the bank, reached down for her, and after some effort, both lay breathless on the moist earth, shaking so with cold that neither could speak but only clutch the other like one creature made of two. But after a while he said, "Come, Joan. We can't stay here, no matter how precious solid earth may be again. We'll die of cold, and there's work to be done—even tonight."

She groaned at the thought. "But where, Matthew?"

"To the Temple. It's close by—it and fire and dry clothes, and a fiery hot drink to warm our innards—and then to Bishopsgate, where we will serve Master Leyland as he would serve us."

The gates to the Middle Temple were closed for the night, as they knew they would be, given it was near twelve o'clock. Matthew rattled the door of the porter's lodge, and presently Jacob opened and looked at Matthew and Joan with amazement. He told them that Master Hutton was probably not gone to bed, for several gentlemen of the Court had come to the Temple, one to see Matthew, and

they were all assembled in the Treasurer's office confer-
ring on some great matter.

Joan looked at Matthew. "Sir Robert, do you think?"

"If so, he's timely come."

"Oh, but you're both half-drowned," Jacob said, as
though just noticing their condition. "Did you fall into the
river?"

"In a manner of speaking," said Matthew, "but do let
us in before we freeze." They went into the lodge, and
Matthew asked Jacob for fresh water and a kettle to heat
it in.

"Water, sir? Have you twain not had sufficient of *that*?"

"For washing, Jacob," Joan explained. "And we shall
need soap. If scented, all the better, for I shall not endure
another half hour stinking like a cod." Kneeling by the
fire, she was still trembling, fumbling with her cloak. She
needed dry clothes, she said. Matthew too. Else they
would catch their death. Alarmed, Jacob said he would
fetch Matthew's other suit from his chamber. As for the
woman, he said, shrewdly appraising Joan's height and
girth—she was somewhat shorter and fuller than Jacob—
he thought he might have something to replace her sodden garments, but no female dress. She would have to
content herself with a man's garb. That was the long and
short of it, he said. And for added warmth, his spare gown.

"Yes, yes," Joan said impatiently. "But please hurry."

"And what of the gentlemen come from the Court?"
Jacob asked, turning to Matthew, who was now stripped to
the waist and drying himself with a rough towel. "I was to
tell them when you returned. Master Hutton was most explicit as to that point."

"I won't be seen like this," Joan said. "Not until I've
washed."

"First hot water, then dry clothes, then to Master Treasurer and the gentlemen," Matthew told Jacob, making

his instructions as emphatic and plain as possible. "And make haste, please."

Jacob went about his work, fetching water from the well and putting it on the hob, then finding the clothes for Joan, and the scented soap, and then out again into the night for Matthew's second suit. In his absence, Joan scrubbed her body, bemoaning the filth it had endured. Meanwhile, they talked of what had happened and what it meant.

"Leyland's our man, without a doubt," Matthew said. "And the Templar conspiracy made plain—this laudanum prepared by him and sold, doubtless with the same intent as poor Alice confessed, to make thralls of them all."

"But why murder them—and Phipps, who wasn't on the list?"

"The cause can be known when Leyland is taken. He'll confess willingly or otherwise. Since his guilt is certified by our own experience, it will little profit him to keep silent."

But Joan looked worried; he asked what was the matter. Wasn't she pleased now that the mystery was solved?

"I fear for Nan Warren. What danger she must be in, living in the very house. She must be warned and saved, Matthew. As for your understanding of these matters, I think we only know part, Matthew. We are seeing through a glass darkly, as the Scripture says."

Washed and dry, Joan felt like a new woman and was at the moment struggling to get into the clothes Jacob had provided. "We know the *who*," she continued, "but not the why. For myself, I shall not be pleased until we know what moved the man to kill the geese that laid his golden eggs. Phipps's death is easily explained. Like us, he stumbled upon fatal knowledge. Thank God we missed his end—and wretched Alice's, whose screams I even now hear in my head. I only pray to God we can prevent Nan's coming to a similar fate."

"For which death and the others Leyland and his companions will pay with their lives," Matthew said, unsure as how to answer her objections.

She said amen to that, but still she wondered. The identity of the fifth Templar continued to elude her, and until she had given a truer name to Giles's "Prideaux," she would not consider Matthew's case settled.

Men's voices came from outside the door, and the next minute Master Hutton appeared, all bundled and red-faced. He was immediately followed by a small, well-dressed man with a hunched back, a finely trimmed beard, and a silver chain of office hanging around his neck and just visible through the parting of his cloak.

Matthew greeted the Queen's Principal Secretary with a reverential nod while Joan, her face to the hearth, turned slowly at the door's opening and the sound of boots on the floorboards.

Sir Robert Cecil greeted the both of them warmly and thanked God for their safety. He looked Joan up and down and smiling said, "By Heaven, Joan, you look every inch the man in that gown. With your back turned to me just now, I took you to be some Templar wandered in to keep Matthew company before the fire."

"Oh, I am woman despite these things that the ancient porter gave me," she said, but at the same instant Sir Robert's statement of confusion sent such a thunderbolt of revelation to her brain that she remained stone-quiet during all of Matthew's report of their false imprisonment, the grisly discovery of Phipps's body, and their near drowning by Leyland's henchmen.

"Two of the rogues are taken!" exclaimed Hutton, grinning broadly with satisfaction and looking toward Cecil for approval. "Osborne gave me your message. But unfortunately, not until after his play, which was foremost in his thoughts, hence our delay."

"Both your men, Flynch and Simmons," added Sir Robert, seating himself on a rickety stool by the fire and pulling off his gloves to warm his hands. "Of course, neither admits to assaulting you, Joan—or, for that matter, even to knowing you."

"They're liars every one," said Matthew. "They know her well and would have murdered the both of us had Heaven not decreed otherwise. But what of Hodge?"

Cecil answered, "The barkeep was there when we arrested the others, then fled into the night before we could question him further."

"Then he'll warn Leyland," Matthew said grimly. "He's your murderer, Master Hutton, not Keable, as you supposed. And if Hodge has alerted him, as I suspect, there's no chance in hell that he's still in London."

Matthew quickly summarized the case against the physician, interrupted from time to time with mild protests of disbelief and dismay from his friend Hutton, who was finally forced to accept the evidence against his favorite physician.

"Laudanum, is it?" said Cecil when Matthew had finished. "I have heard of the stuff and can well understand how a clever and unscrupulous apothecary could profit by its most remarkable effects." Then he stood up suddenly and thrust his long, white fingers back into his gloves. "But there's no time for speculation now. Matthew is surely right. There may be but one chance in hell, but at least it is a chance, and my wagering instincts drive me to hazard all for what it may be worth. Come, let's proceed to Bishopsgate at once. If Heaven's with us, we'll rescue your friend Nan Warren, who lives in his house, and catch Leyland before he can escape."

23

Not one hour later, the three were on their way in Cecil's coach to Bishopsgate Street, with a troop of armed men of Cecil's household following on horseback. It was the second or third hour of the new day; the streets were dark and deserted, and over the clatter of hoofbeats before and after and the cracking whip of the coachman, Joan tried to explain her new understanding of the Templar murders. She would address a remark to Cecil, then to Matthew, and then to Cecil again. The trouble was that Matthew knew so much, and Cecil so little about the case; and yet both needed to be told. The seating arrangement in the coach was awkward for her purpose, she crunched up against Matthew; the both facing Cecil opposite, he having naturally taken the side with the plushest cushions and the velvet armrests. But there had been such a rush to be off, no time for more talking then, when her deepening suspicion, so repugnant and painful in its implications, had yet to harden into conviction.

"Oh, don't you see?" she said to Matthew, twisting toward him. "The mysterious Prideaux, the stealth with which the murderer came and went. Strange that it was Sir Robert himself who set me on the right track."

Cecil expressed amazement. "Why, Joan. Surely you give me more credit than I deserve. What was it I did? I hardly said a dozen words of greeting before we were in the coach and on our way."

"You mistook me for a man," Joan answered. "Upon entering the porter's lodge. Oh, sir, it was most reasonable, your assumption, for I was dressed so, and because my back was turned, you were easily deceived. So was Keable."

She paused, turning to her husband. Seeing the confusion in his face, she was about to make another effort to explain when Cecil asked who this Keable was and what deception she spoke of. She answered, then continued with her own line of thought, somehow addressing both men at once. "The name Prideaux was the key, just as I supposed from the first. Naturally I thought Prideaux was a man, for the others were."

"Yes, the apothecary of Norwich," Matthew interrupted.

"Not him, but his *wife*," Joan said.

"His wife?"

She spoke quickly, trying to control her impatience. There was so much to explain, to clarify—in her own mind as well as in the minds of her husband and especially Cecil, who knew so few of the details.

"Prideaux had a wife," she said, as much to herself as to either of her companions.

"He did," Matthew answered. "Never heard of again."

"I put it to you, for mere argument's sake, that she lived, came to London, a fugitive—a fugitive with revenge in her heart for wrongs she believed done to her husband. There was a dead child as well—and another mighty cause for vengeance, for it is an ill mother who will not fight tooth and claw against those who take her child or cause him hurt."

"Imagined," Matthew said guardedly. "And so proceed."

She warmed to her theme. "Well, suppose she conveys her husband's art to another apothecary—who then puts his skill to an illicit purpose, gulling his victims of their money by making them mere slaves to this . . . this elixir, this hope of earthly heaven. Leyland's alchemy must have had a part in it. What better field for mischief than the Inns of Court, a crop of ninnies with more money than brains? What better victims than lawyers, for whom doubtless she has nothing but hatred and contempt? What better accomplice than an impoverished physician-alchemist, who comes and goes freely in the Inns, plying two trades, honest medicine and subtle fraud?"

But Matthew was not entirely persuaded; Joan could see it in his eyes. Was his resistance masculine stubbornness, or had she overlooked some contradictory detail? She glanced at Cecil; he seemed more receptive. She directed herself to him, believing that only the whole story would convince her cautious husband or the dignified knight.

"But say," she continued, "the pious Giles became a member of the laudanum ring—by design or happenstance. Remember that his sister had been a victim too. Remember that he knew Prideaux and wife by sight, having been present at the trial."

"And recognizing the wife, he put her true name on the memorandum—Prideaux," Matthew said.

"Yes, her husband's name."

"Because she was disguised as a man—to gain admission to the Temple. Keable saw her back only and was taken in by her disguise, but Giles saw her face to face, knew her for the woman she was."

"But it was really Mistress Prideaux," Cecil put in.

"You don't mean Mistress Browne?" Matthew asked.

"Prideaux was a young man, not above thirty, by all accounts," Joan continued. "The broadside in Giles's chamber said his wife was fair to look upon and of good family. None of this fits Mistress Browne, an ill-speaking woman in her fifties if a day."

"Alice, then?"

"Not Alice," Joan said, and then she paused. She held back the tears of betrayed friendship, the humiliation of admitting that she who prided herself on her ability to tell an honest heart from a fraud had failed so miserably in this instance. Then she said it; it was to this end that her persuasions had led. "Not Alice, Matthew, but Nan Warren. She who rescued me and first put into my mind the trick of disguising myself as a man. She who once told me she had been in London five years, who speaks like a gentlewoman and is Leyland's bedfellow and accomplice. She who in all her discourse to me never once asked after a child of mine, as though the subject was distasteful—or too painful to endure. Nan Warren *is*, or was, Prideaux's wife."

For a moment Matthew made no reply to her theory. Then he nodded slowly and looked at Cecil, who nodded back. So Joan had persuaded them both. But her victory brought her little joy. Within she felt a vast desolation of spirit, an emptiness more profound than grief.

She was grateful that Matthew spared her any of his

scolding. Instead, he took her hand in his and held it gently. No, he would not censure her, and at that moment she loved him more than she had ever done; her eyes welled with tears.

Cecil asked if they would find this woman Joan referred to in Leyland's company, and she said they probably would. And then they rode in silence until minutes later they jolted to a stop, the horses all lathered and wheezing and Joan flung forward practically into Cecil's lap for the suddenness.

"Now I shall give you both all the proof you require," Joan said. "You shall see that every word I have spoken is true."

Matthew advised Joan to wait in the coach until the conspirators were taken, but she insisted on accompanying the men. What danger was there with such a multitude to seize but two? She wanted more than anything to confront Nan, to fling the girl's false professions of loyalty and gratitude and love in her face. To proclaim her the fraud she was. But in her haste, Joan stumbled as she stepped down from the coach and nearly broke her ankle, while already the troop behind had dismounted and were preparing to advance the hundred or so paces to the apothecary's shop.

Although the upper parts of the house were dark, a dim light could be seen in the street, and after half the distance had been gained, Joan saw there was a horse and cart in front of the shop door with a lantern hanging from its side. The cart was already loaded with barrels and crates, and at the very moment two men were coming down from the upper story of the house lugging a big chest. Both were short, thick men, shabbily dressed.

Until this moment, Cecil and his troop had been advancing silently upon the apothecary's. Now they rushed forward to surround the workmen, with Cecil shouting out for them to stand where they were in the Queen's name.

The laborer in front dropped his end of the chest in surprise, but the other held on and flung a curse in Cecil's direction. Before the knight could respond, Leyland appeared in the doorway. Apparently grasping what was going on, he darted in again, slamming the door behind him. "There's Leyland," Matthew cried.

About half the men rushed forward to seize the laborers, and the other half followed Matthew and Cecil in an effort to break in the door that Leyland had evidently bolted from the inside.

The storming of the house was quickly accomplished. The door gave way after but a few onslaughts by Cecil's men, who used nothing but their shoulders in the effort. Joan followed the men up the stairs. When she reached the top, the door to Leyland's study was already open, and she could see upon entering herself that the physician had been taken, with two officers on each arm and Matthew trying to wrench something from Leyland's right hand. Three of the officers who had gone to search the opposite chamber now returned to report that it was empty, nor was there any sign of a woman ever having occupied it. Cecil asked Joan to provide his men with a description of Nan Warren, which Joan was glad to do, and then about a dozen of the officers were dispatched to search the immediate neighborhood, for Cecil said it was likely she was nearby.

The whole company now went downstairs, where they were met by what seemed half of the neighborhood all come outdoors to see what the uproar was about. Among these was Mistress Browne. Still dressed in her nightclothes and cap despite the bitter cold, she was demanding to know who had invaded her house and under what pretext. When she saw it was her son who had been arrested, her fury intensified and she so abused the officers who held her son with foul language that Cecil ordered she be bound and gagged herself.

While this was happening, Matthew demanded that Leyland tell him where Nan Warren was, but Leyland said he would see him and the officers in Hell first before he would say another word. This remark incited several of the officers to fall upon the prisoner and begin beating him until Cecil's orders called them off, and a bloodied Leyland said that they could beat him all they willed, for he had taken a draft that would prevent him from feeling aught but pleasure and would presently say farewell and be damned to the whole world and all the damned souls upon it.

Cecil ordered Leyland to be taken away to his coach, and his mother too, and then turned his attention to the two laborers who were being held close prisoner by Cecil's coachman. Joan listened as the one who had cursed Cecil explained in a fearful voice that he and his brother—the other laborer—were honest men and that he had not realized who Cecil was or that his men were officers but supposed them common thieves. He said that he had been hired by a woman of the neighborhood—Nan Warren, by his description—to transport the goods in his cart to a house in Wapping. He said she had offered to pay them extra for doing the work by night and gave them no reason she should want it so but that she feared her valuables inside would be stolen otherwise.

By this time many of the barrels and crates in the cart had been removed and were being examined by Cecil's men. They contained, as Joan surmised, equipment from Leyland's study, his books and manuscripts, and a number of personal articles, man's and woman's. "Ah," Matthew said, seeing the female clothing. "This proves Nan Warren intended to flee with her accomplice."

"Was the woman in the house when you arrived?" Matthew asked the brothers.

The first of the men, who up until now had let his brother do all the talking, answered that she was not. He said there was only her servant.

"Servant?" Joan interjected. "But Nan had none."

The laborer said that there was indeed a servant—a dark-skinned young man, amiable and smooth-faced . . . perhaps a Spaniard or Portuguese. "It was he who let us in and told us what to take and where."

"I think they're lying, the both of them," Matthew said. "No one was upstairs but Leyland."

At this the older brother wrestled free of the officer who held him and dashed into the darkness, and in the confusion of orders and pistol shots that followed, his brother bolted in the opposite direction. Matthew joined Cecil and the officers who had not been sent to search for Nan Warren in pursuing the two men, leaving Joan in front of the shop with only the curious neighbors for company.

Joan had not been as skeptical of the laborers' story as Matthew had, and she now wondered who the servant might have been. One possibility, of course, was Hodge, yet to be captured. But Hodge did not begin to fit the description the men had given, nor could a disguise have done anything to make the burly and bearded barkeep smooth-faced or youthful.

Having no torch, Joan took the cart's lantern to guide her and went upstairs to Nan's rooms. They were as she remembered them, but devoid of any personal possessions that had been Nan's. She opened the little wardrobe and found it empty. Except for the boot marks recently made by Cecil's troop, there was no sign of recent occupation. Yet despite all the evidence of abandonment, Joan felt she was not alone. Remembering the priest's hole Nan had showed her, she went to the adjoining room and, setting her lantern on the floor, kneeled down to pull aside the cloth that concealed the recess.

The sight of a crouched figure in the hole made her start, but seeing the swarthy stranger's face, she knew at once it was both servant and mistress. "Nan?"

Nan looked as though she had seen a ghost, and Joan realized that to Nan, a ghost was what Joan now appeared to be. "I'm no spirit, but a living woman," Joan said, hoping to draw Nan out and talk with her before Cecil and his men returned. Strangely, given what she now knew, she had no fear of the huddled figure who seemed so vulnerable and innocuous in her hiding place.

"Won't you come out?" Joan asked.

Nan crawled from the hole and stood before her. She was much changed in appearance. It was not only her garb, but her expression, which, beneath the veneer of stain and false black hair, had lost every trace of the feminine and been replaced by grim resolve and masculine hardness.

"So you *are* alive," Nan said after a moment. She even reached out and touched Joan's shoulder. Then Nan sighed heavily and sat down near the hearth. She stared at Joan blankly.

"Yes, despite the best efforts of Master Leyland—and you."

Joan's measured response was not the response she had intended when she first realized how thoroughly she had been fooled and betrayed by Nan. The fullness of her anger and resentment did not come; instead, she found herself simply curious. What had Nan wanted of her? What lay behind such evil machinations to wreak destruction and confusion among men who, for all their faults, seemed not mighty sinners but merely wayward youths?

Joan's calm invited a similar tone in Nan. She spoke

slowly, as though she were suddenly past caring. "I suppose it will do no good to ask you to forgive. I never hated you, Joan, but loved you, rather—as close a friend as I have had since my husband was taken. You were good, and generous to a fault. But you proved too zealous in your husband's cause. You learned too much . . . there was too much at stake."

"So he *was* your husband, Prideaux, I mean."

"Yes."

"He was a scoundrel, by all accounts—a cheat and deceiver."

Nan's eyes flashed angrily at these words, and suddenly Joan was reminded of the woman who had risked her own safety to save her. Nan said: "Christopher Prideaux was a great and learned man who dispensed medicine to idiots."

Joan said: "He begat a child on one of his patients—on another woman. He was an adulterer. How can you defend him?"

"Lies, all lies," Nan cried, rising with such suddenness that Joan's heart leaped into her throat. "Inventions of the girl's family, who wanted to hide the fact she had been undone by some groom or perhaps the girl's pasty-faced brother."

"You mean Hugh Giles."

"A skulking traitor."

"You poisoned him."

Nan seemed hardly to take notice of Joan's sudden accusation. Her face was implacable in its hatred. She spoke as one possessed.

"I gave him no less than he deserved, for he came among us as a friend, and was a spy after all."

Afraid of what her accusations had unleashed, Joan decided to temporize. "Juries sometimes err. Reputable families have been known to resort to shifts—lay blame elsewhere to avoid it themselves."

"By God, they have," Nan declared. "Her father was a subtle lawyer of Norwich. As for myself, I was run out of town like the vilest of criminals. My child—" And here Nan's voice broke; her face contorted as though a sword had been driven into her bosom. "My child, stillborn. I had my husband's books and a smattering of his knowledge, for he treated me with the respect one man has for another and not as an inferior creature without brain or will. I came to London, where, having neither friend nor money, I faced starvation."

"And became—"

"Whore, doxy, Guinea bird, name me what you will."

Tears filled Nan's eyes; she spoke with great bitterness. It did not seem to Joan self-pity, but something more noble. It was passing strange: Nan had tried to kill her—her and Matthew. She had killed God knew how many others, Hugh Giles by her own admission. At her orders Theophilus Phipps and poor wretched Alice had been drowned. And yet Joan felt a great swelling of compassion.

"There are a hundred names for what I was and am, and none is very pretty," Nan continued. "Nonetheless, such a life kept my bones together, until rage and proximity to the Inns of Court and lawyerly arrogance and greed, already my downfall, taught me that triumph was sweeter than mere survival."

"You made and sold laudanum—at a tidy profit."

"Nothing unlawful in that."

"At exorbitant prices; the men became obsessed with pleasure."

Nan laughed. "Ah, men! I learned quickly what men were made of—the four elements and a concupiscent soul. Even the lawyers who think so much of themselves. I knew well from my husband's practice the effects of laudanum, knew it could do more than ease pain but also deliver such an ecstasy that, once enjoyed, the enjoyer would not soon forgo the experience. I became a queen of pleasure, satisfying every sense. I created a ring of worshipers, all convinced that laudanum was as good as the philosopher's stone to bring infinite happiness."

"But you saved my life," Joan said.

Nan turned and walked to the window. She looked out into the night, although surely she could see nothing but her own reflection in the glass. "I had no enmity toward you, another woman. At first you were merely a victim of men's wrath, like myself. Naturally I took your part, helped as I could. When I realized it was your husband who had been sent to the Middle Temple, it served my purposes to maintain our friendship, nor was your generosity unappreciated."

Joan said: "Tell me, then, what I have been ignorant of from the first. I can understand your hatred for Hugh Giles, the son of your worst enemy. And Phipps and Alice. Each knew too much. But what of Litchfield and Monk? And Braithwaite? What reason for such a massacre of youth and promise? Were they all murdered because they were lawyers and you hated every one?"

Nan turned from the window, a subtle smile on her lips.

"They were gulled because they were lawyers—and because they had more greed than justice or common sense. The ancient Knights Templar were often accused of being sorcerers by their enemies, of whom there were many. An old legend had them possessors of the magisterium, or philosopher's stone. You can't believe how little it took to persuade our dupes that we had somehow come upon old writings in which all the means of concocting the stone were plainly set forth. We represented the laudanum as the first fruits of our prospective riches. It was not only laudanum that took them to paradise, but the thought of fabulous wealth."

Joan said: "Well and good, but my question remains unanswered."

"Really? You disappoint me, Joan. Isn't it obvious? We had laudanum, but we had no stone or magisterium but in our heads. Alchemy is no simple matter. All the world knows as much. There's costly ingredients, tools, equipment. None comes cheap. Laudanum and its delights was mere earnest money for the rest."

"Which you used for your own purposes."

Nan nodded. "Now you understand the game."

"They couldn't live on promises forever," Joan said. "Sooner or later something more was needed, something more than pleasant dreams."

"Litchfield was first to break ranks. He was the most zealous disciple in the beginning, but he would not stay for the long-promised conclusion. He wanted his money back, threatened to tell all."

"And so his own chamberfellow killed him."

"On my suggestion—and for a greater share of the profits. You see how greed triumphs over friendship?"

"And made the death appear to be suicide."

"Monk's idea. Ingenious, wasn't it?"

Joan couldn't resist remarking that it was a transparent device after all. Even Hutton had suspected the truth. "You hanged Monk and scrawled upon the wall to make his death seem to be by his own hand."

"Monk killed himself," Nan said. "He was a timid soul at last, for he could not face what he had done. Place the blame on a repentant spirit. Had he been devoid of conscience, he would still be alive—and possessed of what his friends are now bereft of."

"But no richer."

"Alive, at least."

"You claim to be innocent of both deaths, then?"

"Completely," Nan said. "For I never told Monk what

to do. Murder sprang from his own brain. I only had to tempt him with a larger share. Of course, I also mentioned how dangerous to our enterprise Litchfield's loose mouth might become."

"What of Giles?" Joan asked. "Surely you recognized him from Norwich?"

"As a matter of fact, I did not. Monk brought him in. I didn't think to connect the names. But he recognized me—from my husband's trial—and then threatened to expose us all after Monk and Litchfield were dead. I sneaked into the Temple as I had often done, dressed as you see now, a whore's trick. I adulterated his drink with enough laudanum to send him leaping into paradise. And so he did and our secret safe."

"And Braithwaite?"

"His wounding was not in the reckoning," Nan continued, seeming almost pleased to have Joan for an audience. "Yet it worked to my advantage. By that time we had milked our calves dry, and he, the last remaining, was at the point of sheer distraction—all his fellows dead under sinister circumstances and as ready to blab out our secrets as to make water after dinner. Yet he was glad to see me the night I stole into his chamber. I told him the elixir had been achieved that very day, and that as sole survivor of our society, he should take all shares save mine and Leyland's. His last thoughts were of lucre. I gave him his laudanum, inducing such a state of lassitude that smothering him with his own pillow cost no more effort than to press down hard."

"On that same night you nearly killed my husband," Joan said accusingly.

"He and Phipps interrupted me before I took my leave. I didn't mean to hurt your husband. I didn't know whom I struck. Besides, the wound was a trifling thing. I inflicted it only to prevent his following me."

Joan thought of the horrible dungeon beneath the Gull,

the frigid river, the desperate escape. "You tried to murder me as well."

Nan hesitated before answering Joan's new charge; she cast her eyes down. "It was necessary. I had no choice."

"You *had* a choice," Joan declared with conviction. "You could have made an honest life, forgiven those who had wronged you. I gave you a chance."

"It was too late then—and later now. Besides, I'm not sure I would have taken it, this honest life you speak of. London hasn't been that bad for me. Gulling the lawyers gave me considerable satisfaction. After a while killing them caused me no more grief than squashing an obnoxious fly. I would have gulled and killed twice the number if I had a chance."

For several moments the two women, both dressed as men, stared at each other as though the other's very existence was incomprehensible. Whatever love and friendship Joan had felt for Nan, whatever compassion for her loss, was now vanquished in these cold-blooded confessions of fraud and murder. Never had Joan felt so betrayed. What a fool she had been to allow her generous impulses to blind her to the truth. She said: "You have revealed all these things with wondrous candor. Aren't you afraid I'll tell all to my husband—and he to the authorities?"

Nan laughed. "Should you relate to another what I have told you, I will deny it. There are no witnesses against me. It will be your word against mine."

"We shall see," said Joan.

Joan turned to leave; as she did, she glanced toward the hearth. There stood a pair of andirons she had not remembered, and they were in the shape of lions' heads. Remembering her dream of the threatening blackamoor, she swiveled around to face Nan.

Nan was clutching a dagger; her face was twisted in malice. "You won't tell anyone what I've told you."

Joan dodged the flashing blade, swinging the lantern at her adversary. She screamed, "Help-ho murder!" uncertain if any help was within hearing. Nan advanced for a second lunge while Joan kept swinging the lamp.

"You won't escape . . . you won't," Nan said between clenched teeth, looking determined and merciless.

Her heart in her throat for fear, Joan backed slowly into the adjoining room, keeping her eyes fixed on Nan, who wielded the dagger with the skill of a tavern brawler and was only inches beyond arm's reach. Nan moved swiftly to put herself between the door and Joan. Joan darted behind the bed. Then she screamed for help again, louder this time.

"It's useless. Your husband and the knight are gone," Nan said. "There's only the two of us now, and soon there shall be but one."

Suddenly from below there was a sound of men's voices and heavy footsteps on the stairs. Out of the corner of her eye Joan was aware of the door opening, and in the next second, as Nan made a second quick thrust, Joan was nearly deafened by a thunderous explosion.

Through the haze of gunpowder, Joan saw Nan jerk violently and then fall forward on the bed, where her body continued to convulse for a few seconds as though it were possessed by a demon.

Joan felt herself losing consciousness. She slumped to the floor and the next thing she knew, Matthew was looking down at her, her head was resting on his knee, and he was calling for someone to bring water to douse her with.

"Joan, Joan. Are you hurt?"

Her nostrils were filled with the acrid odor of gunpowder. She heard Cecil's voice giving orders and other men shouting and a thunder of footsteps. Her lamp lay beside her, its light extinguished. There were torches lighting the room now. "Help me up, Matthew. What's happened?"

"No, stay where you are."

She got up under her own power, saying she was all right, not hurt, only bruised. It was the second time in one night she had narrowly escaped death. Was there to be a third?

While Matthew berated himself for leaving her unprotected, Joan looked around her. Cecil's coachman stood in the doorway, smoking pistol in hand. He was trembling and explaining to Cecil that he had never killed a man before and that it made him sick to think on it.

"You've saved my wife's life," Matthew said.

Cecil assured the coachman he had done the right thing and took the pistol out of the man's shaking hand. He walked over to look at the body on the bed. "So there was a manservant after all."

"No man, but a woman born," Joan said. "Although perhaps female devil is a better word. See for yourself, sir."

When a cursory inspection of Nan's body proved Joan's words true, the coachman, who had remained in the doorway, cried out that he was damned for having killed a woman, even if it was in defense of another. To console him, Joan went over to assure him that without his timely firing, she would be a dead woman herself at that moment. He had taken a life and saved another.

"And a better," Cecil added. "Am I right in assuming that this thing on the bed is Leyland's accomplice, Nan Warren?"

"More than his accomplice," Joan said firmly. "His inspiration, his guide. She confessed. Her part and its reasons are all now as plain as day, and when convenient, I'll report every word."

"And we shall gladly hear all," Cecil said. "As for now, let her body be removed from this place, and we too shall go. It is very late, and Master Hutton will be beside himself to know how all has turned out."

As Joan and Matthew were leaving, Matthew paused to look at the dead woman. The final convulsions of the body had caused the wig to rest askew, and beneath the false black hair of the Spaniard appeared the yellow strands of Nan's own true hair.

"So this was the Nan Warren you spoke so glowingly of."

There was no mockery in Matthew's voice. He made the statement as a fact, and indeed it was a fact Joan could not deny.

"I thought you said she was fair to look upon. Death and discovery of her wrongs have made her most hideous."

Joan wanted to tell him just how hideous Nan had been during the minutes before her death, while her full lips were twisted in scorn and hatred and while all her discourse was a record of such cold-hearted malice that Joan could hardly believe one of her own sex capable of it. But that was a part of the tale she would reserve for later. For now, she wanted only to leave the presence of the bloody corpse, for somehow she imagined at any moment Nan would spring to life again, seize the dagger, and finish the evil work of silencing Joan's testimony against her.

"She *was* fair," Joan said as they passed out the door and started down the stairs. "But only to the outward eye. My judgment was too readily blinded—by friendship, kindness, and trust. Such emotions that she was beyond feeling."

"Because she was wronged," he suggested. They had reached the street. All quiet now.

"That doesn't explain it, Matthew. Many in this world are wronged and are well satisfied to let God avenge them. It was more."

She was glad he didn't ask him *what* more it was as he helped her into Cecil's coach, for she herself could not say. *There* was the great mystery.

She heard Cecil give the coachman directions to Cooke House. He said there was no point in their returning to the Middle Temple, not tonight. Then Cecil climbed in and the coach moved forward.

"I was gulled, just like the others," Joan said, directing the remark to both men in the coach, and expecting no answer from either.

But Matthew answered. "They were taken in by greed, their false ambitions and lust for power. You were betrayed by love, no fall from grace. Nan Warren had you *there*."

"She said she loved me well," Joan said simply, feeling a terrible grief swell up in her.

"And so perhaps she did, Joan," said Cecil, leaning forward and taking Joan's hands in his. "Don't be ashamed of love, Joan. It's the purest thing we know, and another's treason cannot sully it. In the Judgment it will shine forth in such splendor as to hide a multitude of sins. Believe me, it is so."

Matthew said he believed the same, and Joan felt comforted.